Brace for Impact

Becky Harmon

BELLA
BOOKS
2019

Bella Books, Inc.
P.O. Box 10543
Tallahassee, FL 32302

Printed in the United States of America on acid-free paper.

First Bella Books Edition 2019

Editor: Medora MacDougall
Cover Designer: LJ Hill

ISBN: 978-1-64247-008-6

PUBLISHER'S NOTE

Other Bella Books by Becky Harmon

Tangled Mark
New Additions
Illegal Contact
Listen to Your Heart

Acknowledgments

As always my first thanks is to Linda and Jessica Hill. Without them there would be no Bella Books. I love my Bella family. Each and every author at Bella makes us better and better.

A big thank you to all the folks who work behind the scenes at Bella. Thanks for making each book a work of art. And, of course, to Kathy—thanks for another perfect title.

I guess this is the part where I mention that I do own Lucy, the moose, on the cover. And yes, it was a Niagara Falls purchase. I jokingly mentioned how fun it would be to have it on the cover and my amazing cover designer made it happen. Thank you so much!

Once again, Medora MacDougall, your editing has managed to make my story into a real live book. You wave your magic wand and the proper words fall into place. You are the best!

My two favorite Generals—DB and Rose—thanks for sharing your military knowledge.

About five years ago, while waiting for my morning Yogi tea to brew I noticed the teatag. "Love is an experience of infinity." Being a romance reader, the word love drew my attention. Most of us have a fascination with love and at some point in our lives we have believed we found it only to find it was fleeting. Putting love and infinity in the same sentence touched me in a way I haven't been able to forget. That same teatag still sits in the windowsill over my kitchen sink. I look at it every day.

A big final thanks to every reader who takes a chance on one of my books. Without you, I would only be entertaining myself and that would be very lonely.

About the Author

Becky Harmon was born and raised just south of the Mason-Dixon Line. Though she considers herself to be a Northerner, she moved south in search of warmth. She shares her life with her partner, two cats, and Manny the dog. If you haven't seen Manny before, you can check out plenty of pictures on Becky's Facebook page.

Romance has always been Becky's first love and when she's not writing it, she's reading it. Her previous published works, *Tangled Mark*, *New Additions*, *Illegal Contact*, and *Listen to Your Heart*, are available from Bella Books.

You can reach Becky at beckyharmon2015@yahoo.com.

Dedication

For DB
You brought love and infinity together.

CHAPTER ONE

Dex pushed the blaring music to the back of her mind as she focused on the instrument panel in front of her. Following the instructions from the Wacasaw County Airport ground control, she changed the heading of her C-26 Metroliner. The large United States Army airplane leveled out as she searched the horizon for the runway markers. From behind her, she heard the music switch from Def Leppard to Black Snake and she held back a grimace. Staff Sergeant Blakely had warned her that the soldiers had prepared a compilation of Private First Class Ryan's favorite songs.

The hot mid-July air in southern Kentucky shimmered as the airplane wheels touched the concrete runway. Her mind flashed back to so many identical but random nights in Afghanistan. There the sandy terrain stretched in front of her so far she could only find her location by the glowing panel in front of her. She could feel the resistance from the humidity in the air as it wrapped around the helicopter, forcing her to push the accelerator harder. To pray that the tiny lights in the distance would guide her back to safety for another night.

"How much longer, Captain Alexander?" a voice behind her asked, pulling her back to the present.

She glanced quickly at the young face cloaked in the darkness that stretched behind him. She carried nine soldiers on this flight along with her co-pilot and the cedar oak coffin holding PFC Ryan. Normally she only carried one or two soldiers with a body, but this was a special trip. PFC Ryan's death had been the result of an unselfish act of heroism.

His company had been at Camp Charlie in the southern province of Kandahar, Afghanistan, for over seven months and was due to rotate back to the States. At an afternoon pickup game of football, PFC Ryan and his teammates heard the gate sentry's warning cry about explosives. Rather than run away like so many around him, he ran toward the threat and jumped into the driver's seat of the car in question, throwing the car in reverse, and getting away from the camp. His quick action had saved the soldiers standing sentry duty and potentially many more inside the camp. Due to the special circumstances, the company commander had granted forty-eight-hour leave for the entire squad to escort PFC Ryan's body back to his family.

Dex landed the plane and taxied to the outskirts of the airport, where a group of people waited beside a black hearse. After the plane rolled to a stop, the soldiers behind her lifted the flag-draped coffin and descended the ramp. She slowly made her way to the tarmac following them. She had seen way too many soldiers returned to their families in this manner; she was thankful this would be her last.

As a military pilot tasked with returning soldiers' remains to their families, she had forced herself to keep a distance from the grieving families, emotionally and physically. Survivor's guilt was a monkey on every soldier's back and one that she was not immune to. Those like her who departed before the job was finished carried the bulk of the burden, leaving behind friends and fellow soldiers to continue the battle while they returned to the safety and security of family.

Dex pushed aside her thoughts and joined PFC Ryan's squad in saluting him one last time before stepping back into the shadows of her plane to watch their departure. The handful of family members and friends who had arrived to honor PFC Ryan as he was returned home was a somber group. Not the flag-waving, cheering crowd most soldiers were lucky enough to see when they returned. The woman in the middle of the crowd, probably his mother or maybe an aunt, watched closely as the soldiers secured the coffin inside the waiting hearse.

Most soldiers' remains were transported in an aluminum case rather than a traditional coffin. The case would be adorned with a special cardboard cover embossed with an American flag and created to fit on top of the airline industry's standard air tray for coffins. Since PFC Ryan was being given special honors, he was prepared for burial and clothed in his full dress uniform at Dover Air Force Base, then placed directly into his specially made coffin for burial. He would be going directly to his place of rest with no stop off at a funeral home. Unfortunately she saw this a lot. Many families didn't have a lot of money to spare and now there would be one less paycheck coming in. Paying a funeral home for several days of services was not in their budget.

She watched as the soldiers piled into a nearby SUV to make their way to the gravesite. There they would pay their final respects to their fallen comrade and his family. She, on the other hand, would wait patiently for them to return and then fly them back to Delaware. From there they would catch a ride back to Afghanistan and rejoin their company.

Before she left them, she would study each of their faces, placing them in her mind with those of all the brave young men and women who had gone before them. War was hard and they would never gain back the years of their lives they had lost fighting the battle. She wanted never to forget the courageous soldiers she had transported to places that would change their lives forever. Or the relief on their faces when she flew them to safety.

She knew there was probably some relief showing on her face as well. Tomorrow, after eight years in the service, she would sign the paperwork to leave the United States Army and prepare to enter the world of civilian flying.

CHAPTER TWO

"Hello, everyone. My name is Tamika."

US Air Marshal Lucy Donovan listened to the mumbled greetings from the other passengers around her. She knew from experience that Tamika would not be happy with their response or lack thereof. Keeping her head down she tried not to smile.

"Now." Tamika stepped to the side of the check-in desk at Gate 17 and pulled the microphone closer to her mouth. "I don't know how things are done at the rest of the gates but here at my gate when someone offers you a greeting it's only polite to respond. So, let's try that again." She paused dramatically. "Hello, everyone. My name is Tamika."

The response was larger this time. A few people even added Tamika's name in their greeting.

Lucy grinned as she met Tamika's eyes. Apparently Tamika was pleased with the response because she continued her normal script welcoming them to Toronto Pearson International Airport. To Lucy and the other travelers at Gate 17, Tamika's next words brought immense pleasure. Their departing flight to Atlanta, Georgia, was currently on time.

Lucy made a final trip to the bathroom and remained standing when she returned to the gate. She didn't usually fly Eastern Airlines, but Jan had asked her nicely to switch assignments. She liked staying on Jan's good side and all the perks that went with it. Neither she nor Jan liked commitment, but an occasional hookup when they were in the same city worked well for both of them.

Her original assignment would have taken her to San Francisco and then back to Atlanta. This way she was arriving home a day early and Jan was spending the weekend with a babe on the beach before flying back to their base in Atlanta. It was a win-win situation for both of them.

Tamika's voice interrupted her thoughts again. "Would passengers Lucy Donovan and Mason Tygart please see me at the podium? Thank you."

Lucy didn't have to look for Mason. He was easy to spot due to his over six-foot frame. She liked working with him. Not that two air marshals on the same plane really ever worked together unless there was an emergency. Two years ago, she and Mason had worked a spring break flight filled with drunken college students. It was a memory she wasn't sure she would ever forget. Mason's cool head and laid-back demeanor had certainly made the flight easier than she expected.

Her eyes met Mason's as they approached Tamika. His sandy hair was covered with a blue ball cap and she knew she would find several more in multiple colors if she looked in his travel bag. He had told her once that no one looked at his face when he wore a ball cap. They knew the man in the red or blue or green hat but remove the hat and they couldn't identify his face. He gave her a cursory nod and she returned it. No need to let anyone see they actually knew each other.

Tamika leaned across the podium and whispered, "You guys want to board first?"

"No, I'm in Zone One anyway," Lucy said. It was hard to be upset with Tamika or other gate agents who were only trying to be kind, but she really hated having attention drawn to them. Their job was to fly under the radar unless needed, not to be identified and given special perks. She didn't, but she knew some marshals took advantage of skirting the system.

She was pleased when Mason declined the offer as well. He was in Zone Six so he would be one of the last to board, but he didn't seem to mind.

"Okay. I wanted to give you the option." Tamika nodded at Mason, dismissing him. As he walked away, her intense brown eyes focused on Lucy. "I tried to call you last night."

Though it sounded like a statement, Lucy knew it was a question. One of the hazards of her job was returning to the locale of her latest one-night stand too soon. Tamika's creamy dark skin and her overzealous personality had placed her in Lucy's sights only two weeks ago. She tried to be honest with all of her encounters, but sometimes she screwed up and messed with a sweet one. Tamika was a sweet one and she had a tender heart that Lucy did not want to hurt.

"I'm sorry. I was really tired and went to bed early." That was partly true. Tamika didn't need to know she wasn't alone when she went to bed.

Tamika nodded, but Lucy could see her feelings were still hurt. This was the last place she wanted to have this conversation, which was why she normally never did so, but this time she made an exception. She didn't want to drag Tamika along or say something harsh to help her get the hint faster.

"You're really sweet, but I thought you understood that I don't do relationships?" Lucy made her tone as gentle as she could.

"I know. I didn't realize that meant we couldn't hook up again."

She tilted her head. Had she misunderstood Tamika's call last night? No, she should stick to the game plan. Jan was the only person she trusted enough to meet on a repeat basis. It was a risk with other women. Though they said they were okay with a no-strings arrangement, they seldom really were. Tamika had been fun, but some things were best left alone.

"Maybe we can get a drink next time I'm in town," she said, praying she wouldn't be back in Toronto for a while and feeling terrible about it.

Tamika looked at her for a second and then nodded, picking up the microphone in front of her. "Ladies and gentlemen, I'm happy to say your plane has arrived at the gate. If you could please clear a path for the departing passengers, we'll get started with your boarding shortly."

Lucy felt the brusque dismissal but was relieved Tamika wasn't whining or crying. Oh, crying. That was something she couldn't take. She tried really hard to choose women who weren't that emotional, but sometimes she was caught by surprise. She leaned against the huge round pillar that blocked the seating area of Gate 17 from the aisle filled with anxious, fast-moving travelers. She watched Tamika and the other gate attendant make their boarding preparations while greeting the departing passengers. Tamika was an attractive woman. Her black hair and dark eyes accented the definition in her cheekbones and around her mouth. She knew she would be lucky to settle down with someone like Tamika, but the thought of doing so made her nauseous.

Using "settling" and "down" in the same sentence was like cursing and she would never say them out loud together. Even as a teenager, she had never taken any relationship seriously, and because of that she didn't have any close friends growing up. After her father's death, things in the emotional arena had only gotten worse. The hole he left in her life was only made bigger by a mother who was still there but unable to continue living. She realized very quickly that it was better to not get attached to anyone. Depending on herself gave her the confidence and security to face whatever life threw at her.

She always felt like she was playing a role in the world and never really living her own life. The switch from dating men to women in college had definitely helped her feel more at home in her own skin, but it didn't help her ability to cultivate a relationship. She would try to listen to a lover talk but their words didn't reach her. Caring about herself was all she could manage. She didn't feel a tug on her emotions toward anyone else. Relationships were a burden and she just didn't have it in her.

When Tamika called Zone One, she made her way toward the entrance to the walkway leading to the plane. She didn't like to be smothered within a group, so she hung back letting everyone else push and shove for a position. Finally approaching, she gave Tamika her brightest smile.

"I hope you have a wonderful day."

Tamika shrugged. "I will. Thanks. You too."

She didn't feel the sincerity in Tamika's words, but she was confident Tamika was strong enough to bounce back. She was glad for that. She liked her. She really did. And she wasn't lying when she said she didn't have a relationship in her. Yes, she had a reason for closing the doors around her to anyone else, but the truth was it probably wasn't in her DNA. People came and went in her life, and she wasn't interested in asking any of them to stay.

The line in front of her stopped as she approached the door of the plane. She watched each person slowly disappear through the opening and into the body of the aircraft. She glanced behind her, hoping Tamika wouldn't call the next zone. Her eyes flew back toward the group of passengers blocking her entrance. Biting her lip, she hid her anxiety at being trapped in the jetway with a bit of impatient foot tapping.

"Excuse me," a voice said behind her as she felt a hand placed gently on her shoulder.

She spun, ready to put a stop to the pushy passenger behind her.

"Hey." Her next words froze on her tongue as she took in the pilot's uniform.

The woman took a step back, raising her hands in the air. "I didn't mean to startle you. I'm running late. May I pass, please?"

Without a thought, Lucy bowed slightly at the waist and used her arm to guide the woman toward the open door. "Your chariot awaits."

Even she was surprised sometimes at her own words. She liked to blame it on being a Gemini. Flirting was her first—and second—nature. A huge grin spread across the woman's face, and Lucy felt her gaze slide across her body. She was used to being scrutinized by strangers since she knew few people in her profession and her workplace changed every day. This was different, though. She felt naked and unprepared. After a few seconds, she seemed to have passed the appraisal. The woman continued on, disappearing to the left into the cockpit.

Lucy took a deep breath. She couldn't remember the last time a woman had stopped her from taking in air. In fact, she really couldn't remember if that had ever happened before. She glanced at the flight crew welcoming the passengers onto the plane and was disappointed to see that she didn't recognize any of them. If there had been someone she knew, she would have asked for the name of the pilot and maybe found out more about her.

As she located her seat and placed her bag into the overhead compartment, she replayed the scene. Did she imagine it or had she been perused like a sculpture sitting in a museum?

She laughed at the thought. She wasn't prone to having such an active imagination. It seemed more likely that the woman really had studied every inch of her in those few seconds. There wasn't a lot of ground to cover. She was barely five foot five and the pilot was at least an inch or two taller than she was. Her long brown, almost black, hair had been pulled back in a ponytail, but Lucy could imagine it loose. She liked letting her fingers get lost in thick, long hair, and this woman fit the perfect profile in so many ways.

She held back the small smile playing at the corners of her mouth. Pilots were off limits. At least, they normally were. Being selective was being smart. She didn't like to think about boarding a plane flown by someone she had pissed off. Her job held too many other risks. She tried not to worry about things she couldn't control, but in a sense this was one she could. She might have to deal with the unknowns of a passenger or their behavior, but she didn't have any influence over them beforehand. Unless you count, the silent prayer she said each morning on her way to the airport. She did believe in a higher being that had protected her all her life. Although, she still wondered where He had been when so many died on September 11, 2001.

The death of her father had driven her to this profession. He had been killed on 9/11. He was a passenger on one of the planes that crashed into the World Trade Center. She was a few weeks into her second year in college with no solid major and no real direction in her life. The tragic loss of her dad turned her world upside down, and after a few months she returned to school with a plan. She changed her major from art appreciation to criminal justice and began applying at every federal law enforcement agency, with the air marshals being at the top of the list.

By the time she graduated, the air marshal division had been transferred from Immigration and Customs Enforcement to the Transportation Security Administration as a part of the new Department of Homeland Security. She was one of the three thousand plus recruits hired in the years following the September 11 attacks. Becoming an air marshal was her way of regaining control of the small portion of the world she lived in. She knew she couldn't be on every flight, but on the flights she was on she would do everything in her power to ensure the passengers returned safely to their families.

She stood, allowing an older woman to take the window seat in her row. She watched the woman pull out a magazine and situate her bag under the seat in front of them. Magazine readers were normally chatters, and she regretted not getting her earbuds in sooner.

Adjusting the pistol resting in the small of her back, she settled back into her seat. The cool leather holster fit perfectly inside her jeans and she never felt uncomfortable. If anything it gave her reassurance that she was always in control of any situation. She had only ever pulled her weapon once and after careful assessment she had realized the passenger was mentally ill and didn't really want to open the door while they were in the air.

Even though air marshals were required to be excellent marksmen and women, firing a weapon inside an airplane could be extremely hazardous. She could choose instead to use the expandable ASP baton she had clipped inside the front pocket of her jeans. She liked to wear her jeans a little loose so it was easy to conceal. Although at five inches collapsed, she did have to cut off the end of her pocket sometimes to make a better fit. The remaining piece of equipment she carried was a set of handcuffs that slid onto her belt in a quick snap leather case.

"Hi, I'm Ruth. Most of my friends call me Ruthie, though. I don't mind so much anymore. It makes me feel younger." The woman settled her large hips into the seat as she spoke. "Are you headed to or leaving home?"

Lucy forced her enthusiastic fake smile onto her face and faced the woman. Her gray hair was pushed up in the center by the sun visor cap she wore and there was a faint streak of lipstick clinging tightly to her lips.

Hoping a few disclosures would make Ruthie happy for now, she jumped right in. "I'm headed to visit my family in Iowa. I have to fly through Atlanta, though. It was the cheapest flight I could find. I can't believe how expensive they've gotten." She shrugged, giving Ruthie the opening to take back the conversation. As she expected, Ruthie did not miss a beat as she ranted about the price of airline tickets.

When the flight attendants began the safety briefing, she focused on them to discourage Ruthie from continuing their conversation. When they finished, she quickly plugged her silent earbuds into her ears and rested her head on the back of the seat. As she felt the plane leave the runway, her thoughts drifted back to the attractive pilot, imagining her hands as they moved across the buttons and levers that kept them in the air. Watching a woman's hands had always been very arousing to her whether they were doing something sexual or only typing on a keyboard. She loved it when they moved with confidence and grace, asserting control of whatever waited at the end of their fingertips.

When the fasten seat belt light finally went out, she stood and rummaged around in her bag, taking a moment to observe the people around her. Two men in suits and ties were directly behind her. A man, woman, and teenager were across the aisle. Her eyes quickly took in multiple rows in both directions as her mind analyzed each passenger and conducted a rapid risk assessment. She kept an open mind about her profiling. The modern-day terrorist came in many sizes and colors. Single travelers always drew her attention first and then she branched out.

When she felt familiar and confident about the area around her and that there were no obvious potential hazards, she made a trip to the rear restroom and checked out where Mason was positioned on the plane. He sat a few rows from the rear in an aisle seat. The man beside him and the one across the aisle carried on an enthusiastic conversation. His head bobbed back and forth between them as their tone grew louder.

"Seriously, man, how can you even suggest Brady was involved?" Mason antagonized them.

"How can you say he wasn't? He runs the show and the footballs were his," one of the men responded.

Lucy didn't look at them as she passed. She would never understand men and sports. If she didn't know that Mason hated football, she might have been concerned with the tone of his voice. Mason was a golf man. He liked a sport he could play by himself, he had told her that on many occasions. Grown men reliving their high school or college football glory days weren't his favorites to be seated by, but he followed enough sports radio to carry a conversation. And quite persuasively, she might add.

She was quickly in and out of the bathroom, casually bumping Mason's shoulder as she passed. She worked hard to avoid being lackadaisical at her job and she liked that Mason would play with her. They never did anything that would draw attention to them so it was a challenge to think of something to annoy each other with. Once he had dropped his heavy overcoat over her head when he pulled it out of the overhead bin. She had to work hard to avoid laughing and pretend to be aggravated.

Their job had a lot of hazards, but the worst in her opinion was being overconfident to the point of carelessness. Flight after flight with nothing ever happening could lull a weary air marshal to sleep. She returned to her seat and pretended to study the *Us* magazine on her lap. She purposely bought magazines that didn't hold her interest to avoid getting lost in an article. This magazine was one of her least favorites. To her it was nothing but a bunch of gossip. Crappy magazines were also another reason for the earbuds. A nosy seatmate could strike up a conversation regarding what she was reading and she wouldn't be able to hold up her end. Most chatty people carried the conversation on their own anyway, requiring only an occasional head nod of agreement from her.

Turning the page of her magazine, she glanced up and noticed the serving cart blocking the walkway between first class and the cockpit. She was ready for a nice sugary soft drink, but she also knew flight attendants often used this maneuver to block the aisle when one of the pilots was leaving the cockpit during a flight. She returned her eyes to the magazine, glancing up occasionally to see which option would occur. She caught a glimpse of a dark ponytail disappearing into the first-class bathroom. When the woman emerged a few minutes later, Lucy was watching. The pilot hesitated before quickly returning to the cockpit. Lucy returned to her magazine, but her thoughts still lingered on the sexy hands in control of the plane.

* * *

Dex Alexander slid into her chair in front of the console and glanced at the pilot beside her. Grant had several years on her in age and experience.

"Thanks for the break. I was running so late to catch the flight I didn't have a chance to stop off before I boarded."

"No problem. I know they sometimes schedule us too close to make flights comfortably. No change to report here."

She glanced at all of the gadgets in front of her and settled back into the co-pilot's seat. Grant hadn't removed his double-breasted black jacket, but he had unbuttoned it, so she followed his example. She was still learning what was acceptable on the job and what wasn't. After two months of training, she had been in the cockpit for barely a week. Being back in a classroom hadn't been fun, but lucky for her Eastern had sent her through an accelerated program. She had her Airline Transport Pilot certification and with another five hundred hours of flying time, she would be eligible for promotion to captain. She would gain a wreath around the star on the pilot wings she wore above her left breast.

"So how are things working out for you with Eastern?" Grant asked.

"Good."

In so many ways civilian flying was easier and yet still harder than the military. There had been a comforting consistency in the military. Expectations were clear there, unlike with Eastern Airlines. The off-of-the-job freedom was something she would have to get used to after eight years in the military, as well as the planes. A turboprop engine was nothing compared to the twin-engine jet she was flying today. The up- and the downside was she still wore a uniform. She had traded the army flight suit for an Eastern Airlines suit. Black pants and double-breasted jacket with a black tie over a white button-down shirt. Neither uniform was shorts-and-T-shirt comfortable, but she also didn't have the dilemma of what to wear each day.

Grant glanced at her. "So you like it so far? I know it must be a big change. Never really understood why the military used turboprop planes. They aren't very efficient."

She hated this quandary. Do you correct a senior officer? Often she let her opinion of the officer influence whether she offered correct information or not. If the man or woman was a jerk then she didn't care if they continued to show their stupid side. With a good officer who had a future in the military, she wanted to make sure they were properly informed. She had mastered the ability to pick the necessary situations and the proper technique to administer it. If she was about to fly with a superior officer who didn't know the required fuel amount for the trip they were making, she would make the correction as respectfully as possible whether she liked him or not. It was a life-or-death situation.

She took a chance that Grant would be open-minded rather than let his ego call the shots.

"Actually props are more efficient at shorter distances," she explained.

"Really? I didn't know that."

"Yeah, it's a misconception most people have. Props are good cargo planes or for drug enforcement. They fly slower for better ground visuals, and they can land on smaller runways. And they're much quieter."

"Learn something new every day."

When it was clear Grant was finished with their conversation, she let her thoughts drift. She found herself unable to push the woman in the chance encounter from her mind. The woman's dark hair was cut in a jagged bob style—longer in places and shorter in others. It flowed freely around her face, especially when she spun quickly. Dex's thoughts had been on the flight and the rush to get to the gate, so she had been more than a little surprised by the way her body had reacted when they met.

Impulsive ideas didn't really hit Dex in her personal life. Work life, yes. She could make a split-second, accurate, life-or-death decision with precision. Anything to do with emotions and feelings, however, needed time and planning, which could be why she was always single. She was surprised at her own actions then when she ripped a piece of paper from her notebook and scribbled down a note.

"Coffee?" she asked Grant, as she stood.

"Yeah, that'd be great."

She flipped the light for the flight attendant and waited until they gave the all clear before opening the door.

She smiled at Olivia, the head flight attendant. "I'm sorry to be such a bother today. Could we get some coffee when you brew it?"

"Sure. Hold on a second. I just made a pot and can grab it right now."

Dex folded her note into a small square and passed it to Olivia when she returned with the coffee.

"Can you give that to the dark-haired woman in 12D? She's wearing a blue Boston Red Sox shirt."

"Sure." Olivia tilted her head. "Should I wait for a response?"

"No, that won't be necessary. Thanks." Dex handed Grant his coffee and secured the cockpit door before sliding back into her seat. Not knowing the woman's flight information, she didn't know if she would even be able to meet her. Hell, there was even the chance her gaydar was off or the woman was already in a relationship. She tried to convince herself it didn't matter either way. But deep down, she felt like it did.

CHAPTER THREE

Lucy glanced up at the flight attendant as she leaned low over her.

"From the First Officer," the attendant said softly as she dropped the folded note onto Lucy's tray table.

"Thanks."

She waited until the attendant walked away, then checked to make sure she didn't have any unwanted attention around her. She looked at the small square of folded paper. There was no writing on the outside. She unfolded it and stared at the words scrawled across the page.

Gate A33 at 8 p.m.

Dex

She liked the name, Dex. It seemed to fit the woman. *Dex. Dex. Dex.* She enjoyed saying the name several more times in her head before allowing her mind to switch to the logical. She had traveled through Atlanta enough to know Gate 33 was beside the Eastern Airlines first-class lounge and the Southern-cooking restaurant. She was almost curious enough to hang around, but she really wanted to get to her cabin before dark.

Besides, she didn't like to be summoned. She was normally the one calling the shots. She glanced up to find the flight attendant who had delivered the note watching her. Lucy gave her a shrug. If the attendant was waiting for a return response, she would have to wait because she wasn't prepared to give one.

While she nursed her Coke she tried hard to keep her mind from wandering through the what-ifs of a meeting with Dex. Wasn't the situation that had transpired with Tamika fresh enough to keep her from breaking her own rules? Their flight was scheduled to land at five and she hoped to have groceries and be at her house long before eight. She was looking forward to sleeping in her own bed tonight.

"Is that about your flight? Is something wrong," Ruthie asked.

"Oh, no," she answered, flipping through her mind for a convincing story as she pushed the note farther under the napkin on her tray table. "I asked the flight attendant about her shoes and she wrote down the website she had purchased them at. I thought they were so pretty."

"I didn't notice them," Ruthie said as she leaned toward the aisle trying to see the flight attendant's shoes. "I thought everything they wore was part of their uniform."

Oops. She should have thought of that.

"That's probably true. Maybe we shouldn't mention it further so she doesn't get in trouble."

"Right. Good point." Ruthie settled her hips back into the seat again and picked up her magazine.

Lucy returned to planning out her evening. She mentally added carrots to her grocery list in case the neighbor's donkey decided to make another appearance while she was home. He had to travel through quite a bit of thick vegetation to get to the fence line that joined her property and deserved a reward when he succeeded. His rounded stubby nose and chunky body were extremely adorable and she couldn't help but hope she would see him again.

This would be her first consecutive four days off in several months. Though considered by her co-workers to be a true workaholic, she was really looking forward to it. She shook her head. This desire for consecutive time off was the second "first" of the day for her. Normally, she didn't even turn her head to glance at pilots. They held no appeal for her. She wouldn't deny Dex had caught her interest, but the draw of her cabin in the woods was greater than the chance of sex. *Yikes*. Had she really just thought that? She was getting old, or maybe her mantra that pilots were off limits was starting to register. She would blame the lingering image of Dex on the way they had met and nothing more.

Pushing Dex from her mind again, she found solace in the memory of her new house. It had been barely three months since she had purchased the cabin on the outskirts of Madison. It was a perfect location, away from the noises of the city and only a short distance across the Florida line. An easy drive on the interstate and less than four hours from Atlanta, Madison had all the amenities of a high traffic town without the size.

She knew the moment she had seen the cabin that she would buy it. The thousand-square-foot house had a sturdy frame even if the interior had seen better days. It had allowed her remodeling imagination plenty of room to grow. She probably hadn't spent more than two weeks there total, but she had started with the creature comforts. She spent the first days of construction remodeling the bathroom with the help of a local contractor. She would have liked to do everything herself, but she recognized her limits when it came to plumbing and electric. The three-bedroom cabin was now a one-bedroom with a large master bath and walk-in closet. Decorating wasn't important; the bedroom contained only her bed and two nightstands.

She felt the plane touch down as she mused about the next steps in her renovation. When passengers began to disembark, she stood and grabbed her bag from the overhead compartment. Sliding into an empty row in first class, she pretended to search her bag while she waited for Mason.

"Enjoy your visit with your family," Ruthie called as she passed.

"You take care too," Lucy said lamely, realizing she couldn't remember where Ruthie was headed. It was a bit disconcerting to her because her job was to pay attention. Too bad she couldn't have told Ruthie that she had been distracted by the pilot. She smiled. That might have shut Ruthie up for the entire flight. She made a point, though, to never tell a fellow passenger anything with any truth behind it. She was a career actress in so many ways.

The flight had been quick and quiet, as the majority of flights were, and she was eager to be back behind the wheel of her truck. Mason finally reached her, giving the all clear that the rear of the plane was empty and she followed him down the aisle. At the door of the plane, Dex stood greeting the passengers as they departed. Lucy couldn't help but smile at her friendly face, but she didn't linger. As she passed, she read the name on Dex's chest tag, Alexander. *Dex Alexander.*

She pushed aside the possibilities of a night of great sex and moved with the flow of passengers headed to baggage claim and the exits. She took the bus to the B long-term parking lot and easily found her blue Toyota Tacoma. Back in the driver's seat with control of the wheel, she wasted no time getting away from the airport. She left the rush hour traffic on Interstate 75 and took back roads away from Atlanta. The stop-and-go traffic off the interstate might be slower, but she didn't care. At least she was looking at more than the car in front of her.

* * *

Dex followed the server to a corner table where she could watch the travelers pass by. It was almost a quarter after eight and she was sure the woman wasn't coming, but she decided to get something to eat and wait a little longer. She stretched her legs under the table and played with the menu. This restaurant advertised Southern cooking and that's what she needed today, a little comfort food.

After weeks of ground training to learn the ins and outs of Eastern Airlines, she'd finally gotten the chance to get in the air. She'd made it through her first day as a civilian pilot, and tonight she would sleep in a hotel bed, the first of many. Tomorrow she would fly to New York and then to Los Angeles. By Saturday, she would be back in Toronto to sleep in her own bed. At least for a night or two. She wouldn't know her schedule for the following week until she returned from this rotation.

She knew it would take a while to get used to this line of work, but she knew when she left the service that this would be the best alternative. She could have stayed in and tried to get her twenty years, but she wasn't going to second-guess her decision now. Her army assignment had taken a toll on her even though she had never been on the front lines. She couldn't even imagine what the men and women in direct combat went through.

In the beginning, she had liked the excitement and adrenaline of flying troops all over the world, but the thrill had quickly worn off. Watching young men and women go into battles they weren't prepared to fight gave her a sick feeling. The memory of the young, eager faces on those she dropped off and the shadowed eyes she saw on those she picked up would haunt her forever.

She couldn't help feeling responsible for the ones she dropped in remote locations. The ones she deposited were hardly ever the ones she picked up, so there was rarely any closure. She knew the troops each had a mission to conduct and she tried to convince herself she wasn't leaving them behind, but sometimes that was what it felt like. The majority of her flights were without a lot of risk, but her nerves were still frayed and she needed a life away from the smell of fear and death. Her last flight back to the US she had transported eight bodies and it made her stomach churn thinking about it. The young men and women who gave their lives were only a quick announcement on the local news, but their families felt the loss forever.

She had spent countless hours hashing and rehashing her most harrowing missions. Everyone said time was the only healer. She knew what they really meant was time away from it all. It had taken signing separation paperwork and moving into her apartment in Toronto for her to even come close to a good night's sleep. She knew there were soldiers who had the ability to push past their own emotions and do what needed to be done and she was thankful for them. She, on the other hand, had survived by building a wall around herself. Allowing herself to do anything more than mourn the loss of a fellow soldier would have opened up the floodgates to a potential emotional breakdown. And now she was thankful she had recognized her own limits and left the army behind. She was confident she could separate whatever baggage she had returned with from her current profession. Now that she wasn't facing it day after day, she felt like she had a handle on controlling the emotional trauma she previously had repressed. That she would be able to move past all of it.

She pushed aside all thoughts of the military and allowed more pleasant images to take over. Images of one Lucy Donovan. After everyone had left the plane, she had asked the flight attendant to see the passenger manifest and looked up her name, discovering, to her surprise, in the process that the occupant of 12D was identified as an air marshal. The flirtatious woman had already gained Dex's attention, but now she had her interest too. Maybe it was Lucy's attractiveness. Or maybe it was the idea of ships passing in the night. That made sense. She wouldn't have to think about interacting with Lucy in her daily life. She wouldn't have to share emotions or get to know this woman. She could appreciate her in the moment and then move on. And that—that was an attractive thought.

She had to admit, though, that she was disappointed Lucy had not chosen to accept her invitation. She knew realistically that Lucy may have been booked on another flight. It was hard to miss the fact, however, that she could have easily given Dex that information when they had passed after the flight, but she had chosen not to. Oh well, Lucy certainly wasn't the only fish in the sea, even if she was the first one who had caught her eye in a long time. Besides, she was still getting her feet on civilian ground again. She didn't need a distraction. The server brought her Salisbury steak and macaroni and cheese with the token vegetable she wouldn't indulge in, and she dove in with gusto. She would make time for the gym tomorrow. Tonight she was splurging and it felt good.

* * *

Lucy slowly maneuvered her truck down the sandy road toward her cabin. It was later in the evening than she had hoped to arrive. The last rays of sun were starting to fade. Acres of green pasture on each side of her merged into a heavily wooded area. Big, tall pines and old oak trees lined the sides of the road. A tunnel of limbs covered in Spanish moss hung low, blocking out the bit of light left in the sky. Then all the vegetation parted and opened up into the little nook where her cabin sat. The road ended at her house, which was bordered by pastures on two sides and thick vegetation on the other.

Using her phone to turn off the house security alarm, she carried the heaviest of her bags onto the porch and unlocked the door. The room was a comfortable seventy-four degrees, exactly what she had requested when she dialed in and set the digital panel earlier. She loved being able to check on her house while she was away. She knew it was stupid, but it almost felt like communicating with someone waiting at home for her. She hadn't installed any cameras yet, but she was thinking about it.

She dropped her bag and stepped back outside. Standing on her porch, she looked around at the small yard and then up at the night sky. Soon it would be covered with bright stars, which looked so much brighter here without all the city lights. She quickly retrieved her duffel bag and the last couple of bags of groceries from her truck before heading back inside. She put all the perishables in the refrigerator but left the canned food on the counter. The small kitchen didn't have a lot of cabinet space and the majority of it was filled with dishes and other items she would never use.

She dumped beef stew from a can into a pot on the stove and then unpacked her duffel bag, throwing her dirty clothes into the hamper. She did a quick walk-through of the house, settling in and feeling the comfort of being home. She didn't have any buyer's remorse, but she had been afraid she would. She had moved so many times in the last ten years that she wasn't sure she would ever feel comfortable anywhere. She wasn't sure if it was the house or the location that spoke the most to her, but something certainly did.

She turned the stove off and dished a bowl of stew, taking it out on the porch. She didn't have a swing or any chairs yet, so she sat on the steps, reminding herself of the to-do list she had for tomorrow. The new boards on the steps and porch needed to be weatherproofed, but she should probably build the hand railings first. The porch stretched the length of the house so it would take her most of tomorrow to build them. Then she could paint them on Friday.

The contractor would be working on the laundry room Friday, which meant she would need something to work on outside the house anyway. He didn't like people hanging over his shoulder while he worked. The final interior repair would be the kitchen. She had a design she wanted to use, but she needed more than four days to pull it off. She didn't like to do a partial job, leave, and then come home to a mess. It would require taking a week off from work, and she couldn't remember the last time she had done that. Maybe after the upcoming holidays she would take some vacation leave.

The sound of running hooves and then crashing of nearby bushes drew her attention to the tree line beside her house. She ran into the house and grabbed a carrot from the fridge. Given the amount of noise being made, it sounded like a herd of elephants coming to visit, but she knew it was only one black donkey. He gave a couple of snorts to let her know he was there and she laughed.

"I hear you, boy," she said as she walked across her yard.

The full moon provided enough light for her to cross to the fence. She couldn't see the donkey's black face, but the white tip of his nose seemed suspended in midair as he waved his head around impatiently. She put her legs through the wooden split rail fence, sitting on the middle board. His round nose began to push at her immediately as he searched for the treat.

She held the carrot out to him and he bit off a chunk. Munching happily, he leaned his shoulder into her legs and she petted his neck, talking softly to him.

"Did you miss me, boy? I missed you."

He swung his head around and nuzzled her arm before biting off another chunk of carrot.

"It's nice to have you here to welcome me home."

She heard the roar of a four-wheeler and saw headlights coming down the road. She stood and gave the donkey a pat before returning to her porch. She hadn't changed clothes yet and was glad her pistol was still in the small of her back.

The covered UTV, a modified golf cart, squealed to a stop beside her truck. She watched as a shadowy figure climbed out and slowly approached, talking quickly.

"I hope I didn't scare you. I heard Bogarts take off like a bat out of hell, and I was afraid he was spooked. Have you seen him?"

Relieved to hear a woman's voice, Lucy stepped into the yard to meet her.

"Is he furry with a black face and white nose?"

"He is."

Lucy thought she could hear the woman smile. "He's over at the fence. I gave him a carrot. I hope that's okay."

"Oh yeah. That's fine. I'm Karen, by the way. Sorry I flew in here like that. I didn't expect to see your vehicle. Or you for that matter."

Lucy took a step closer and shook Karen's hand. "It's okay. I just got here. So, his name is Bogart? I like it."

"Bogart. Bogarts. Hard head." Karen waved her hand in the air. "He'll answer to pretty much anything, especially for a carrot. That's his favorite."

"I did give him one last week, so I guess I've created a monster."

As if on cue, Bogarts brayed.

"He probably shouldn't have more than one or two a day, but we don't give him any on a regular basis so you're free to spoil him when you're here. If you want," Karen offered.

"Thanks. It was nice to be greeted when I got in tonight."

"He must've heard or seen your truck and that's why he came running. I'm surprised he stopped at the fence." She laughed. "I guess I should head back home. If he becomes a burden let me know. Do you have something to write on? I'll give you my number. I'm sure you figured it out, but I live in the white house you pass on the way in. My wife works from home, so she's around during the day if you need anything."

Lucy stepped into the house and grabbed a pen and notepad from the counter. She met Karen at the door, curiosity covering her face as she quickly looked around the combined kitchen and living room. Lucy hesitated for a second before jotting down her own number and then handing the pad to Karen. She didn't know this woman and she hated giving out her number, but having a local contact was a plus if something went wrong at the house while she was away.

"Sheila, that's my wife, will be sorry she missed meeting you. You should expect a dinner invitation. Will you be here long?"

"Until Sunday."

"Great. I'll let Sheila know."

As the UTV roared away, Lucy felt the quiet return like a heavy, old-fashioned quilt covering her body. Rustling in the trees at the fence told her that Bogarts was following Karen back to the house. She sat down on the porch and looked up at the sky filled with stars. For a moment the silence felt empty, and then she reminded herself how much she liked being alone. Sharing a space with someone else felt confining, especially when the space belonged to her. This was her house and she had no intentions of ever inviting anyone to visit. Well, Karen and Sheila might be an exception, even though friends were a luxury she had never indulged in. She liked Karen's curiosity.

CHAPTER FOUR

Dex groaned as she rolled over to silence the alarm at six the next morning. She wasn't really a morning person, but this was her penance for the meal she had eaten the night before. She dressed in the dark and headed for the gym. The light in the hallway was blinding and she squinted her eyes. She sincerely hoped she didn't meet anyone she knew because she looked a mess. Her hair was pulled back in a ponytail, but she could already feel wispy strands escaping confinement.

The gym was empty, she was glad to see. She chose the treadmill farthest from the door, inserted her earbuds, and began a slow walk, trying to convince her body to wake up. After ten minutes, she increased to a jog and slowly increased her speed every few minutes. Thirty minutes later she began her cooldown and then returned to a walk. There was no denying she felt better for having forced herself to endure this torture. She grabbed a banana and a yogurt from the continental breakfast and returned to her room to shower.

Dressed in her Eastern Airlines uniform, she caught a cab in front of the hotel. The hotel provided a shuttle to the airport, but she didn't want to share a ride. She wasn't in the mood for small talk. She also wanted to leave when she wanted to leave, and standing around waiting was not in her personality. The cab would take her straight to her terminal rather than a general drop-off location.

Hartsfield-Jackson Airport was crowded as always, but she quickly moved through the security checkpoint and made her way to the Eastern Airlines office. There were no changes with her departure schedule, so she grabbed some breakfast and waited with Grant until their plane had landed. Grant didn't seem to be in a talkative mood either, so they both kept their faces buried in electronic devices. She was content to focus on one of the new romance novels she had downloaded before her flight yesterday.

Flipping through the summaries of each book made her think of Lucy Donovan. Alluring women with lots of lust seemed to be the theme. Lucy's image had been dancing around on the edge of her thoughts all night, and she fought again now to push it away. No matter what her parents had told her, she had never believed in love at first sight and all that mumbo jumbo. Attraction was only attraction and lust was only lust. She had no problem calling her feelings what they were.

Sure, her palms had begun to sweat and her heart to race when they met, and that had never happened to her despite the hazards of her work. As for the nervous twitch in her stomach when she was writing out the note and the fact she had even written a note—well, it was possible Lucy had brought something to the surface in her. She didn't want to dwell on that. She had never met a woman she had instantly wanted to get to know rather than sleep with. And she wasn't ready to admit Lucy was that woman.

Clearly, though, she had been intrigued and the physical attraction she had felt toward Lucy wasn't going to go away quickly. It was probably only because it had been way too long since she had given in to such feelings. She prided herself on not being a shallow person. She had always been an equal opportunity non-dater. For her the military had been all-consuming; it hadn't been the best place to explore a dating lifestyle. Not that she had wanted to. DADT, the "Don't Ask, Don't Tell" military policy, was in effect when she joined. She had been relieved to hear about that at first. Then she learned that it hadn't stopped the witch hunts. All it took was one commander who didn't agree and a soldier's career could be over.

When news of the implementation of the repeal of DADT reached her unit in Afghanistan in 2011, she was no longer interested in dating. In companionship maybe, but for her a war zone wasn't compatible with romance. Even though most minds were broader than when she had joined, she had never felt comfortable drawing unwanted attention. The few women who had asked her out in the last few years had barely held her attention through the first date. If they even made it that far.

The twinge she felt in the back of her mind told her Lucy might be different. She could still see the smile dancing in Lucy's dark eyes while she flirted with her outside the plane. It was possible they could run into each other again one day, but realistically the chances of that happening were slim. Air marshals weren't assigned to specific airlines, and unfortunately not every flight contained any.

She felt Grant stand from his seat beside her and she glanced at the airline board, noticing their flight had landed. She gathered her belongings and followed him into the flow of people moving from one gate to another. Grant seemed more alert now, and they chose to walk rather than ride the underground tram.

"How was your first day?" he asked as they passed Terminal B and headed to C where their plane waited.

"Basically uneventful." She thought of Lucy. Unfortunately, that situation had been uneventful as well.

"We pray for every day to reach that level, right?" he asked.

"Absolutely."

They walked the rest of the way in silence. This was Dex's favorite area of the Atlanta airport. Light and dark green cut-out leaves hung from the ceiling with a few spots of blue sky between them. Birds tweeted and crickets chirped in a soothing cocoon around her. The unexpected design was impressive if not something you would expect to find in an airport terminal. She enjoyed seeing the expressions of wonder on the faces of children as they walked into the underground forest for the first time. Their parents, walking with a purpose, were often oblivious to what was above them or even to the sounds around them.

Dex stepped onto the escalator first, pulling her airline suitcase behind her. At the top, restaurants and coffee shops called out to her.

"Would you like a cup of coffee?" she asked Grant.

"Sure. I'll go ahead and get started. If you don't mind." He dug in his pocket for cash, passing her a couple of bills. "Black is fine."

She turned left into the food court as he headed down the concourse toward gate C35. There were several people already in line at the coffeehouse so she studied the menu while she waited. All the flavors and options were mind-numbing. When it was finally her turn, she simply requested two black coffees. The barista didn't seem surprised by her simple request and quickly filled two paper cups, securing their lids and placing them in front of Dex before taking her money.

Dex stacked one cup on top of the other and carried them with one hand while she pulled her bag with the other. It was a balancing act to maneuver around the mass of harried travelers. The gate agent at C35 wasn't busy when Dex arrived and she quickly held the jetway door open for her to pass. She walked slowly toward the plane, flashing back to yesterday when Lucy had been waiting at the other end. It was an involuntary thought, but a pleasant one. She wondered how long it would be until walking a jetway didn't make her think of the woman and the feelings she had evoked.

The few words they had exchanged didn't really constitute a conversation and she had no right to feel such a connection. She should stop trying to figure it all out. Yes, Lucy was attractive. She could even use the word "cute" to describe her.

Her face was round and her cheeks were slightly plump. Not really overweight but more like the baby fat had never left. She guessed her age between thirty and forty. She was never good at that.

She was glad she had left the military when she did. At thirty-four, she still had plenty of time for a civilian career and then the pleasure of retirement. Making plans for what she would do with her life when there were no longer demands placed on her was what she had done in her free time with the army. Some days there was a lot of free time. Standing around and waiting was unfortunately the life of a soldier, no matter the rank or position. It was also the main reason she didn't have any patience for it now. She probably would have made major within the next year, but she had no regrets with leaving. Her life was her own now. Well, at least when she wasn't at work.

* * *

Thirty minutes later, Dex slid into her seat and was happy to find her coffee was still warm.

"All okay, Bridge Master," she joked to Grant.

She had checked the exterior of the plane and the cabin to ensure everything from the bolts holding the plane together to the seat belts were ready for their flight. Now she would complete the pre-flight checklist with Grant. ACAR, the aircraft communications addressing and reporting system, would do most of the calculations for her once she entered the runway and wind conditions. Over the last eight years, technology had changed the way planes were flown so much. In many ways the amount of work required was less, but in her opinion the stress and responsibility had increased. Environmental threats were the easy ones. She knew what to do and could handle a storm. People, on the other hand, were an unknown entity. Gauging someone's intent when they were risking others' safety was not her forte. Flying was what made her happy. At least she didn't have to worry about being shot down anymore. On most days at least.

She had started her career in the Army Aviation Branch flying helicopters, as all army pilots do. Ninety-nine percent of the branch is helicopters and that is the certification every aviation soldier graduates with. Her first three years were spent flying a Blackhawk in and out of combat zones, which was the assignment she had requested. She wanted to help. To make a difference. She did that until she couldn't do it any longer. The emotional toll on her body and mind was more than she could have ever imagined. Five years later, the nightmares had started to fade and she had more nights of sleep without interruption than with.

She had almost gotten out of the army at the three-year mark. If not for her commanding officer, who had seen Dex's potential and was willing to do the work to avoid losing a combat veteran. Brigadier General Rose Loper had pushed through the paperwork for Dex to return to training on a fixed-wing aircraft. The army didn't do any combat missions with fixed-wing aircraft, only surveillance flights and transports. Dex had moved to combat support, starting with the UC-35A, a medium-range, small utility jet with a range of only fifteen to eighteen hundred nautical miles and limited passenger space. There was no more dropping baby-faced soldiers into situations even she couldn't imagine.

She had been relieved with her change in assignment until the last year. Almost worse than dropping troops into combat was transporting the killed in action. Her assignment to work with the Army National Guard flying the C-26 Metroliner turned out to be an emotional challenge for her. The twin-engine turboprop with accommodations for a pilot, co-pilot, and nineteen passengers or cargo was mainly assigned to work drug control operations, but she only handled transports. Flying soldiers from one airport to another and bringing home the ones destined for their final resting place. It was heart-wrenching.

Flying commercial airliners was different. She didn't connect or even talk with any of the passengers. She did what was expected of her, offering a friendly greeting as they departed the plane. She was gradually getting back to the serenity of being in the air, which was what had attracted her to flying in the beginning. Once in the air, everything else in the world faded away.

Realizing that Grant had been talking, she focused her attention back on their flight preparation.

"Our flight path looks clear. No weather anywhere. We should be in New York in less than two hours," Grant informed her.

She nodded, thinking ahead to the twenty-five hundred miles to Los Angeles that would follow. Probably about seven hours. Grant would be replaced by a pilot she didn't know when they reached New York. She liked Grant's easygoing manner and hoped the next pilot would have one as well. She knew she would face opposition eventually, being one of the less than seven percent of women commercial pilots in the United States. She couldn't imagine that it could be worse than anything she had faced in the military.

It was estimated that the major airlines would be replacing as many as eighteen thousand retiring pilots in the next seven years; she hoped that meant the percentage of women would increase. Not many people could afford the cost of the education to learn to fly commercial airliners, though, not unless they took the military route as she had. Even then the certifications and licensing were still expensive. She knew she was one of the lucky ones. Eastern Airlines had hired her even before the ink was dry on her army discharge.

* * *

Lucy dropped the hammer, dug her phone from her pocket and glanced at the screen. It was her new neighbors. True to Karen's word, Sheila hadn't even waited twenty-four hours to call. She swiped to accept the call, placing the phone to her ear.

"Hello."

"Hi. Lucy?"

"Yes."

"This is Sheila. Karen's wife. You met last night."

"Right. Bogarts's parents."

Her statement made Sheila laugh and Lucy liked the way it sounded. She could already tell Sheila was the opposite of Karen. Karen was hyper and bit on the rambling side of a conversation, but Sheila was more hesitant and seemed to choose her words carefully.

"Yes, we are parents to one fuzzy black donkey and a few other barnyard animals," Sheila joked. "I'm calling to see if you would like any fresh vegetables from our garden?"

Lucy hesitated. She didn't normally cook much when she was home, which was why most of her purchases were in cans or frozen.

"I'm not…I mean…I don't."

"I didn't mean to put you on the spot. I thought you might like something fresh."

"That sounds great, but I'm not really much of a cook."

"Oh, no problem. I'll be right over."

Lucy's eyes widened at the silence in her ear. Sheila had hung up. She pocketed her phone and picked up her hammer as the roar of the four-wheeler grew louder. Sheila had clearly been poised to descend on her even before the phone call was placed.

Sheila was the opposite of Karen in appearance as well. Karen's dark hair was wavy and cut short all over her head. Sheila was fair-skinned with shoulder-length blond hair pulled into a Pebbles-style ponytail on top of her head.

"Forgive my appearance. I've been working in the garden all morning," Sheila said as she jumped off the four-wheeler.

Lucy laid the hammer on her newly built section of railing and held out her hand. Sheila's grip was firm and quick. She grabbed a plastic bag from the cart and motioned toward Lucy's cabin.

"Can we step inside?"

"Yeah, sure." Lucy pushed the door open and stepped aside, allowing Sheila to enter first. She smiled when she heard Sheila gasp.

"Wow. It's amazing." Sheila glanced at Lucy with surprise. "I was here less than a year ago and it was downright scary."

Lucy glanced around at her small but comfortable living room. The floor was covered in a swirled gray ceramic tile with a gray and maroon area rug. Two squishy mint-colored chairs formed an L on both sides of the room with a matching loveseat between them. The furniture faced a small stone fireplace that was centered on the right wall with a television mounted above it. She hadn't purchased any type of cable plan yet and she wasn't sure she would. She had a DVD player and some movies if she really wanted the noise.

"Is that gas or wood?" Sheila asked.

"Gas."

"I love it. I've been begging Karen to replace our wood one with gas, but unfortunately she likes to chop wood." Sheila shrugged. "Crazy. I know."

"I didn't want the mess of wood or the need to gather it."

Sheila nodded as she stepped into the kitchen area and deposited her bag on the counter. "I brought everything you need except spices. Do you have any?"

Lucy opened the cabinet above their head and displayed the thirty little jars her mother had sent as a housewarming gift. The gift was one more sign that she hadn't bothered to get to know her adult daughter. Her mother had never visited any of the places she lived, and she had no reason to expect this one would be different. Not that Lucy had put in much effort either. She couldn't remember the last time she had visited her childhood home in the northern panhandle of West Virginia. She had met her mother at a hotel in Pittsburgh for one night several years ago. Christmas, maybe. Lucy had been passing through and whatever the reason, maybe it was the holiday, her mother suggested they meet for the night. The fact that her mother had been willing to drive the two hours north from West Virginia had made Lucy feel guilty enough to change her plans for the one-night layover.

"That's quite an impressive display," Sheila said, pulling Lucy from her thoughts.

"Thanks," she mumbled. Maybe her mother had done something right, and she should make an effort too.

"Okay, dice up the onion and red pepper and sauté them in chicken broth. Add a bit of these spices," Sheila explained as she pulled the spices from the cabinet and set them on the counter. "These are plum tomatoes. Dice them and add them last. Let it simmer until the tomatoes are the consistency you want. It's the best tomato soup you'll ever have or you can add ground beef or turkey and make it into chili."

"That sounds delicious," Lucy said sincerely. She really didn't know how to cook, but it sounded easy enough.

Sheila smiled, stopping at the door and turning. "Can we expect you for dinner Saturday night?"

"Well, uh, sure, I guess." Having a few friends wouldn't hurt, she supposed. Especially since she wasn't around much. It would be hard for them to become a nuisance.

"Great," Sheila said, ignoring Lucy's hesitation. "Come on over anytime, but we'll eat about six."

Lucy nodded. "I'll see you then."

She watched Sheila climb into the UTV and drive away. Even though she had just met them, she had to admit she liked Sheila and Karen already and a part of her was looking forward to dinner with them. Having friends was not something she indulged in, especially moving as much as she did. It felt good to put down roots, and friends were a good way of doing that. Besides anyone who kept a donkey like Bogarts around must be okay.

CHAPTER FIVE

Dex leaned against the railing on the balcony and gazed down at the glimmering blue water below her. Normally the draw of a refreshing pool would have her neck-deep within minutes, but one too many screams from the abundance of children was pushing her away. She flipped a page on the hotel directory, which showed nearby attractions, and took another sip of the caramel macchiato she had grabbed in the lobby on her way in. Eastern Airlines's contract with Marriott ensured she always had a clean, comfortable room. Usually they were booked at the lower ends of the chain, but the airline did splurge when necessary to keep them close to the airport.

On the way to the hotel, she had been surprised by the willingness of the cab driver to swing through the drive-through so she could get one of the famous cheeseburgers she had heard so much about. Maybe it helped that she bought one for him too. She wasn't a picky eater, but the juicy burger had been delicious. She especially liked the luxury of eating in her room. Balancing her burger bag, coffee, and suitcase had been a challenge, but it was well worth the peace and quiet.

If she wanted to she could spend most of the next morning exploring Los Angeles, but it made her too nervous to do something like that before work. With a noon departure to Albuquerque before heading back to Atlanta, she didn't want to risk getting caught in traffic too far away from the airport. Tonight would be her best option for seeing the sights. She closed the directory and quickly changed into shorts, a T-shirt, and running shoes. Walking a short distance from the hotel, she purchased a ticket for the Ocean Express Trolley. Manhattan Beach looked like a nice place to explore.

The trolley was a bright, cheery red and decked inside and out to look like a real old-fashioned trolley. Inside, wooden benches running along both sides faced the center where there was plenty of standing room if it was needed. Only three people were riding when she boarded, two male teenagers in swimsuits whom she wished were still in school and an elderly lady. The lady wore a purple and white cover-up over her swimsuit and clutched a large beach bag on her lap. The boys sat in the rear, laughing and occasionally punching each other. She sat near the front with the lady to avoid their frolicking. She clung to the brass pole at the edge of the seat to keep from sliding back and forth on the slick bench.

She was the first one off the trolley and the smell of salt water invaded her senses. The long stretch of sandy, white beach was inviting and she almost wished she had worn her swimsuit. Next time. The number of people around was surprisingly low. Not at all what she was expecting. She walked the length of the pier, carefully avoiding the men and women fishing from the end. From the pier she could see bike and walking paths stretching in both directions, miles and miles of barely populated pavement. After only a few minutes walking along the path, she ditched her coffee cup and rented a bicycle, riding south to the end of the trail and then back north as far as Marina Del Ray.

The white concrete bike path was separate from the walking and jogging lanes so she only had to dodge an occasional pedestrian. The view was amazing in either direction and her attention was split between it and the piles of sand on the path that threatened to pitch her from the bike. Huge, million-dollar houses lined the beachfront along with smaller condominiums and a few camping parks. The beach side was filled with sunbathers, swimmers, and volleyball players. Riding along the path was tranquil, and she was able to leave the occasional screaming children behind rather quickly.

She wished she could go farther and see Venice Beach and Santa Monica, but the bicycle rental office would be closing soon. Not to mention her skin was turning pink from the sun, reminding her, way too late, that she had forgotten to put on any suntan lotion. She returned her rental and found a drugstore, where she purchased aloe lotion to apply after her shower. She caught the trolley back to the Marriott and was settled back in her room by ten p.m.

She enjoyed the luxury of no alarm clock the next morning before taking a quick swim in the pool. The area was quiet and absent of children at this hour, so she was able to swim a couple of laps without interruption. After a quick brunch in her room, she headed back to the airport. She had flown with Carlos from New York to Los Angeles but had heard a rumor before leaving the office the previous night that she would be flying with Captain Mueller this morning. She hoped the rumor was true. Miranda Mueller was on the verge of retirement and had flown with Eastern since its creation eighteen years earlier. She was the first female pilot Eastern had hired and Dex had enjoyed learning about her career during her training.

She arrived at the airport almost two hours before her flight. The time change had her awake before nine Pacific Time so she felt like she had already been awake for a day. She checked the flight manifest as soon as she arrived and saw she would be flying with Captain Mueller as far as Albuquerque. Her eyes quickly scanned the rest of the list, locating the names of the two air marshals flying with them. She knew how unlikely it would be to see Lucy's name, but she couldn't stop herself from checking.

The Transportation Security Administration, otherwise known as TSA, would not release the exact number of air marshals, but they liked to brag about how many were actually in the air each day. The number sounded large, but when you compared it to the number of flights it amounted to an estimated barely one percent. Most were larger international flights, but some covered planes flying in and out of major hubs. Eastern was one of the three largest airlines operating in the US. With over eight hundred active planes, they flew almost five thousand flights a day. Combine that total with all airlines and she was looking at about forty thousand commercial flights a day. Finding Lucy again was starting to look like finding a needle in a haystack.

"Good morning."

She turned at the voice behind her and smiled at Miranda Mueller. "Good afternoon, for those of us based on the East Coast."

Miranda gave her an acknowledging nod. "Have you reviewed the flight reports yet?"

"I didn't pull anything but the weather. Looks like a little turbulence over the Midwest but it's clear into Albuquerque."

Miranda nodded again as she pulled the flight packet from her in-box and began flipping through it. "Everything looks in order. Our plane has just touched down. Shall we head that direction?"

Dex quickly fell into step beside her. She was glad she had been ready with coffee in hand before Miranda arrived. She glanced at her as they walked through the airport. Miranda was several inches taller than her even with the flat-heeled shoes she wore. She had her own class of style. The Eastern Airlines pants and blazer she wore had clearly been altered to fit her figure. Her dark hair had a few gray strands, but that was the only sign that she had reached sixty several years earlier.

Miranda's career had started with an extremely wealthy father who believed his daughter could do whatever she set her mind to, including flying airplanes. He spared no expense with her education and possibly lining whatever executive pockets were necessary to put Miranda in the cockpit. Miranda had flown with a few different airlines before finding her home at

Eastern. Her forty years of experience made Dex feel young and inexperienced. She found it sad that the travelers they passed had no idea of the icon in their midst.

"So you're new," Miranda stated.

"Uh, yes." Interrupted from her replay of Miranda's life, she struggled to find her words. "Uh, yes, ma'am."

Miranda laughed. "Please call me Miranda. At my age, you hear ma'am way too much."

"You can call me Dex."

Miranda tilted her head. "Military nickname?"

She felt her face blush as she realized Miranda had looked into her background. She guessed that was understandable since she was new.

"It's a combination of my first name, Diane, and my last name, Alexander. My dad thought it was cute when I was little, but I think he really just wanted a boy."

"Don't they all?"

She wanted to ask Miranda more questions about flying planes in the seventies, but they had arrived at the gate and it appeared the attendants had been watching for them. Dex stood back as Miranda joked with them, waiting as they unlocked the jetway door. Miranda was friendly with a sophisticated style. Classy. Yes, that was the only word Dex could think of to describe the woman walking in front of her. The way she walked and interacted with others gave her a magnetic appeal. Everyone wanted to have her attention if only for a few moments. She looked forward to having Miranda to herself in the cockpit for the next several hours.

"You good with outside?" Miranda asked. "I'll head in and get started."

"Yes, sure. That's fine. I can handle it."

She left Miranda standing in the airplane doorway and trotted down the steps to reach the tarmac. She hoped before she returned to the cockpit that she would regain her ability to have a conversation rather than stuttering and rambling. She slowly began walking around the plane. A quick look underneath told her there were no fluid leaks coming from the plane. Running her hand along the smooth, cool aluminum and steel, she focused her thoughts on the job ahead.

She checked the turbine blades to make sure there was no damage and that they spun freely. She looked between the tires at the brake wear indicator and then checked the tread on the tires. So far so good. All the hatches except the luggage storage were closed and the little wicks along the plane wings that drained static electricity and prevented a large static discharge were all in place. She checked the vents in the rear of the plane to make sure they could expel air properly once the engines began passing it through to the cockpit and the passenger cabin. She finished her checks and then spent a few minutes walking around the plane as she enjoyed the warm Los Angeles weather.

She liked living on the East Coast and the humidity wasn't too stifling if she stayed in the northeast. She had grown up in Michigan, but her family had moved around every few years. Her mother wanted to be near the ocean and her father seemed to have a wandering spirit. Together they had drug their family through six states before settling near Ocean City, Maryland. Her mother had passed away during her early years in the military and her father had moved back to his native Canada. He claimed it was because he wanted to, but she had soon learned it was for the universal health care. Neither she nor her sister could have foreseen how fast his condition would deteriorate. Apparently their mother had hid more than her illness from them.

Dex's sister, Deidra, had followed their father to Canada and now had her own family settled outside Toronto. It seemed right that Dex return to Canada as well when she left the army. Her small condominium in Toronto wasn't really home, but it was comfortable and in the snowy season everything she needed was available in the underground mall beneath it. She didn't even own a vehicle. Public transportation took her everywhere she needed to be, and if it didn't Deidra was only a phone call away.

She climbed the steps, slowly clearing her mind to everything but the task of flying. She wanted to be focused and efficient so Miranda would have no doubt Eastern had invested well. She tossed her coffee cup in the trash as she made a last pit stop in the restroom before heading to the cockpit. She greeted the flight attendants and then joined Miranda. Secured behind their cockpit door, they completed their paperwork and pre-flight checks. The passengers boarded quickly and before she knew it they were in the air.

Miranda relaxed back into her seat. "Nice work."

She smiled. "Thanks. You too." She hesitated for a second and realized she might never have another chance to talk freely with this woman. "It's a pleasure to fly with you."

Miranda chuckled. "Thank you. I can't imagine that this is the most exciting flight of your career, especially with your background."

Dex shrugged. She didn't want to talk about her past. She wanted to explore Miranda's history. "What was it like when you began flying?"

"Besides scratching and clawing the administration?"

"Were they worse than the close-minded men you flew with?"

Miranda chuckled again. "Sometimes. Even though I was in the co-pilot seat I was asked by senior level management not to make the PA announcements. They were afraid the general public would be afraid to know a woman was flying the plane."

"Wow." Dex couldn't think of anything else to say.

* * *

Lucy was drinking her coffee on the porch when the contractor arrived at seven. The sun was barely peeking through the morning sky, but she could already feel its warmth. While summer was fading in Florida, the nights were seldom below seventy. She propped open the front door and watched as Dan carried his supplies inside. Her design for the laundry room was simple—a table to fold clothes on and a bar for ones that needed to be hung, along with a few shelves for supplies.

Dan would be replacing the drywall and laying down a new floor. She had learned during his first day working for her that he didn't like to be watched or even helped. She thought he might have a touch of Attention Deficit Disorder. The way he jumped from one task to another would have driven her insane, but it seemed to work for him. It was probably why he didn't have an assistant helping him. In the end, he had finished every task and done an excellent job. She couldn't have been happier with the finished product or the time it took him to complete them.

"Morning, Dan. Coffee?" she asked as he made his third trip past her.

"No thank you. Had a cup on the way in."

"Okay. Let me know if you need anything."

"Roger that," he said, disappearing into the laundry room.

Lucy sat back down on the porch and finished her coffee. She leaned against the step behind her as she thought about a future living in this house. She had always lived in the moment, never really planning for tomorrow. Watching how distraught her mother had been after she lost Lucy's dad, she quickly decided that planning a future and losing it was more painful than never planning one. The therapist she saw in college would have said she was projecting her mother's loss on her own life. And maybe she was, but she couldn't see a reason to risk it anyway.

She did get lonely sometimes, which was why she sought out women, but they never really filled the emptiness. She had considered getting a dog, but leaving it constantly would be hard on her and no life for the dog. A few of her fellow marshals had cats and she had heard their horror stories. Coming home to a urine-stained bed or clawed-up furniture was not something she could tolerate. In fact, it was almost worse than sharing a house with someone, and she hadn't done that since college.

Except during her air marshal training, that is. There were only four women in her class of fifty. So, for eight weeks at the Federal Law Enforcement Training Center in New Mexico, she had shared a bathroom with another woman. Thankfully they each had their own small, attached bedroom.

The training centered on basic law enforcement techniques and included a lot of physical exercise. She had used her exhaustion as an excuse to close her door every evening and block the others out. Was she sorry she had never cultivated even a friendship? Not really. Okay, maybe sometimes. People wanting to get to know her stressed her out. The thousands of strangers in an airport were okay, though. They didn't care who she was and didn't even want to know. They didn't ask questions about her past or her career. She could make up any story she wanted to about what she did for a living. And she didn't have to pretend to care about someone else's life drama.

She pushed herself off the steps. Analyzing her life was not something she needed to do today. She gathered her paint supplies and began applying protectant to the porch. By noon she was starving, so she threw the ingredients Sheila had suggested into a pot and let it cook. She enjoyed the first dish so much she had a second and then took a bowl to Dan. She had never really cooked much so she didn't have much confidence when she was in the kitchen. Sheila's recipe had been easy and certainly worth the small amount of effort it had taken to create it.

She finished the porch late in the afternoon and wandered around outside until Dan finished. After he left, she stood in her new laundry room and admired his work. The shelves were all accessible and held everything she needed them to. The floor was a white and gray tile that matched the light gray walls. She grabbed her dirty laundry from the bedroom and started the washer. Occasionally she would be called in early for work, so she went ahead and packed her suitcase for another five days. After eating the last of the tomato soup, she made popcorn and started an old DVD. She liked the no-brainer comedy from twenty years ago, and Sandra Bullock was the perfect date for the evening.

* * *

"Thank you, Miranda," Dex said as she pocketed the card with Miranda's cell number on it. "I really enjoyed our conversation."

"I did as well. Don't let the few close-minded people in this industry scare you off. You are perfect for this job."

Dex smiled. Miranda had heaped praise on her throughout the flight, and she found it hard not to school-girl crush on the amazing woman. Miranda gave her a wave as she headed to lunch. Dex returned to the airline office to gather the details for her flight to Atlanta. She tried not to be disappointed by Tom, the gray-haired man she was being teamed with for this leg of her trip. He seemed nice enough and didn't try to micromanage her tasks. It was all she could really ask for. Not every pilot could be Miranda Mueller.

The flight to Albuquerque had been quicker than she would have liked, her time with Miranda making it seem much faster than it really was. Miranda was a wealth of knowledge. Not only about their colleagues but also about the airplanes they flew. They weighed the pros and cons of each aircraft and joked about the experiences Miranda had been faced with. She realized quickly that Miranda liked to laugh and Dex knew she would be smiling for a while.

She turned her attention back to Tom. He was no Miranda Mueller, but he was efficient. He was also nosy. Once they were in the air and the cruise control was set, he began a barrage of personal questions. She quickly invented a spouse and pushed every question back to him. She had discovered quickly in the military that most guys backed off quicker if she mentioned a male spouse rather than saying she wasn't into men. Each one always believed they could be the one who changed her.

She sighed as the airplane finally touched down in Atlanta. The conversation with Tom had exhausted her, and she couldn't wait to get to her hotel. It was almost midnight and she blamed jetlag as she quickly signed out in the Eastern Airlines office. She left Tom checking out the other women in the office and hurried through the airport, her mind flashing to Lucy as she passed the gate they might have met at.

She replayed the thoughts she had had that night. Clearly Lucy had chosen not to meet and to not even share an explanation. If there had been any interest at all, she would have offered something. Maybe Lucy had a partner. Or maybe Dex's gaydar was off and Lucy was straight. Though she didn't think so. Or at least, she hoped not. Her mock chivalry had been adorable and was perhaps one of the things that had endeared her to Dex.

Frustrated for not ridding herself of the hold this stranger had on her, she forced herself to avoid searching the faces of every passerby for Lucy's as she left the airport. Grabbing a cab on the curb, she gave the driver the hotel information and settled in the seat. She couldn't believe it, but she was looking forward to getting back to her little condo in Toronto tomorrow.

CHAPTER SIX

Lucy dried her hair with a towel as she danced around her bedroom. She wasn't sure why she was excited to visit Sheila and Karen, but she was. Maybe it was time for her to make some friends; this would be a good test for her.

She grabbed her phone as it rang and glanced at the display. She agonized for a moment and then swiped to accept the call.

"Hi, Mom. What's up?"

"Only checking on you."

"I'm fine." She hopped on one foot as she slid her leg into cargo shorts.

"How's the new house?"

"Fine."

An uncomfortable silence stretched between them. Was her mom looking for an invitation to visit? She definitely wasn't ready for that.

"And the remodeling?"

"Almost finished."

"I could help decorate if you want."

She hesitated. Her mother did want to visit. She resisted the urge to ask why.

"I'm good. Besides it's really small. Only one bedroom."

"Okay. Well, if you change your mind I could stay in Madison. They have a few hotels."

She hesitated again. Apparently her mother had already looked at hotels in the area. Why? Why was her mother reaching out to her now?

"I'm headed out again tomorrow," she lied. "And I'm not sure how long I'll be gone this time. Maybe when I know I'll be home for a few days." She knew as she said it that she wouldn't invite her mother to her house, and it hurt a little to know her mother knew it too.

"Stay safe and call if you need anything." Her mother's voice faded. "Anything at all."

"Okay. Bye." Lucy disconnected the call before her mother could say anything else. Connecting with her mother was not on today's agenda, but making new friends was and she was going to be late if she didn't start walking now.

She walked the quarter mile down the road with Bogarts on the other side of the fence. Once she cleared the trees along the road and the view of the pasture opened up, he had caught sight of her. He didn't have anything to say this evening, but she occasionally stuck her arm through the fence and petted his head. He seemed to like to have his long ears scratched after he realized her hands didn't contain carrots.

Sheila met her at the door before she could even knock. "Come in."

Lucy stepped into the small mudroom and slid off her running shoes before following Sheila into a large open kitchen. Cabinets and counter space ran the length of both walls. A work area with a sink was in the middle island. Through the breakfast bar, she could see Karen at the kitchen table leaning over a laptop with a cell phone pressed to her ear.

"The food's ready and Karen should be finished soon. Would you like a drink? Alcohol or non-alcohol?"

"Non, I guess."

"Sweet tea, lemonade, or water?"

"Sweet tea is fine."

Sheila poured them both a glass and then motioned for her to follow. They stepped out onto a screened-in porch off the back of the house. A small in-ground pool was enclosed on one side and a long rectangular glass patio table was on the other. Sheila took a seat on the swing and Lucy turned around a chair at the table, sitting across from her.

"I'm sorry Karen's working, but sometimes her hours are sporadic."

"No problem." Lucy smiled. "You're very understanding."

Sheila returned her smile. "Not always, but I do try. She's doing a good thing so it's hard to fault her."

"Oh, what does she do?"

"She's a social worker. Seems there's always a kid somewhere that no one wants."

"That's a hard job. Emotionally, I mean."

"It is. That's why Karen is so good at it. She has a good heart, but she can separate herself from the pain she sees every day."

"She's lucky to have you to come home to. Karen said you work from home?"

"I do. In a former life I did website design and I still dabble a little, but mostly I tend to the farm. Animals, plants, and stuff like that."

"Hey, where's the food? I'm starving," Karen said as she stepped onto the porch. "Hi, Lucy. Glad you could make it."

"Food's waiting for you," Sheila said, standing. "Want to eat out here or in the house?"

"Out here, I think," Karen said, glancing around to make sure everyone agreed.

Lucy helped carry out the dishes of green beans, corn on the cob, coleslaw, and barbeque chicken. She listened to Sheila and Karen banter about everything from the kitchen appliances to the food preparation. It was entertaining and not at all uncomfortable. Neither woman was upset or angry nor were they short-tempered. It was easy to see they had lived together for a while.

"This all looks great," Lucy said as they sat down at the table. "Is it all from your garden?"

"Yep," Karen and Sheila said together.

Lucy laughed.

"I heard Sheila giving you the rundown on my job, so what do you do?" Karen asked, looking at Lucy.

She had already played in her head how she would answer this question. It was normally the first question people asked when they met you—after "where do you live," of course. She could lie, but if she did she would always be building on that lie. So, she took a leap of faith.

"I'm an air marshal."

Sheila raised her eyebrows. "Wow. That's not what I was expecting."

"How exciting," Karen added.

"It has its moments, but mostly it's a lot of travel."

"That explains why you're gone so much," Karen said, looking at Sheila.

Lucy caught the look that passed between them. A look that said so much without any words. A look that meant years of living together didn't require anything more than a meeting of their eyes. She considered letting it pass, but she felt the twinge of wishing she had someone to share things with. Wishing she had a friend who understood and knew her. She pushed past her normal surface acquaintance guidelines and smiled at them both. "Okay, what?"

Karen laughed. "We'd made a game out of guessing what you did for a living."

"Why would you tell her that?" Sheila groaned.

"Why not?" Karen glanced at Lucy. "It wasn't mean or anything."

"I'm not offended," Lucy said with a grin. "Tell me your guesses."

"Oh, we had everything from sales to secret agent."

"Really, Karen. You can't stop talking, can you?"

Karen gave Sheila a scathing look. "What? Lucy isn't upset and it was all in fun."

Sheila scooped a spoonful of coleslaw onto her plate and passed the dish to Karen. "Fill your mouth and then I won't have to wonder what you'll say next."

"Gladly." Karen gave her a big smile.

Lucy helped herself to some of everything and made appropriately appreciative noises. The food was really good and it wasn't hard to give many compliments.

"Having this area screened is great," Lucy commented as she enjoyed her last bite of chicken and coleslaw.

Karen shrugged and Sheila swatted her arm.

"Karen's blood is sour, so she isn't bothered by insects. I spend more than enough time battling the gnats and mosquitoes in the garden. I didn't want to continue that when I was relaxing too."

"It is nice and we spend a lot of time out here when it's cool enough," Karen added, swatting Sheila back. "And my blood's not sour. It's just I'm tougher than you are."

"Right. I'll remember that the next time we see a spider in the house."

Karen shivered. "Spiders aren't natural. Especially those little black ones with the white eyes that move in all directions. I'll take a snake outside any day to a spider."

Lucy laughed. "I don't want either so keep them over here."

"You can see our roles are clearly defined," Sheila added and then glanced at Karen checking her phone display. "Are you going back out tonight?"

"Maybe. Deputy Watkins confiscated a baby earlier, but she's still trying to decide what to do with it."

"Confiscated?" Lucy asked.

"Yep. She was called to the house for a domestic dispute. Apparently a young unmarried couple had given birth and the grandparents were fighting over the baby. Neither of the parents were present so she took the baby. She's giving them two hours to produce a birth certificate and a parent with identification. She called to give me a heads-up in case they don't show up."

"Wow. Poor kid," Lucy said.

"At least people want this kid. Normally I'm called out because there's a kid no one wants."

"What do you do?" Lucy asked. She was enjoying hearing Karen talk about her job and Sheila was starting to pass around dishes of raspberry pie with ice cream.

"There's a group home in the next county over and we have a couple locally who will take kids for a night or two in an emergency."

"And sometimes she brings them home," Sheila added.

Karen nodded. "If everywhere is full, then someone from my office will step up. It depends on the situation though. I won't bring any risk home with me. If a violent parent might show up or if the kid has violent tendencies then the sheriff's department will use a holding cell. It's a last resort, but it keeps the kid safe until we can deal with the situation."

"That's a lot of pain to deal with."

Lucy could imagine how easily she might have ended up in foster care if she had been younger when her father died. Her mother wouldn't have been able to take care of a young child. She took another bite of the warm raspberry pie with ice cream and let it dissolve in her mouth. The tartness of the berries was quickly smothered by the sweetness of the melting ice cream. "This is delicious."

"Thanks. It's because of you that I found this patch."

"Me?"

"I walked the fence line to see what Bogarts was up to when you were here last."

Lucy laughed. "Where is my buddy?"

"You can't see him from here, but he's probably already in his stall waiting for dinner. Want to go feed him?"

"Oh yeah. That would be great."

Lucy followed Sheila and Karen across the yard to a small red pole barn. Karen opened a large bin beside the fence and pulled out a cup filled with pellets. When they entered the gate and moved into Bogarts's view, he began to bray.

"He has a lot to say," Lucy observed.

"Always," Karen and Sheila said together.

He seemed happy to see them all, but the food was too hard to resist so he stuck his head in the bucket as soon as Karen dumped the cup. Lucy took the opportunity to stroke his neck without him head butting her. His fur was thicker than she expected and extremely soft.

"He's starting to grow his winter coat. Even though it doesn't get really cold here, he still grows it," Sheila explained.

"I love the shaggy look. He's adorable," Lucy said.

Apparently aware he was the topic of conversation, Bogarts pulled his head out of the bucket with a mouthful of pellets and nudged Lucy's stomach. She stroked his nose, avoiding the saliva-squished food oozing from the corners of his mouth.

"His manners are the best," Karen laughed as Lucy stepped away from his swinging head.

They left Bogarts to his dinner and walked back toward the house.

"No one else gets fed now?" Lucy asked as she glanced across the field at the other donkey and a few goats.

"No, Bogarts is special," answered Karen.

Lucy waited, expecting Karen to elaborate and was surprised when she didn't. "Should I not ask why?"

Sheila groaned. "Karen rescues everyone and everything in need, but it's a long story. We'll save it for next time."

Lucy laughed. "I'm getting invited back. Woo-hoo!"

"Of course," Karen and Sheila said together.

Lucy was sure that was at least the third time they had spoken together. She had to admit she was a little jealous of their relationship. They seemed so relaxed and comfortable with each other. The level of confidence they showed in each other and their relationship was what she admired the most. Confidence the other wouldn't leave. It was something Lucy had never had in any relationship, even with her mother. Her dad left and her mother checked out behind him. Though she had still been around, she wasn't dependable, and probably still wasn't. Lucy didn't have any confidence she would see her again, or even if she wanted to.

Lucy joined in with clearing the table even though Karen and Sheila both said no. She did leave once everything was moved into the kitchen but not before Sheila made her a to-go container. She tried to relax when they both hugged her and extracted a promise that she'd let them know when she was returning. Karen wanted to drive her home, but she refused, insisting she needed the walk after all the good food.

She waved at their silhouettes in the lighted doorway and followed the sidewalk back to the road. Two Ford vehicles, an SUV and a truck, stood outside the gate like sentries protecting the quiet home. She was surprised at how comfortable she had felt here tonight. A part of her wanted to remain inside and maybe curl up in front of the television. She understood the difference between a house and a home now.

She enjoyed the moonlit walk along the quiet road but stopped when she moved into view of her own house. She looked at it like it was the first time. It still looked a little worse for wear on the outside, but some paint would help. Her focus had been on making the inside comfortable. With everything but the kitchen finished, she looked forward to fixing up the outside on her next visit. Maybe she would get Karen's and Sheila's help picking some flowers and vegetation. Something that wouldn't need her attention on a regular basis. Something that would help make her house feel more like a home.

* * *

Dex rolled over as the ringing phone brought her out of a deep sleep.

"What?" she answered a little too harshly.

"Love you too, sis."

Deidra.

"What time is it?" Dex groaned.

"You missed breakfast with Dad. If that's what you're asking."

"I'll make it up to him with lunch. Or maybe dinner."

Deidra laughed. "I'll send Trevor to pick you up in an hour."

She groaned again, this time for multiple reasons. After being away eight years, she had missed Deidra's sons growing up and their relationship had withered. Trevor was half Deidra's age, almost twenty. He had grown from a child who loved Pokémon to an adult while she was gone. Dillon was barely seven when she left and was now in the midst of the rebellious teenager stage. She held no hope of connecting with him for a few more years.

"Dex?"

"Okay."

"Trevor still thinks you walk on water, you know?"

"Really?"

"Really. Just talk airplanes and helicopters and before you know it, you guys will be best friends again."

Dex said goodbye and disconnected the call. Now that her father, Russ, had been officially diagnosed with Alzheimer's, she wanted to see him as much as she could before he got to a point where he couldn't remember her at all. Right now, it was hit or miss and he was still able to leave the nursing home. Because of her time in the military, Dex knew she was the favorite daughter—even though Deidra had more than earned the title. Every Sunday like clockwork, Deidra made the time to pick up their father and take him to breakfast at the Senator Restaurant on Victoria Street, his favorite for as long as Dex could remember. There he'd always consume the same thing—two fried eggs and potatoes, bacon, toast, and baked beans, their specialty. Along with a cup of delicious coffee Dex longed for right at this moment. She sighed. Though it was only a short subway ride from her condo, it was too far to go if she was going to be ready before Trevor arrived.

* * *

Dex glanced over her shoulder and smiled. "Thanks for coming along for the ride, Dillon."

Unable to pull his face from the smartphone glued to his fingers, he mumbled something incomprehensible. She looked at Trevor for explanation.

"Mom told him we would stop at Tim Hortons."

Dex almost squealed with delight at the thought of visiting the Canadian version of Dunkin Donuts, with even better coffee.

"Coffee sounds great," she announced to the car.

"And a donut?" Trevor asked.

"I'll let you know when we get there."

Trevor laughed as he signaled to change lanes and take the exit. Tim Hortons wasn't too crowded and they were back on the Queen Elizabeth Way without much delay.

"How's college going?" Dex asked Trevor, seeing no hope in making conversation with Dillon. Though the younger boy had placed a donut order, his fingers continued to move across the keyboard on his phone.

"It's okay. A lot different than high school. I miss driving every day. Mom makes me ride the train."

Sheridan College, located in Oakville, Ontario, was only about twenty miles from Deidra's house in Hamilton. A thirty- to forty-minute trip on the Go train was often much faster than driving in traffic, which could take twenty minutes—or two hours.

"I know riding the train probably seems like a bore, but you don't have to find parking and you can study during the commute."

Trevor nodded his head. "Yeah, it's nice to have most of my work finished before I get home in the evening. I'm hoping to convince Mom and Dad to let me move to Oakville next fall. There isn't any student housing on campus, but I have some friends who rented a place nearby. There are six of them in the house and two will be graduating in the spring."

Dex took a sip of coffee as she listened to Trevor talk about the potential housing options and his digital animation classes. She and Trevor had had a close bond before she left for the military, and she had assumed being away eight years would diminish it. She had felt uncomfortable with the adult beside her, but she could see now that it wouldn't take much to get to know him again. He was open and social like his mother, exactly as he had been as a kid.

"How's civilian life?" Trevor asked, pulling her thoughts away from analyzing their relationship.

"I'm adapting?" she said with a chuckle.

"You were in the air this week?"

She glanced at him and he shrugged.

"I listen to Mom talk."

"I was. Atlanta, New York, LA, Albuquerque, and back to Atlanta."

"Wow, that's a whirlwind."

"I guess that's what my life is going to be now. Traveling all over but never really seeing anything." *Wow*. She hoped that didn't sound depressing to Trevor. Because she really was looking forward to her new life. It would bring a lot of opportunities her way, and she didn't have to stay with Eastern forever. Especially not if something better came along.

She sighed as Trevor turned the car into his driveway, parking in front of the two-car garage. The two-story, brick- and beige-sided house filled the one-acre lot. Deidra had wanted space inside and as little to mow outside as possible. Her husband Tony was in agreement. Deidra was born in Canada but had met Tony at Fairmont University in Michigan. It had taken little to persuade him to move to Toronto, and both were happy with their house near Lake Ontario.

Dex greeted Curly, their hyperactive cocker spaniel, at the door and then crossed to kiss her dad on the cheek. He squeezed her hand but didn't acknowledge her presence with any words. She knelt beside his chair and ran her other hand absently through Curly's fur.

"How are you feeling today, Dad?" she asked.

He grunted a response that told her today would not be filled with conversation. She had learned in the last couple of weeks that he was starting to withdraw, but his eyes still seemed to follow discussions around the dinner table. She was thankful for each day she had with him. She knew the time was coming soon when he wouldn't remember them or anything around him.

"I'm fine, Mary."

His irritated tone and the reference to her mother surprised her.

She rubbed his shoulder as she stood. "That's good."

Deidra stood by the sink in the kitchen, and Dex could tell by the flush on her face that she had been crying. She crossed the room and pulled her into a hug.

"It's been a tough morning," Deidra explained.

"I spoke with him."

"I heard." Deidra sighed, pushing Dex away. "I made him leave the television to eat lunch with Tony and me and he wasn't happy about it. I guess I annoyed him as much as Mom always did because he was calling me by her name too."

Dex took the sandwich Deidra offered and sat at the table. It was going to be a long day. Deidra sat with her and they reminisced until their eyes were filled with tears of laughter. She was thankful for her sister and remembered to tell her that many times before Deidra dropped her off at her condo that evening.

CHAPTER SEVEN

Lucy had to admit she was a little relieved to be returning to work. Four days off had been nice but also long. Keeping her mind occupied took more than keeping herself busy. This week's assignments would take her to New York, to Florida, back to Atlanta, and then to Paris with a one-day layover. Unfortunately that would be her time off between workweeks and then she would return to Atlanta to start a new week. Still, she enjoyed international flights, especially if she wasn't too tired to see a little of the city she landed in.

For speed and convenience, she parked in visitor parking and walked through the glass doors into the Atlanta Air Marshals office. She showed her badge to the officer at the reception desk and passed into the secure area. The room was painted a horrifying shade of yellow-beige and white cubicle dividers were crammed into every available space. She acknowledged the few faces that were familiar and made her way to her desk. She quickly cleared the paperwork from her in-box and logged into her email. There was nothing pertaining to her current assignments, so she cleared the spam and left the rest to read later.

She knocked on Deputy Avila's open door and stepped inside. His black hair was peppered with gray, but the tight T-shirt he was wearing displayed his fit upper body. An impeccably pressed suit hung on the coatrack behind him waiting for him to officially begin his day. Over the years, Lucy had gotten used to seeing him in the office hours before his schedule demanded. As he had when he was her training officer, he always made a point of knowing where and when she was on the job.

"Headed out?" he asked, looking up from the paperwork covering his desk.

"Yes, sir."

"Okay, have a good week. Don't forget you have a week of vacation that you need to use before the end of the year."

"There's still plenty of time. I'll plan it later."

He grunted and gave her a dismissing wave.

Returning to her car, she thought about when she might take her vacation time. Between Thanksgiving and Christmas was a busy time for travel, and there was a significant uptick in the number of flights. She preferred to receive a monetary payment instead of taking the time off, but she seldom said that out loud because few people really understood that. With her new place, though, she had a need for time off so she could do her kitchen remodel. She could feel the muscles in her neck and back begin to relax as she thought about what she could do with vacation leave.

She parked in long-term Lot C and rode the bus to the departure terminal. Finally settled at her gate, she surveyed the crowd already waiting and took a seat with her back to the wall. She pulled out her iPad and opened the romance novel she had been saving for a long workweek. Inside the airport terminal she could lose herself in the words of her favorite authors and not worry about anything happening around her. She was only another passenger until she stepped on to the plane. That's what protocol said, anyway. For her, work began when she arrived at her departure gate. Anything that happened here wouldn't be her responsibility, but she could still be observant and watch for suspicious behavior.

There had been great controversy several years after two air marshals failed to assist a TSA officer who was shot inside the airport and later died. The marshals involved had followed their training, which emphasized avoiding airport disturbances. They were instructed to leave all disputes to local police officers in order to maintain their anonymity. She tried not to second-guess other marshals' decisions because it was hard to know how she would react until placed in any given situation. She always tried to follow basic human instincts, though, even if it drew attention to her. If someone needed assistance anywhere outside of a plane and she could offer it, then she would.

A man's voice rose above the usual crowd chatter and Lucy glanced down the row of seats in front of her to locate him. The man wore gym shorts, flip-flops, and a T-shirt that barely covered his emerging stomach. His words were directed at a woman in a sundress seated beside him. She didn't seem concerned at his tone or elevation of his voice so Lucy discarded him as a threat.

Her eyes moved next to the travelers closest to her—a gray-haired man in a business suit, a teenager in polka-dotted pants that could only be sleepwear, and a woman in jeans and cowboy boots. She often played a game of trying to determine where people were traveling to and from based on their clothing. She knew in the past there had been a dress code for flying but in the last ten years she had watched the level of what was considered appropriate drop precipitously. Now it seemed anything was acceptable.

She herself seldom wore anything other than jeans and a major league baseball shirt. She had begun collecting T-shirts representing the local team in each city she passed through and now it was kind of her trademark. Like Mason, she could put on a ball cap for quick disguises if she needed to or pull her hair into a ponytail, but the real talent of doing her job was to remain under the radar. To look like every other passenger and disappear into the background. She always carried a business suit as well in case she ended up on a back-to-back flight that might reveal or allay suspicion about her identity. She had had only a few occasions where another passenger had recognized her. Her fake professional story for other passengers, which always centered on a job with lots of travel, usually fixed that.

She nodded at the gate agent as he scanned her ticket. The flight to LaGuardia wouldn't take long, and she would be in Orlando for the night. She would have most of the morning to enjoy the sun and warmth and then a short flight back to Atlanta. Another hotel and then an early morning flight to Charles de Gaulle Airport in Paris. Sometime in the next forty-eight hours she would do some research and identify the sights she would like to see while in Paris. Over the years, she had exhausted most of the popular tourist attractions in all major cities. Now she looked for something off the beaten path. Something only a local would know about. Fortunately for her that sometimes required a local tour guide. Finding the perfect one was part of the fun.

Once in the air, she finished her usual routine of checking out the surrounding passengers and then made her trip to the restroom in the rear of the plane. Thomas Ballard, her coworker, was working a crossword puzzle in the very last row. There was no one in the single seat beside him and he gave her a nod as she passed.

When she returned to her seat, she placed her earbuds in her ears and opened her magazine. She shifted in her seat so the leather pistol holster slid comfortably into that perfect spot in the small of her back. She looked up when the flight attendant stopped beside her seat.

"The captain would like to see you," she whispered, leaning close.

Lucy frowned. She knew this wasn't an Eastern Airlines flight, but she couldn't stop her heart from racing. Was Dex behind the controls of this plane? Was she being summoned by her? She stood, placing her magazine in her empty seat, and followed the flight attendant to the front of the plane. Another flight attendant slid the beverage cart across the aisle, blocking all passengers from the front of the plane.

The flight attendant knocked on the cockpit door and it opened immediately. The uniformed man ducked his head as he stepped through the door. He nodded to the flight attendant and then addressed Lucy.

"Marshal Donovan? I'm Tim."

"Lucy's fine."

"Okay, Lucy. Here's the situation. A suspicious package has been found at the gate we just pulled away from. Airport security has cleared the area and they're waiting for the bomb-sniffing dogs to arrive."

"Any identification on it?"

"Not yet."

"So we're in standby mode. Are they making us return?"

"I'm pushing not to." He motioned toward the cockpit. "We're both at the edge of flying time and won't be able to depart again."

She nodded. She didn't want to return either, but her priority was passenger safety. Being back on the ground would allow her more options. "Can I talk with someone on the ground?"

"Sure. We'll connect you with Captain Terry from the Atlanta Police Department. He's the incident commander." He turned to the flight attendant standing nearby. "Meredith, can you connect her with Captain Terry?"

"Of course." She turned her back to them and picked up the wall phone. After a few minutes, she handed the phone to Lucy. "Captain Terry."

"Thank you." Lucy followed Meredith's example and leaned forward into the wall to shield her conversation.

"Hello, Captain Terry?"

"Yes."

"This is Lucy Donovan. I'm one of the air marshals on Flight 2406. Can you give me an update?"

"Of course. I was about to contact you. We were able to zoom in on the luggage tag with binoculars. It's labeled as belonging to a Beatrice Meyers. My bomb squad is moving in now so I haven't had a chance to check your manifest. I'll call you back in a few once they clear it."

"Okay. Thanks."

She hung up the phone and faced the captain and flight attendant. She looked at their eager faces while she considered her options.

"Can I see the flight manifest?"

"You have a name?" Tim asked.

"I do. Beatrice Meyers."

Tim caught himself before he laughed out loud. "That's a terrorist name if I've ever heard one."

Meredith flipped through the printed pages. "Seat 31C. It's on the aisle," she said unnecessarily.

"Anyone else on the plane with the same last name?" Lucy asked.

"Nope. Nothing to identify anyone flying with her."

"Or him. Keep an open mind," Lucy reminded her.

Meredith had already prepped both carts and was clearly getting impatient to begin the drink and snack service.

Lucy continued. "Keep the cockpit blocked. I'm going to talk with my colleague, Marshal Ballard. I'll be back in a minute. If Captain Terry calls back, let me know."

Meredith nodded as she slid the beverage cart to the side enough for Lucy to pass. She stopped at her seat and opened the overhead compartment. She stuck her hand in her bag and pretended to be looking for something. Then she closed the compartment and headed for the restroom. She counted the rows so she didn't have to look up at the seat tags overhead.

Beatrice Meyers appeared to be in her seventies. Her gray hair was piled on top of her head and the glasses she wore were perched at the end of her nose. She was pulling yarn from a bundle and rolling it into a ball. Her seatmate was a female and in her twenties. Thomas was still alone in the last row and didn't even look up when she stopped in the aisle outside the restroom. She mumbled loudly about how long people took in the restroom, even though it wasn't occupied.

"Excuse me, sir. Do you mind if I sit while I wait?" she asked Thomas.

"That's fine," he grunted.

She sat down beside him and leaned back in the seat, slouching down behind the seat in front of her. She leaned toward Thomas and, speaking softly, filled him in on the situation. "I'm going to pass her and then come back. I want to get her isolated now. If she comes with me without a fight, hold your position."

"Okay. I'll keep eyes on you. Motion if you need me."

Lucy took a deep breath. She wasn't going to assume this little old lady was anything but a threat to her and the safety of everyone on board. At least until she knew otherwise. She passed 31C and then turned.

"Ms. Meyers?"

The woman looked up at her with a quizzical look. "Yes, yes, I am."

"There's been a mistake in the seating arrangements. You're supposed to be in first class and I'm supposed to be in your seat. The flight attendant said we should switch so their passenger list is correct."

"Oh no, honey. You go ahead and stay up there. I don't care where I sit."

She shrugged. "It's for safety reasons, you know."

She had made a quick assumption that Beatrice wouldn't be the type of woman to want to break the rules.

"Oh, well, in that case, I guess we better do as they asked. Which seat are you in?" Beatrice asked as she stuffed her yarn into the bag she held between her feet.

"Just follow me. I'll show you."

Lucy glanced behind her as she made her way to the area between business class and first class. She stopped at the boarding door and quickly closed both curtains blocking the view into the space from each cabin.

She turned and faced Beatrice, quickly pulling her badge from her pocket and holding it up. "Ms. Meyers, I'm US Air Marshal Donovan. Can I ask you a few questions?"

"Of course," Beatrice said, blinking several times before becoming wide-eyed. "I'm very sorry. Have I done something wrong? I'll move right now to the seat you requested."

Ignoring her question, Lucy moved right to the matter at hand.

"What's your final destination?"

"Little Rock, Arkansas."

"Who are you visiting?"

"My granddaughter and her family."

"When was the last time you visited them?"

"It's been almost a year. Right before Christmas. Really, what have I done wrong? I'll make it right. Whatever it is?" Beatrice's voice was starting to quiver.

"It's okay, Ms. Meyer. I only have one more question. When was the last time you took a flight?"

"When I went to see Amy last year. She's my granddaughter."

Lucy stood. Instinct told her Beatrice wasn't a terrorist trying to blow up the Atlanta airport. She didn't want Thomas to identify himself, but protocol dictated she keep Beatrice under surveillance until the officers on the ground cleared the bag. She moved the curtain and motioned for Thomas to join her. Without introducing the two of them, she asked Beatrice to take a seat in the rear of the plane with him. Once again, Beatrice followed without asking questions.

Meredith was waiting for her when she returned and slid the cart to the side again, allowing her to pass.

"Captain Terry," she said, handing the phone to Lucy again.

"Captain?" she asked.

"Lucy. Are you ready for this?"

She heard laughing in the background. Even though she was anxious to hear what the captain would say, she waited patiently for him to clear his throat.

"Vibrating bedroom slippers!"

"What?" Lucy asked. Not sure she had heard him correctly.

"Yep. You heard me right. We just cleared the airport for vibrating bedroom slippers."

"Okay, Captain. Thank you for the update. We're all clear then, right?"

"Carry on. Have a good flight."

"Thanks." She hung up the phone and motioned to the cockpit. "Just buzz him. He doesn't have to come out for this."

When Tim answered the phone, she quickly relayed the information. She could still hear him laughing as she hung up the phone. She made her way back to Thomas's seat and knelt in front of Beatrice.

"Are you missing a bag, Ms. Meyers?"

"Well, I don't believe so."

"The Atlanta Police Department believe they found a bag belonging to you at our gate at the airport."

"Oh my. Is that what this is about? I thought I had it." Beatrice stood. "Can I check?"

Lucy knew she didn't have it, but it was best to let Beatrice confirm this information on her own. There was absolutely no reason to argue or put any additional stress on the woman. "Of course."

Lucy followed her back to her seat and helped her open the compartment above her seat.

"Oh my, it's not here! And I bought new massage slippers just for this trip." She turned to Lucy. "How will I get them?"

"Contact your airline and they'll be able to make arrangements to get it back to you."

"Okay. Thank you, dear," Beatrice said, collapsing into her seat. "Oh, wait. Do I still have to change seats?"

Lucy laughed. "No, you're fine here."

Beatrice sighed and immediately pulled the yarn ball from her bag. She seemed to find comfort in the winding motion and Lucy left her explaining to her seatmate how her slippers were lost at the Atlanta airport. She was pretty sure Beatrice had no idea how airport security reacted to an unattended bag.

She gave Thomas an all-clear wave and headed back to her seat. She would fill him in later. It was one of those humorous stories that would be told for years. She casually glanced around at the other passengers. No one seemed interested in what she had been doing, and she settled back into her seat right as the beverage cart reached her. A cold Coke over ice and a few pretzels later, her stomach was finally beginning to settle. An interruption to a quiet day was nice now and then, but she was looking forward to getting to the hotel later that night.

* * *

Dex listened to the automated voice count down their height above ground level as she pushed the button to slow the Boeing 737. She was more than a little excited about her first landing at the Charles de Gaulle Airport in Paris. She had hoped to see the Eiffel Tower from the air, but Rick had informed her that wasn't possible coming in from the US. Some flights leaving to the south would fly over the city and have a view of the tower, but for her coming in and out wouldn't provide that opportunity.

Rick Portis gently touched the wheels of the airplane to the runway and guided it to the directed gate. He was a few years younger than Dex and single. She knew this because she had spent the last four thousand four hundred and forty miles fending off his advances. He wasn't shy about his desires but had been extremely careful to remain slightly above the sexual harassment line. He wasn't the first man to pursue her, but Dex wasn't sure she would ever get used to it.

She quickly left the cockpit before Rick had removed his headset. Standing in the doorway, she greeted the passengers as they departed, wishing them a pleasant stay in Paris. When everyone had exited and the cleaning crew had boarded, she grabbed her bag and gave Rick a wave. As the senior officer, Rick would handle most of the paperwork, but Dex carried her portion with her. She wasn't willing to spend another minute alone with him inside the cockpit. Once they were inside the Eastern Airlines office, they would be surrounded by others and Rick would be on his best behavior.

An hour later, Dex closed the door on the airline office and swung her bag over her shoulder. Two days in the great city of Paris. She was really looking forward to seeing the Eiffel Tower in person. Her only regret was that she would be alone in the "City of Love." An image of Lucy flashed in front of her again and she shook it away. The chance of anything ever existing between them was nonexistent and she was starting to come to terms with that truth.

Her gaze swept over a woman sitting alone at an empty gate. Her head was bent over the device she held in her hands. As Dex passed her, something inside her stirred. *Was that Lucy?* She slowed her pace. *Unbelievable!* Now she was imagining she saw this fantasy woman everywhere she went. She needed to get laid. She hated to admit it, but that's really what she needed. Something that would curb this insatiable desire that kept rising up in her. She lengthened her stride and picked up her pace.

After a few steps, she slowed to a stop. She couldn't walk away without knowing for sure that wasn't Lucy. She quickly walked back to the gate. The woman in a navy blue Milwaukee Brewers T-shirt and faded jeans still sat there alone. Dex stood for a second watching her, trying to decide if she was prepared to make a fool out of herself to confirm this wasn't the woman of her dreams.

"Lucy?" Dex asked as she approached. She froze as her eyes met Lucy's. "Please tell me you just arrived."

Lucy shook her head.

"Do you remember me?"

Lucy shook her head again, but Dex could see the recognition in her face.

"When do you leave?"

Lucy glanced at her watch and back at Dex. "In about two hours."

Dex took a step back. What was she supposed to do now? Here was her chance to connect with Lucy, but she couldn't help remembering that Lucy had blown her off the first time she had tried. Maybe the interest was completely one-sided. How much was she willing to risk to find out?

She took a deep breath. It was now or never. "Look, I know you say you don't know me—"

"And yet you know my name."

"I looked at the passenger manifest." Dex stopped talking. Why was she explaining? Clearly she was the only one who wanted to pursue anything. She turned her back to Lucy and then quickly spun back again.

Lucy stood in front of her with a devilish grin on her face.

Dex had never acted on impulse with a woman and she certainly didn't kiss them without an invitation, but at the moment kissing Lucy—pressing her lips to the pink succulent ones on the adorable face right in front of her—was all she could think about.

"Come with me," she said as she grasped Lucy's arm and pulled her through a set of double doors into a maintenance hallway. Relieved to find it empty, she turned to face Lucy, dropping her bag at her feet. She pushed Lucy against the wall and elatedly fulfilled her desire.

At the first contact of their lips, Lucy gasped and pushed Dex away. Her brown eyes flashed as she studied Dex's face. A second passed and then she placed a hand behind Dex's head and pulled their lips together again.

Dex surrendered to the pressure of Lucy's lips as their kiss deepened. She had never felt the instant arousal that now engulfed her. Her hands slid under Lucy's jacket and found the warm flesh between her jeans and T-shirt.

Lucy pushed her away again. "I don't sleep with pilots," she stated.

Dex chuckled softly. "So you do remember me."

Lucy's face spread into the grin that made Dex's heart race as she looked Dex up and down.

Dex blushed as she realized she was still wearing her uniform. "Can I get your number?"

Lucy shook her head. "I don't sleep with pilots and I don't do relationships." She pushed open one of the doors and turned back before stepping through. "And I can see that *you* are both of those." Lucy let the door fall closed behind her.

Dex collapsed against the wall and sucked in a breath. Kissing Lucy had been everything she had imagined. How could anyone walk away so easily after that? Remembering Lucy's flashing brown eyes, she knew she wasn't the only one who had felt the fire between them. She picked up her bag, sliding the strap over her shoulder, and pushed through the doors. She resisted the urge to look toward the departure gates, instead striding in the opposite direction. With two days alone in the City of Love, how was she supposed to forget the most passionate kiss of her life?

* * *

Lucy darted into the closest family bathroom and quickly locked the door behind her. She needed a few minutes to catch her breath without the risk that Dex could follow her. She dropped her bag on the floor and leaned over the sink. Splashing cold water on her face, she ran her wet fingers through her hair. She looked up and stared into the mirror, looking into her own eyes. Dex had really done a number on her. It was only a kiss. "Only a kiss," she chanted softly to herself.

After a few minutes, she threw the strap of her bag over her shoulder and left the restroom. She didn't look around to see if Dex was waiting. She knew her resistance wouldn't survive another encounter. She went straight to her gate and buried her face in her iPad. No romance novel this time. She needed a nice murder mystery with lots of blood and guts.

CHAPTER EIGHT

Dex leaned her head against the back of the couch and ran her fingers through Curly's fur, watching her dad sleeping in the recliner across from her. At a glance, a stranger wouldn't realize there was anything wrong with him. He looked healthy, though she could see he had dropped a few pounds in the three weeks since she had last seen him.

Deidra squeezed her shoulder as she dropped onto the cushion beside her.

"He almost fell asleep during dinner," Dex said stoically.

"I don't think he recognized me when I picked him up this morning."

"I got that idea too. I told him I was his daughter so he wouldn't have to ask who I was."

"Yeah, me too. The nurse said we won't be able to take him out of the nursing home once he passes that point," Deidra explained. "She said he will need constant supervision to keep him from wandering off."

"Are you about ready? I'm exhausted." Dex sighed.

Deidra patted her leg. "I'm ready to take you home, but I wish I could keep Dad."

"I know. It's hard to wake him only to make him leave."

Dex helped her sister wake their dad and get him into the car. They drove the distance to the nursing home in silence. He had dropped back to sleep as soon as the car started to move. They woke him again and with the help from a nursing home attendant they managed to get him into his bed.

"Thank you for the help," Deidra said. "I'll bring him back earlier next week."

"We put most of the residents to bed by eight because of that issue."

Dex didn't feel like the nurse was chastising them, that she was only stating a fact. Deidra was here a lot and seemed to know her.

Dex closed the door to their father's room and stepped closer to hear the soft conversation between her sister and the nurse.

"Are you guys seeing a big change in him?" Deidra asked.

"We did notice his memory loss is more of a constant rather than intermittent as it was in the beginning." The nurse smiled at them. "But he hasn't forgotten food yet. He grabs his fork as soon as we place the tray in front of him."

Deidra hugged her. "I'll see you on Wednesday to check on him. Call me if I need to come by sooner."

Dex slid into the car and buckled her seat belt. She didn't want to think any more about death and loss. When her mother had passed away, she had had the military to distract her, but how would she cope with the loss of her father? Seeing how frail his body had become in the last year was as much of an emotional toll as she could handle. Today anyway.

Deidra seemed lost in her own thoughts as well so Dex stared out the window at the passing traffic. The high-rise buildings of Toronto loomed in the distance like steel monsters reaching toward the sky. She liked living in Toronto. It was a city bustling with excitement, and yet it had a feeling of peace. She liked the convenience of subway travel as well as the elevator ride to the grocery store beneath her building.

Deidra shifted in her seat and cleared her throat. "Do you want to talk about Dad?"

"Not really."

"The nursing staff has started making little comments every time I visit. Like they're trying to prepare me for the day his mind will be lost inside his body."

"I said no, Deidra."

"I heard you."

Dex could see Deidra fighting to remain silent. And then she couldn't.

"You act like my children. Not talking about it won't make it go away. Soon he'll only be a shell and our father won't be in there anymore."

Dex stared longingly at the city, mentally trying to pull it closer. Deidra was wrong. Not talking did make things go away. Some things, anyway. She pushed away thoughts of the man she had spent the day with and called to mind earlier years when he had taken her to baseball games and for ice cream. When her mother had been by his side and it seemed like the world would never change. Back before she had even considered joining the military and never even thought about how a modern day war would be fought.

"So have you met anyone date-worthy yet?"

Dex turned to glare at her sister.

"What? I was only trying to find a new topic of conversation."

"Really? And that's what you came up with. I've barely been out of the military for two months. The last thing I'm thinking about is who to date."

As the words left her mouth, Dex could feel her cheeks flush. She had thought plenty about Lucy, but even more so since the kiss they had shared in Paris. She had analyzed every second of that most pleasurable moment in her life. Had Lucy felt everything she had felt? Had she felt the promise of more to come?

A huge grin spread across Deidra's face.

"What?" Dex demanded.

"You have. You've met someone."

"Honestly, Deidra. Can't we talk about something other than my love life? Why would you even think I've met someone or that I'm even looking?"

"That's the beauty of love. I know you're not looking and that's when love hits you." She shrugged. "You've been different today. Distracted but not sad. Even Trevor mentioned he had seen you lost in thought with a smile on your face."

"Trevor noticed." Dex groaned.

"So tell me about her."

"We only met in passing and I can't imagine that I'll ever see her again."

"Why not? Track her down and plant yourself in front of her."

"Real life doesn't work like a romance novel. I can't just track her down. And that's called stalking anyway. Besides, the airline world is bigger than you think. We don't even work for the same company."

Deidra pulled to a stop in front of Dex's building.

"Okay, but I haven't seen you interested in anyone since the fifth grade when you chased Julia Perez across the playground."

"Why do you always bring that up? We were playing chase."

"I know. Too bad she didn't know."

Dex swatted her arm as she opened the door. Moving quickly, she avoided Deidra's return swipe. "I'll let you know my schedule when I get it tomorrow."

"Okay. Think about tracking that woman down. She makes you smile."

Dex shook her head as she climbed the stairs into the lobby of her building. Lucy did make her smile. She also made her heart race and her palms sweat. How could a woman she had never even had a conversation with do so much? Clearly it was all her imagination. The farther she got from their meeting in Paris the bigger the kiss became. She needed to think logically about this situation. She didn't know Lucy and fantasizing about her only made her and their interaction larger than life.

Dex had never been one to fabricate or embellish the truth, so why was she letting her mind do that now? Lucy was only a woman. Granted she was an appealing woman. More than appealing, actually, she was adorable. The way she occupied a space, like she owned it. The way she gave the appearance of being relaxed in her environment but was extremely aware of her surroundings. Ready to act in any situation. Even to a kiss.

Dex unlocked her apartment door and stepped inside. The white walls and light blue carpet screamed clean and comfortable to her. It was the reason she had chosen this apartment. After so many years living in an army green world with sand under her feet, she needed clean. She didn't like clutter, so the couch and coffee table were the only pieces of furniture in the living room. A few pictures adorned the built-in bookshelves, but there wasn't anything else in the room that would identify it as hers. The bedroom held even less. A bed and nothing else. All clothing was put away neatly inside the closet. Even underwear and socks, which were tucked into a small shelving unit hidden inside the closet.

She had rented a storage unit to hold the six boxes of army paraphernalia she had brought with her. At least for the moment, she didn't want anything camouflage-colored inside her house or even in her life. Passing soldiers in airports during her travel was more than enough for now. She knew at some point she would have to sort through the boxes and decide what to keep. But right now she needed time away from her previous life. Time for wounds to heal and memories to fade. Time to forget the pain of war.

* * *

Unlike most people, Lucy was happy to work on holidays. Not that she wanted anything to happen on her flights, but the elevated risk that came with them certainly made her more vigilant. Thanksgiving wasn't the biggest holiday of the year, but it was one of the most heavily traveled, and she knew the idea of killing people on a day of thanks would give a sick thrill to a terrorist somewhere in the world.

Sheila and Karen had switched their Thanksgiving dinner to Friday to accommodate her schedule. It was the first time since she'd left home that she would be sharing a turkey with people she knew rather than with strangers in a restaurant. Her schedule had her arriving in Atlanta around nine p.m. Thursday night, but a delayed takeoff in Miami had made her a few hours later. She had planned to drive home as soon as they landed, but now she was considering staying in Atlanta for the night. What was one more night in a hotel anyway?

She walked through the terminal, following the signs to baggage claim and ground transportation. She stepped outside into the cool Georgia night air. When she looked to the left to locate a taxicab, her eyes caught the flash of a dark ponytail. Her mind was instantly transported back to Paris and her encounter with Dex. Her body flushed with heat.

She had tried hard over the last several weeks to forget Dex. The memory of the firm pressure of her incredibly soft lips pressed against her own still haunted her. She had reasoned with herself that she would not give in if they met again, but deep inside she hoped her resolve would not be challenged. She wasn't sure if she could stand strong against the reality of Dex's velvety skin if it was within reach of her fingertips.

The woman stepped from behind the open taxi trunk lid, and Lucy was able to see her face. It was Dex. She watched her slide into the cab and pull the door shut. In seconds, she would be gone and Lucy might never have the opportunity to see or even kiss her again. Maybe giving in to one night would make forgetting easier. The unknown was always made bigger in your mind. If they had one night, then she could hold true to her only once rule.

She liked that logic. Never mind that she was ignoring the pilot issue. Besides what were the odds she would ever end up on a plane flown by Dex again?

Without thinking, she quickly crossed the distance to the cab and pulled open the door. Dex's surprised face was as beautiful as Lucy remembered. She dropped onto the seat beside her and placed her bag on the floor between her feet.

"What are you doing?" Dex asked in surprise.

"Still going to the Courtyard?" the cab driver asked across the seat.

Lucy almost wilted under Dex's intense gaze. She searched her mind for something cool and witty to say, but nothing would come so she just leveled her gaze and stared back into the dark eyes. After a few seconds, she motioned for Dex to answer the driver.

"Yes," Dex answered and then bent her head toward Lucy, speaking softly. "What are you doing?"

"I'm going with you." She leaned back against the seat and gave Dex what she hoped was a sexy, seductive smile. Her heart raced as she waited to see if Dex would turn her down and kick her out of the cab. When the cab was finally able to pull into traffic, she released the breath she had been holding. She was fairly confident Dex wouldn't turn her away now.

Lucy had seen the look of disbelief in Dex's face before she turned to stare out the window. She didn't blame Dex for being surprised. She was shocked at her own behavior too. This wasn't the first time she had openly propositioned a woman, but it was certainly the first time she was giving in to her own desires. Of course, she liked all the women who had come before, but Dex was in a class all her own. Dex made her feel things she had never felt before. She was intelligent, strong, and capable. And the attraction between them was clear. She had worked hard to convince herself that she wouldn't give in, but that didn't matter. Not when the option was right in front of you and within easy reach.

Dex leaned back against the seat and her posture matched Lucy's relaxed demeanor. Up until today, Dex had been the one pulling them together. Now it was Lucy's turn. She had tossed aside all of the logical reasons not to sleep with Dex and placed herself directly within her sights. And she had no regrets.

Five minutes later, the cab pulled under the giant archway covering the sliding glass doors into the Courtyard by Marriott. Lucy paid the driver and climbed out, holding the door for Dex. She wandered around the huge lobby while Dex checked in at the desk. There was a twenty-four-hour market as well as the usual lounge chairs and tables. She joined some people lingering in front of a big-screen television, all the while keeping a watch on Dex out of the corner of her eye. The football game was almost over, but it didn't hold her attention even long enough for her to determine which teams were playing.

When Dex moved toward the elevators, Lucy fell into step beside her. She leaned against the rear wall as the doors of the elevator slid closed. Dex brushed an imaginary piece of lint off her uniform and straightened her jacket. Lucy studied her. Did she detect a hint of nervousness in Dex?

"This is what you wanted, right?" she asked.

Dex's dark eyes met hers, and she nodded.

"Are you sure? I can get another room."

The elevator doors opened with a ding, and Dex reached out, grasping Lucy's hand. She followed willingly behind her, pausing briefly as Dex swiped the key card and pushed her way into the room. Letting the door fall shut behind them, Lucy quickly removed her pistol and other equipment, sliding them into the pocket of her jacket. She set her bag on a nearby chair, took off her jacket and waited as Dex moved around the room.

Dex opened the closet doors and pulled out the dry cleaning ticket, quickly filling in the pertinent information. Lucy could only watch as Dex removed her jacket and tossed it on the bed. With a glance at her, Dex slid out of her shoes and pulled off her pants.

Lucy found herself mesmerized and unable to turn away when Dex began unbuttoning her shirt. If she allowed her imagination to run a scenario of them together this would not have been the way it would have played out. Dex turned away from her as she removed the shirt and pulled on a white robe from the closet.

Lucy took a deep breath and forced her breathing to slow. To keep from crossing the room and grabbing Dex, she laced her fingers behind her back and leaned against the wall. It took all of her restraint to remain where she was. She had no willpower left, nothing to force herself to look away when Dex turned toward her, still pulling the robe closed. A glimpse of a black bra and miles of white flesh burned into her retinas.

Dex pushed her uniform into the laundry bag and attached the dry cleaning ticket as a knock sounded on the door. She avoided Lucy's eyes as she opened the door and handed the bag to a hotel attendant. The door closed and Dex turned to face her, clicking the door lock into place. Dex planted both hands on the wall beside her, trapping her head between fluffy, white robe-covered arms.

Lucy closed her eyes, taking a moment to absorb the closeness and smell of Dex. She couldn't remember ever wanting anything more than she wanted her at this moment. She fought to hold on to the feeling. Her pulse racing, she untied the robe and pushed it open. Sliding her hands around Dex's waist, she pulled her close and buried her face in Dex's neck.

She felt Dex's warm breath on her skin as her lips kissed a path up Lucy's neck and across her jawline. The touch of Dex's lips were familiar when they finally molded to her own. Soft and gentle, they covered and explored every inch of her mouth and neck. Her breathing stopped, forcing her to gasp each time Dex broke the kiss. She struggled to contain the inevitable fire Dex was building as each stroke of her tongue pushed her deeper and deeper into oblivion.

She struggled to remain standing. Dex's kiss and the touch of her hands had shattered every ounce of resolve she had spent her whole life building. The only thing she could do now was give in to it all or run faster than she ever had before. The latter was not an option. She only wanted to give herself and Dex what they were aching for.

She pushed off the wall and forced Dex backward onto the bed. Pulling her T-shirt over her head, she tossed it to the floor and straddled Dex's body. She sucked a black satin-covered nipple into her mouth, groaning as Dex laced her fingers through her hair. Everything she had never known she wanted was in front of her. She wasn't going to stop touching her until Dex made her.

CHAPTER NINE

Dex's eyes flew open as her ears registered the sound of the hotel door clicking closed. She sat up and groaned. Every muscle in her body screamed, and she dropped back onto the bed. Lucy was gone. She wasn't running out to get them coffee or breakfast. The key card lay beneath the television where she had placed it the previous night.

She threw an arm across her eyes to block the first rays of sun from the window beside the bed. It couldn't be much past seven so she had time to hit the gym before her uniform would be returned at nine. Who was she kidding? She wasn't going to the gym. She rolled over and dialed room service. She ordered the deluxe breakfast platter, flipped on the television, and pulled the covers over her head.

She wasn't surprised Lucy was gone, but it still hurt a little. Okay, more than a little. Their connection for one night was bigger than anything she had ever had with anyone she dated in the past. Before last night she could have easily accepted that she felt an attraction for Lucy and that was all, but now she didn't know what to call it. Now she wanted to track Lucy down and admit there could be something real between them.

When room service knocked, she forced herself to her feet and wrapped the robe around her body. Back in the bed, she uncovered the food and found she wasn't as hungry as she had thought. The pancakes were dry, the eggs smelled weird, and the bacon was laced with fat. She fixed a cup of coffee and leaned against the pillows on the bed while she sipped. She felt different. Not only because of the night of amazing sex. And it was amazing. But because she felt alive. For the first time, she felt like there could be a life beyond the sand and sweat of the army. She inhaled deeply, letting the scent of bacon and grease permeate her senses. She had been surrounded by dust and blood for so long that she had forgotten to appreciate other smells when she came home. Today, she felt revived with a renewed hope for the future. She could see the potential of a life that went beyond the killing of war. To a place that could make you feel good rather than bad.

After her uniform was returned, she showered and caught a cab to the airport. Deidra had texted that she would pick her up at the Toronto airport tonight, and Dex knew that couldn't be good. When she had called the nursing home and spoken to the nurse on duty, she had learned her father had missed Thanksgiving dinner at Deidra's house.

Purchasing her third cup of coffee from the airport vendor, she headed for the Eastern Airlines office. She was happy to see Grant there, already filling out the pre-flight paperwork, and she forced her mind to concentrate on the work ahead of her. Grant made the flight to Toronto enjoyable, and before she knew it they were landing at Pearson International. She greeted each passenger as they left the plane, studying their faces. Even though she had checked the manifest and already knew there were not any air marshals on this flight, she still found herself watching for Lucy's face. She had a feeling this was going to be her future. Looking for the one face that mattered in a sea of so many.

Dex spotted Deidra's car easily and hurried across the two lanes of traffic to reach her. Tossing her bag into the backseat, she dropped onto the seat beside her sister.

"What's wrong?" Deidra asked, pulling into the slow moving traffic.

Dex frowned. "I was going to ask you the same thing."

"You first."

Dex thought for a second. She wanted to talk it out, but that wouldn't change anything, and right now she needed to be there for her family.

"No, what's going on here? It's Dad, right?"

Deidra sighed. "He hasn't recognized me all week. Even when I reminded him who I was he would talk about you and me as if we were children."

"We knew this time was coming. What do the nurses say? Is there anything we can do?"

"Nothing, but make him comfortable." Tears started to fall down Deidra's face. "He's still eating, but he doesn't seem to recognize the food."

"Pull over, Deidra."

Dex waited until Deidra had pulled the car to a stop in a restaurant parking lot and then she unbuckled her seatbelt. Pulling her sister into her arms, she squeezed her hard.

"This morning I had to remind him to drink," Deidra sobbed.

Dex said nothing. What could she say? Alzheimer's was a devastating disease. For the family and the patient. She held Deidra until her sobbing slowed and then finally stopped.

"Thank you," Deidra said, sitting back into her own seat. She wiped her eyes and then blew her nose on the tissue Dex dug out of the glove box. "I just can't do that at home. Trevor and Dillon are holding it together, and I don't want to make it harder on them."

Dex swallowed hard. She hated to ask this question, but she needed to know. "Are they projecting how long he'll hang on?"

Deidra sniffled again. "Every patient is different. And he's faded back and forth quite a bit. Before all this started, he signed the papers to refuse a feeding tube, so he won't last more than a couple weeks once he stops eating."

"And if he stops drinking?"

"They're already giving him an IV bag of fluids every day. The real concern is when he forgets how to breathe." Deidra rested her head against the steering wheel.

Dex closed her eyes and rubbed Deidra's back. After a few minutes, Deidra sat up and started the car, pulling them back onto Gardiner Expressway.

"Do you still want to come to dinner on Sunday even if Dad's not there?" Deidra asked.

"Of course. If you don't mind picking me up. Or sending the boys."

"I'll come. We can visit Dad on the way." Deidra sighed. "Want to do brunch at The Senator afterward?"

Dex glanced over seeing the tears starting to fall again at the mention of their dad's favorite restaurant. She squeezed Deidra's hand. "That sounds nice."

* * *

Lucy dropped her dirty clothes into the washer and started the cycle. She still had a couple of hours before dinner at Sheila and Karen's. They had already called several times encouraging her to come on over and visit, but she had begged off with multiple excuses. She had clothes to wash and bills to pay. Basically, though, she needed time to sleep and unwind from her time with Dex.

Dex. She couldn't think of anything else. Dex had given her everything she wanted and still left her begging for more. Her only regret of the entire night was the things she didn't say. The things she hadn't been able to make herself say. She should have reminded Dex that she couldn't see her again or that she didn't sleep with pilots, but instead like a coward she had left while Dex was still asleep. And the memory of Dex, sheets clenched in her fists, was not an image that would fade quickly. If ever.

She returned to her spot on the couch and hit play on the DVD player. She hadn't planned to watch this movie the entire day, but Julia Roberts was always her go-to star when she was feeling wistful. If she was honest, there was a small part of her that was sorry she couldn't see Dex again. Okay, it was a big part of her. She hadn't been eager to leave Dex this morning like all of her other one-night stands. She had stood for a while and watched Dex sleeping. Her peacefulness had touched Lucy, tugged at her, and she had to resist being drawn back into the bed.

Leaving had been her only option, though. Staying would have implied things that weren't true. It would have given the impression that she wanted more, even though her words would have said something different. She had to be careful about sending mixed messages. Clean breaks were her mantra. She didn't stay long enough for women to read something else in her actions. That's why one night was all she could afford to spend with any woman. Even Dex.

The ringing of her phone pulled her from the edges of sleep again.

"Karen?"

"No, it's Sheila this time."

"Am I late?"

"No, you're fine," Sheila laughed. "Dinner is still a couple hours away, but I'm making some appetizers now. Just some easy peel shrimp and mozzarella mushroom bites."

Lucy's stomach growled reminding her she hadn't eaten all day. She rolled off the couch and to her feet. "I'm on my way."

"Karen wants to come get you on the four-wheeler."

"No thanks. I need the walk, but I might take her up on that later depending on how much I eat."

Sheila laughed. "Okay. See you soon."

She took a quick shower and pulled on sweats and a T-shirt. Karen had made it clear that she should come comfortable so they could lounge in front of the television and watch football. Having scrubbed away the last remnants of Dex from her body, she pushed thoughts of her aside as well. Since her early morning departure had ensured they couldn't exchange contact information, dwelling on something she couldn't have wasn't on today's menu. And if she could have her? She would have to face that possibility when it happened.

Bogarts met her at the fence and they walked together down to Sheila and Karen's. He seemed to understand she had a lot on her mind and he only forced her to pet his white muzzle once, sliding it gently through the square holes in the fence. She was happy to oblige his simple request, and it gave her a few more minutes to clear her mind from the previous night. Since Sheila and Karen didn't know her well it seemed unlikely they would question her about last night, but in case they did she had plenty of ideas to quiet their questions. And when all else failed, "it's confidential" would have to work.

She gave Bogarts one last stroke and climbed the steps to the house. Karen met her at the door and ushered her to the living room.

"Seattle's winning by a touchdown. It's been a good game. Sheila, Lucy's here," she called.

"I'm right here, Karen. You don't have to yell," Sheila said, stepping into the living room with two trays of appetizers. "What can I get you to drink, Lucy?"

"Iced tea would be great. Thanks."

She motioned at the couch. "Make yourself comfortable. I'll be right back with it."

"Sit, sit," Karen pulled her down on the couch beside her. "This is the best seat. Right in front of the appetizers," she said, reaching for a mushroom. "Did you make it in last night?"

"No, I stayed in Atlanta. It was almost midnight when my flight got in."

"Oh, bummer."

Lucy filled a plate with shrimp and mushrooms as Sheila placed her drink on a coaster beside her. Sheila filled a plate too and sat down in the recliner beside Lucy.

"Did you get in last night?" Sheila asked.

"I just asked her that. No, it was midnight so she stayed in Atlanta," Karen mumbled around a mouthful of food.

Sheila rolled her eyes. "Watch the game and let Lucy and me talk."

Lucy laughed. Just like before the banter between Sheila and Karen was fun. It didn't make her feel awkward like being around other couples when they bickered.

"My flight out of Miami was delayed on the tarmac, so it was almost three hours late getting to Atlanta."

"You look tired," Sheila said, giving her a wink.

Was Sheila seeing something she thought was hidden? Lucy turned her face away to look at the football game. She managed to mask all emotion when she turned back to her.

"Yeah, I got up early. I wanted to have some time at the house before coming over."

"And then we harassed you all morning."

Lucy laughed. "It wasn't harassment."

Sheila leaned forward. "I'll be honest. I don't really care for football, so Karen has been looking forward to watching the games with someone who does."

"I'm happy to oblige."

Sheila disappeared shortly after their conversation ended and Lucy tried to concentrate on the game. The Seahawks were up by three touchdowns and it looked like they would take the win. Karen didn't talk much other than to yell at the referees occasionally. So Lucy had a hard time keeping her attention on the game. Even though she didn't want it to, her mind replayed the details of her night with Dex. With everything so fresh, she wasn't surprised that she could remember every touch and every sound. She had been pleasantly surprised to learn Dex wasn't a silent lover. She smiled as she remembered one particular moment.

Sheila chose that instant to reappear, of course. She gave Lucy an inquisitive look as she dropped into the chair beside her.

"Want to share? I know that look did *not* come from the football game."

Lucy was surprised to realize she did want to talk about Dex. Well, maybe not Dex exactly.

"How long have you guys been together?" she asked, glancing to see if Karen was listening too. She was glad to discover she wasn't.

"We met in high school so it's been almost twenty-two years."

"Wow, that's awesome. Did you grow up here?"

"Karen has lived her whole life in Madison, but my family moved here my freshman year in high school."

Lucy wanted to ask why she was the only one coming to dinner if both of their families lived locally, but maybe that wasn't a conversation for Thanksgiving. So she asked the other question on her mind.

"Are you guys married?"

Sheila smiled. "We aren't. We talked about it a few years ago and decided we liked things the way they were. We don't need a piece of paper to tie us together. Legally we've done everything possible in the event of sickness or the death of either of us, so for now, at least, we aren't interested in a ceremony."

"Why all the questions?" Karen asked.

Lucy turned to include Karen in the conversation. "I don't know. I guess I was thinking about what it takes to share your life with someone."

"So that was the smile you had when I walked in. Want to talk about her? Or him?"

"Her. Definitely her."

"Just spill it," Karen encouraged.

"My job doesn't leave a lot of room for relationships, and honestly, that's not who I am."

"Not who you were. Until you met her, you mean," Karen teased.

Sheila gave Karen an evil glare before turning back to Lucy. "Just take it slow and you'll know if it's right."

"Well, slow shouldn't be a problem. I don't have a number or any way to contact her. Odds are, I won't ever see her again."

"Well, that's sad," Karen said.

"Or serendipitous," Sheila chuckled. "A chance meeting on a plane."

"No, it's just sad. Why didn't you get her number?"

Lucy shrugged. She wasn't sure how much she wanted to reveal about her personal life. Most people wouldn't understand and would say she used women. She didn't want Karen and Sheila to think less of her.

"What?" Sheila asked.

"I left before she woke up so she couldn't ask for my number."

"And now you regret that decision?" Sheila pursued.

"I don't know. Maybe."

"Do you know her name? You could Google her."

"Karen! That's not the way to find out about someone," Sheila chastised. "You have to talk and disclose stuff to see if someone is trustworthy and honest."

"I'm just saying you could Google to find out where she lives and stuff."

Lucy laughed. "I think that's called stalking."

"I was just trying to help," Karen pouted. "I search for people all the time for work. It's easy."

"We know, and that's for work." Sheila gave her a smile as she stood. "Besides, something tells me Lucy doesn't want to know any more about this woman. Maybe your paths will cross again. Let's eat. I'm starving."

Maybe their paths would cross again. Or not.

She helped Sheila and Karen fill the table with sides, rolls, and a huge turkey. As they were sitting down, her phone rang. A quick glance at the caller ID and she shoved it back in her pocket. She glanced up to see both women watching her.

"My mother."

"Based on the look on your face that isn't a call you want to take," Sheila stated.

"We aren't really close. She's probably only calling to say 'Happy Thanksgiving' and she can say that to my voice mail."

"Ouch," Karen said. "Sounds like our families."

"I wasn't going to ask why I'm the only one here if your families live locally."

Karen spoke first. "My mom passed away a few years ago, and she was the one who held my family together. My brother and sister don't live around here anymore, and Dad was never much of a family person anyway. I visit him when I'm near his retirement village in Tampa, but mostly he hangs with his friends."

"My parents started traveling on holidays several years ago," Sheila added. "They left for Hawaii last Monday and they'll be back in about two weeks. We'll have them over for dinner when they get back, though. I don't have any siblings. What about you?"

Lucy chewed slowly, giving herself a few extra seconds before she answered Sheila's question. "No siblings. My father passed away almost twenty years ago and Mom and I grew apart. Everyone deals with grief differently, and her way was to isolate. With my job, I'm not stationary much, so I've never invited her to visit or anything. Not that she would come."

"Losing a parent that young is tough. Cancer took my mom quickly, but it was still hard."

"My dad was on the first plane that hit the World Trade Center on 9/11."

Karen was silent, but after a small gasp Sheila spoke. "Oh, Lucy. That's horrible. Losing a parent so tragically and publicly is devastating. We're so sorry."

"And I'm sorry if I forced you into that disclosure," Karen said. "It's not surprising to hear that a parent is deceased, but that's certainly not the kind of story you expect."

"Thank you both, but I came to terms with it a long time ago. There were so many memorials and events in New York that it took a while, but when I made the decision to become an air marshal it was like I finally had closure."

"That's heroic, though I'm sure you don't look at it that way," Sheila said.

"I think I like you even more," Karen added, making everyone laugh and lightening the somber mood.

Lucy appreciated Karen and Sheila's attempts to control the conversation for the rest of the evening. They kept her laughing with stories of how they ended up with all of their animals.

"So, the old man was dead when we broke the door down and Bogarts was standing beside him." Karen continued her story of how Bogarts had come to live at their house. "Turns out Bogarts had lived inside the house for most of his life. The old man had won his mother in poker game and didn't know she was pregnant. After Bogarts was born, he sold the mother and moved the baby donkey into the house."

"So how long did he sleep on the screened porch?" Lucy asked, laughing.

"At least two weeks, but in his defense he was a very good boy."

"He was quiet and well-behaved even during meal times," Karen added. "He didn't start braying until we moved him outside."

"Does he like the pasture now?" Lucy asked.

"He does seem to enjoy the freedom if nothing else, but make no mistake, if he gets into the yard, he comes straight to the house," Sheila said with a chuckle. "And just to clear things up, I'm the one who put my foot down about him living in the house. The screened porch was a compromise."

Karen hugged Sheila as she returned from carrying dishes to the kitchen. "And Bogarts appreciated your compassion."

Lucy laughed again. "I feel like giving him a hug. Can I take him a carrot?"

"Absolutely," Sheila said, passing her one from the refrigerator.

Lucy walked across the yard to the fence, watching Bogarts trot to meet her. She felt bad for the change he had had to endure. How was he supposed to understand why he couldn't live in the house with people anymore? No wonder he seemed more attached to humans than to the other animals. She rubbed his nose while he nibbled on the carrot. She remembered the voice mail her mother had left earlier and pulled her phone from her pocket.

"Lucy, I'm at the Hilton Garden Hotel in Madison until tomorrow morning. I know this is a surprise and you might not even be in town, but if you are and you get this message, I would love to see you."

She played the message several times. Why was her mother in Madison? And why did she want to see her? She had willingly given her address so her mother could send the housewarming gift, but that was all she had expected. Did she come here specifically to visit her? She deleted the message and slid her phone back into her pocket. She didn't have to call her back.

"Did she leave a message?" Karen asked as she joined her at the fence.

"She did."

Karen allowed her a few seconds of thought before she prompted her. "And."

"She's in Madison and wants to see me."

"Wow. I'm guessing by the look on your face that's unexpected."

"You're right about that. I haven't seen her in a couple of years. She became a recluse after Dad's death and didn't leave her house much. I'm sorry to say I didn't visit her either."

"Are you going to see her?"

"I'm not sure."

"How long did she give you to decide?"

"She leaves tomorrow."

"Wow. She came to town for less than twenty-four hours."

Lucy shrugged. "I get the feeling from her voice mail that maybe she was here for a couple of days before she called."

"Like she wasn't sure she was going to reach out or that she wasn't sure she would have time to meet with you."

Lucy shrugged again.

"That's tough." Karen patted her arm. "Want to help me feed the animals?"

"Sure." She followed Karen through the gate and into the barn.

CHAPTER TEN

Lucy stared at the clock on the wall in her living room. Was nine p.m. too late to call her mother? She could already feel the niggling of regret. If her mother really did come all the way to Madison only to see her, then she owed it to both of them to make the effort. She located the Hilton's website on her phone's Internet browser and pressed the call button. She impatiently tapped her foot against the footstool while she waited for someone to answer. Then, she waited again while they connected her to her mother's room. The number in her call log didn't match the number she had dialed for the Hilton and she wondered if her mother had given in to technology. She had given up trying to convince her that cell phones didn't cause cancer as had been predicted when they came out over twenty years ago.

"Hello."

"Mom, it's me."

"Lucy! I'm so glad you called. I'd almost given up."

The silence stretched for several seconds as she fought back the biting words hanging on the tip of her tongue. *Why did you come to Madison? And why now?*

"Can I see you?" her mother asked. Her voice was soft and hesitant.

Eileen Donovan had never been a shy woman. In her vibrant years, she gave Dale, Lucy's dad, a run for his money. She had been a woman who spoke her mind, but always stayed more than an inch away from hurting anyone's feelings. It was painful to think about it, but it was clear Eileen wasn't sure if Lucy would be willing to see her or not.

"I can meet you in the morning at the restaurant in your hotel. About ten?" she suggested, guessing that checkout was at eleven. An hour was more than enough time for her mother to say whatever she was here to say.

"That would be perfect. I'll see you then."

Her mother hung up without the usual agony that always left Lucy with a sick feeling and dreading the next call. Normally, she could hear the sadness in her mother's voice, feeling all of the emptiness her mother carried with her. But tonight her mother had sounded good. The child in Lucy longed to go to her now. To see if her mother was really back in the shell of a body that she had been only visiting for years. She forced herself to get out of the chair and stop replaying every past visit. The fact her mother had traveled all the way to Florida from West Virginia was enough for tonight. As she wrapped herself in her flannel sheets, she prayed their visit would be everything she was hoping it could be.

Sleep came and went throughout the night. She was exhausted from getting no sleep the previous night, but that didn't seem to be enough to keep her from dreaming of her mother and Dex. Her mind didn't stop churning all night and she was almost relieved to see the sun coming up. She went for a run and then sat on her porch while she sipped a mug of coffee. Her porch. It was so odd for her to have a place she called her own. A place she actually liked.

After her shower, she slowly made her way into Madison. Less than three square miles in diameter, the town of Madison was filled with charm and heritage. She maneuvered through the streets around the newly renovated downtown area. There were many restored houses with antebellum and Victorian architecture as well as brick sidewalks lined with carriage lights. Her favorite part of the historic town was at the corner of Range Avenue and Marion Street where the Four Freedoms Monument stood. Surrounded by moss-covered oak trees, the four angels stood watch over the town. The monument was commissioned by President Roosevelt after his address to Congress on January 6, 1941. He named the four freedoms as speech and expression, worship, the freedom from want, and the freedom from fear. In 1944, in front of 60,000 people at Madison Square Garden in New York, the monument was dedicated to Madison County's most celebrated hero. Captain Colin P. Kelly, Jr., the first United States hero of World War II. On December 10, 1941, his B-17 Flying Fortress plane had come under attack by Japanese planes as he was returning from a bombing run. Captain Kelly managed to keep the plane in the air until his crew members could parachute to safety.

Located north of town, the Hilton Inn and Suites was only one of four hotels within a twenty-mile radius. Lucy accelerated as the stoplight in front of her switched from red to green. She was within sight of the hotel and her stomach churned with foreboding. Her anticipation at seeing her mother whole again was curbed by the fear that she had mistakenly identified the positive sounds in her mother's voice. She parked in the hotel parking lot and entered through the side door of the restaurant, avoiding the lobby. If her mother wasn't in here yet, then she would find her eventually. She wanted to already be sitting at the table to avoid the awkward hug that always preceded their visits. The hostess seated her in the rear of the restaurant beside the floor-to-ceiling windows that overlooked a grassy area behind the hotel. The view was lovely and not something she was expecting. Pink and white azalea bushes in full bloom dotted the area along with lots of evergreen plants. The green and red leaves added even more color to the display.

"It's beautiful, right?"

Lucy looked up into her mother's face and smiled. She started to stand for a hug even though she hadn't planned on it, but her mother took a seat before she could.

"Yes, it is beautiful."

"They're called Encore Azaleas and they bloom in the spring, summer, and fall." Eileen shrugged. "I was curious so I asked. Did you order yet?"

"No, I told them I was waiting for you."

"Great. Let's order then. I'm starved," her mother said, opening the menu.

Lucy opened her menu and studied her mother over it. Eileen's eyes were bright and clear. Her dark hair looked styled and even her skin was a normal pinkish color rather than the washed-out paleness she had gotten used to. Something was certainly different.

Their waitress approached and Lucy listened while her mother ordered scrambled eggs, bacon, potatoes, and toast. She only wanted coffee, but she heard her voice saying she would take the same. She felt like she was submerged, her mother's voice coming to her from a distance through water. Maybe this was all a dream. She pinched her leg under the table to see if she would wake up.

"So I guess you're wondering why I'm here," Eileen stated as soon as the waitress moved away.

She wanted to find words to make her thoughts seem less condemning, but instead she only nodded. Her mother stared out the window and then took a deep breath.

"I realized I was missing your life."

Lucy opened her mouth and a small squeak came out as she realized she had no idea what to say. Her mother waved a hand to silence her.

"I've been in a fog for almost twenty years and I've missed the milestones in your life. Your graduation from college and from the marshal school, your thirtieth birthday and anything else along the way that a mother would share. I knew I couldn't keep going like that or I was going to die alone just like your father."

"Oh, Mom," Lucy finally croaked. "He wasn't alone and you aren't either."

"I was, but I'm not going to be. I've made some friends and I'm selling the house. I'm thinking about moving to Florida."

"Why?" Lucy couldn't stop herself from asking.

"Why am I moving to Florida or why the change?"

"Yes."

"I woke up one morning a couple of months ago and realized I didn't know where you were or when I would ever see you again. It made me very sad. Sadder even than I had been because I knew you didn't need me in your life." She held up her hand to stop Lucy from interrupting. "You don't. It's clear, but I need you. I didn't want to be a part of your life unless I could contribute and make it better. Not drag you into my darkness. So I found a support group and I've been going to meetings every day. For the first time in almost twenty years, I can see life ahead of me again."

Lucy straightened in the chair as the waitress placed their plates in front of them. She hadn't realized she had been leaning toward her mother as she talked. Her mother immediately dug into the food, and Lucy watched her take each bite. She couldn't remember the last time she had seen her mother eat. They had shared meals at Thanksgiving and Christmas for a year or two after her father passed, but her mother hadn't eaten. She would push the food around on her plate while they sat uncomfortably at the table, her father's empty chair filling the room.

"Eat. Eat. Your food is getting cold," Eileen encouraged.

Lucy picked up her fork and ate all of the food she didn't even mean to order. Her mother talked about the retirement communities she had been looking at online and then listed the pros and cons of each. By the time they finished their meals, Lucy felt as if she had been transported in time. Back to a mother who was able to love and she started to panic. Where would this mother fit in her life? She didn't want to hurt her or crush her newfound spirit, but she was used to living and being alone.

She immediately thought of Dex. If she had the option of having Dex in her life, would she take it? That was a crazy thought. Having Dex in her life was not an option. She knew she would never seek her out and the chance of them running into each other a fourth time wasn't going to happen. They had already defied fate with three chance meetings. She knew she would never *accidentally* run into Dex again. She could contact her through Eastern Airlines, but she knew she wouldn't. That would only make her seem desperate. As well as send a message she wasn't sure she was ready to send. Would she ever want to share her life with anyone? The simple answer was no. She had her night with Dex and now it was time to move on.

She was relieved when she finally managed to get in her car and drive away from the hotel. Her mother had done everything short of begging her to set a date on when they could see each other again. She tried to explain that she didn't know her schedule from week to week and that she would call when she had several days off again. She wasn't sure she meant it and she knew her mother sensed it too. She needed time to process everything she had learned today. Time to adjust to the new woman her mother had become. She was relieved when Eileen finally backed off. With a final promise of keeping in touch, her mother had disappeared back into the hotel.

She had leftovers from Sheila and Karen's, but she stopped at the store anyway and picked up a few additional items. Since she had worked Thanksgiving Day, she wouldn't head back to work until Monday morning. For the first time, she realized she hadn't even considered staying longer with Dex and her mind began to play with scenarios. If staying wouldn't have sent the wrong message, she would have enjoyed eating breakfast in bed with her and continuing their activities from the night. Dex was a passionate woman and she was glad neither of them had held anything back. She chuckled. That thought was kind of ironic. Neither of them had held back physically at least, but they had barely spoken to each other. Maybe it was a good thing Dex seemed to feel the same as she did about a relationship.

* * *

Dex stepped into the nursing home and tried to block out the smell of disinfectant. It was so strong today she could almost taste it. Deidra had already called and they knew their father wasn't coming to Sunday dinner. He sat ramrod straight in the chair beside his bed. The television played an old Andy Griffith episode, but her father's eyes weren't on the television or the food in front of him. He was dressed in light blue pajamas with buttons down the front and thick wool slippers.

Dex knelt beside him and touched his shoulder. "Hi, Dad."

He turned his head in her direction, but his eyes weren't focused on her. They seemed to look through her, and she wondered what he was seeing.

"How's your lunch? Is that spaghetti?"

He glanced at his food and then up at her as if seeing her for the first time. He shifted uncomfortably in his chair. "I didn't realize we had company. Mary, bring our guest a drink," he called to the empty room.

"No, no, that's okay, Dad," Dex said, patting his arm. "I only stopped to say hello. How are you feeling today?"

"Oh, I'm good. Mary's arthritis has been acting up so she's lying down."

Dex wasn't sure if she was supposed to play into his reality or try to convince him what was real. "Did Mary make the spaghetti?"

He looked around again as if he didn't know what she was talking about. So she pointed at the tray in front of him. "That looks good. You should eat it."

He picked up his fork and it wobbled in his hand while he tried to get it into the right position. She could see someone had cut the pasta into smaller pieces and she was pleased when the bite made it to his mouth. He chewed so slowly that Dex thought maybe he had already forgotten about the food he was eating.

She sat with him for about ten minutes coaxing him to eat and drink. When most of his lunch was gone and his eyes were starting to close, she took the tray and placed it in the hallway. She lifted the footrest on his chair and tucked a blanket across his legs. He watched her carefully while she moved around the room, but he didn't speak or even ask her who she was. When she was satisfied he was comfortable again, she left and met Deidra in the hallway.

"He's napping." She shook her head at Deidra's unasked question. "He didn't know me, but he did eat most of his lunch."

Deidra gave the nurse at the desk a wave and they headed back to the car. "Troy called to tell me the boys got invited to an indoor pool party. He's going to go watch the football game with a neighbor so we have the house to ourselves. Do you feel up to going through the two boxes Dad gave us? We could order Chinese and drink lots of wine."

She nodded. The last thing she wanted was to cover her memories from her night with Lucy with the memories contained in her dad's boxes, but she knew it was something they needed to do.

Deidra wasted no time opening the bottle of merlot as soon as they reached the house. She directed Dex to the spare bedroom to locate the two boxes. They were grocery store boxes labeled with case quantity information for paper plates and napkins. They were large enough that she had to carry one at a time, but they weren't heavy. She ran a knife along the top of the first one, splitting the tape, and pulled out several shoeboxes. Each one contained stacks of faded photographs. She took a long sip from the glass of wine Deidra set in front of her and then began pulling out the pictures.

They cried and laughed as they sorted through the boxes looking at memories their father had saved and had wanted to pass on to them. The overhead light was blinding when Deidra finally stood and flipped it on.

"I'm starving. What do you want?" Deidra asked.

"Beef with broccoli."

"Okay, I'll get something with chicken and we can share."

She barely heard Deidra leave the room as she stared at a photograph of her and her mother. At times, if she allowed herself, she could be ashamed of her behavior when her mother passed away. She had arrived in time for the funeral and flown out as soon as it was over, leaving all the responsibility on Deidra's shoulders. Deidra had never complained, but Dex knew she had let her and her father down. She could have easily asked for a week of leave or even two, but she didn't want to. She had thrown herself right back into work, pretending nothing had changed.

Now that she was home for good, she had to admit the loss of her mother had taken a toll on her. Her mother had always been her biggest and loudest supporter. She had been proud when she joined the US military rather than taking advantage of her dual citizenship and choosing the Canadian Armed Forces. Her father had never commented or condemned her decision so she wasn't sure where he stood. Even though she was his favorite, she had always felt it was a matter of contention between them. And now she would never be able to ask him.

"Food will be here shortly," Deidra advised as she walked back into the room.

Dex placed the picture in her stack and stood, stretching. She followed Deidra back into the kitchen and refilled both of their wineglasses. Leaning against the counter, she watched Deidra move around the room. She moved like a mother— distracted but focused. Dex studied her facial features, seeing every detail of their father's French Canadian heritage. Her own high cheekbones came from her mother's Native American background. Their differences in appearance were small in comparison to their personalities. Deidra was outgoing and loved to meet new people. In the military, as she rose in rank, Dex had discovered she could pretend to be a social butterfly, but it was never a comfortable feeling for her.

She loved spending time with Deidra and her family. Their house was comfortable and she always felt at ease here. Tony and the boys were easy enough to be around, but having an afternoon alone with her sister hadn't happened in way too long. Even though they had managed to laugh a lot, she was relieved when Deidra finally drove her home. Her apartment would never feel like home, but it did provide security and solitude.

She went through the box she had brought home with her and pulled out a few pictures to put in frames around the television. Stowing the box on the shelf in her bedroom closet, she changed into pajamas and crawled into bed. The sleepiness she had felt before getting into bed was gone as soon as her head hit the pillow.

The day had been distracting enough that thoughts of Lucy had been pushed to the back of her mind, but now she couldn't seem to get away from remembering every detail. She longed for the chance to experience her touch again. To feel Lucy's arms holding her tight.

Lucy's adamant declaration that she didn't sleep with pilots had been kind of cute, Dex admitted. She also had to confess with a certain amount of pride that she had been able to sway her. Although she also had to concede it hadn't been that hard, since technically Lucy had followed her into the cab.

She didn't want to, but she gave in to her desire to replay their night in her mind. Lucy's dark hair contrasted against the white pillow was a vision of beauty. She liked that Lucy's actions and personality was a mixed box of surprises. She had never given Dex an impression of shyness but maybe "reserved" fit her better. In bed, she was open and sweet. Never taking any advancing step for granted, but not holding back either. Savoring the gentle way Lucy had coaxed her into multiple orgasms, she flung her arm across her eyes. No other woman would ever hold up in comparison to Lucy Donovan. Tonight, she decided, she would enjoy the memories, and tomorrow she would work on trying to forget, since it would never happen again.

CHAPTER ELEVEN

This was the third time in as many days that Lucy was being held captive by a weather delay. Inside the terminal wasn't bad, but being trapped on a plane with over three hundred cranky passengers was not very settling. She had already worn a path between her seat and the first-class bathroom despite the ugly looks she was getting from the first-class passengers for crossing into their area. There was a large man well on his way to intoxication sitting in Aisle 2 and his unruliness grew with every second the plane remained on the ground. So far the flight attendants had managed to contain him, but she had made sure they knew she was close by if it turned ugly.

"Did you see that?"

She glanced at the woman seated on the aisle beside her and shrugged. The woman appeared to be a few years older than her, and she wore what had to be an uncomfortable dress with spiked heels. Lucy had been careful to avoid looking at her legs when they were crossed in her direction.

"He just grabbed her butt," the woman said incredulously. "Seriously, he just grabbed the flight attendant's butt."

Lucy shook her head. She was sure the first-class flight attendant, Michelle, had dealt with worse. Her face must have portrayed disbelief, though, because her seat companion continued.

"I can't believe they're still letting him drink. He's extremely intoxicated already."

She was confident that Michelle had replaced the vodka in his bottle with water, but she would never tell that secret. Flight attendants had to manage whatever was thrown at them and they knew solutions that would never cross most people's minds.

"I'm Heidi, by the way," the woman stuck out her hand.

"Lucy," she said as she closed her magazine, slid it into the seat pocket in front of her and accepted the handshake. "Where're you headed?"

"I thought I was headed home, but if we sit here much longer I'll miss my connection in Nashville. Then I won't have time to go home. I was only passing through for twenty-four hours anyway. My niece has a dance recital and I was hoping to attend."

A ruckus at the front of the plane drew Heidi's attention and Lucy raised her head to look over the seat to see what was happening. The intoxicated man now stood, not too steadily, in the aisle beside his seat. She watched Michelle approach him and guide him back to his seat, his hand firmly attached to her butt.

"I'm constantly amazed by the things people do in public. Especially when they drink." Heidi shook her head. "No one really thinks about what flight attendants have to put up with."

"That's true, but they're trained to deal with all kinds of situations."

"So are you traveling for business or fun?"

She wasn't sure, but she thought she detected a hint of flirtation in Heidi's question. She could play that game too. "I'm always looking for fun."

Heidi ran a finger up Lucy's jean-clad thigh. "Have you been to Nashville before? I could show you around."

Lucy shivered as a chill ran through her body. She could use a night of distraction to take her mind off the unattainable

Dex Alexander. As quickly as the thought crossed her mind it was replaced by the smoldering fire Dex had left her with. Not wanting to dwell or pine for something she couldn't have, she had tried hard to push the night with Dex out of her mind. She shouldn't have slept with Dex. Dex deserved commitment and flowers. Not one-night stands. And that was the problem.

"I'm getting off this plane," the drunk from first class shouted. "Right now."

Lucy jumped to her feet as he ran toward the cockpit and the forward exit doors. "Excuse me," she directed at Heidi as she squeezed past her. Out of the corner of her eye, she saw Frank Roots, the other marshal on the plane, coming from the rear.

She pushed the drunk into the galley and stepped in front of the exit door. Frank blocked the cockpit door. Frank was a thin man, but he took up a wide stance, covering the entire opening. They both remained silent, allowing Michelle to attempt to contain the situation peacefully. As long as the man wasn't violent they would hope for an outcome that didn't involve arresting him. Even though being intoxicated on a plane was against the law, it fell to the local authorities to decide what to do once the plane landed.

"You have to let me off this plane. I have to go to the bathroom," he demanded.

A male flight attendant from the rear of the plane joined Michelle. He held the door to the bathroom open as Michelle directed the drunk man inside.

Pulling the curtain separating the galley from the passengers, Michelle sagged against the wall. "I hope he's emptying the alcohol."

Lucy laughed. "I wish it was that easy. Brew the coffee."

"Already tried that." Michelle looked down at the aisle of the plane. "He dumped it out."

Before anything else could be said, the bathroom door was jerked open and the drunk fell out.

"Back to your seat, Mr. Carey," Michelle said, pulling him along the aisle.

"I need a drink," he slurred.

Lucy groaned, but at least he wasn't trying to get off the plane anymore. Rather than argue with him about his drinking, Michelle pulled an empty vodka bottle from the cabinet and filled it with water. Carrying a glass of cranberry juice to his seat, Michelle let him watch her mix in half of the bottle of water. Michelle returned to stand with Lucy as they watched him happily sipping his virgin drink.

Frank visited the bathroom and then returned to his seat. Lucy chatted a few more minutes with Michelle and then she made her way back down the aisle. She didn't like that she and Frank had both responded and broken their cover. It was always a judgment call when to offer assistance. Normally she wouldn't have been so quick to respond, but a three hundred-pound drunk was stupid enough to unseal the door and fall out onto the tarmac.

She had barely settled into her seat when Heidi's hand found her thigh again. She mentally shifted gears, trying to decide if she could spend the night with Heidi and not feel like she was cheating on Dex. Not likely. Even if she wasn't ready to make any type of commitment, Dex was still there in her mind. She had explained to Dex there would be no repeat before anything even happened between them. So why was she wavering now?

She knew why. It was because Dex was everything she wanted in a woman and everything she tried to avoid. She could still feel the softness of Dex's hair as it lay across her chest, and she longed to run her fingers through it again. Before she had a chance to brush Heidi off gently, she heard raised voices from the front again. She glanced over the seat and saw the drunk man was on his feet again. Mr. Carey had crossed the line. She and Frank would not be able to let him off the hook again.

She gave Heidi a shrug as she squeezed past her again.

In a few strides she reached the drunk man and spun him away from the forward exit doors, pushing him back into his seat. She knelt in the aisle to get face level with him as she explained what was going to happen if he stood one more time. With all the water Michelle had been giving him, he had sobered enough to understand what she was saying.

She looked at her watch. They had been sitting on the tarmac waiting to take off for almost two hours. She could escort him off the plane right now, but it would delay the flight even longer while they taxied back to the gate. Plus they would lose their spot in the departure line. She picked up the cockpit phone to speak with the co-pilot, keeping her eyes on Mr. Carey.

Neither the pilot nor the co-pilot wanted to return to the gate. They both were close to reaching their maximum in-flight time and they didn't want to risk a delay. She relayed her conversation to Michelle and then pushed the drunk into the window seat. She sat down on the aisle to keep him company for the remainder of the flight. She was glad to see Frank had remained in his seat so at least one of them would be in a position to keep an eye on the rest of the passengers. Before the drunk show, there had been rumblings from other passengers, but now everyone seemed content to wait patiently for their turn to depart.

Within ten minutes of their takeoff, Lucy's new seatmate had drifted off to sleep. She wasn't sure which was worse his snoring or his smell. The alcohol combined with his body odor was enough incentive for her to throw him off the plane. Drinking passengers were easier to deal with than drug-related situations or even a passenger who was disruptive for an unknown reason. Once a woman had decided it wasn't safe to fly and had made a thorough attempt to disembark during takeoff. Keeping an eye on the other passengers to make sure she wasn't only creating a disturbance to take the attention off someone else had been Lucy's biggest concern. It turned out the woman had a fear of flying and had mixed a few too many prescription drugs.

Thankful for the short flight and the clear weather in Nashville, she departed the plane first and handed her charge over to the local authorities. She took a seat at the gate to wait until everyone had departed the plane so she could grab her duffel bag.

She watched Heidi emerge from the jetway and glance around. For a brief second, she considered moving out of her line of sight, even though that seemed a bit cowardly. She stood and met Heidi away from the other travelers.

"Not all fun then?" Heidi asked.

"No, sometimes I have to work."

"Are you free now?"

She wanted to say yes. She wanted to hide away for the night and forget all the things Dex was making her feel. The words fell out of her mouth. "I'm sorry, but no."

Heidi shrugged and passed her a slip of paper. "My number. In case you change your mind."

She slipped the paper into her pocket and headed back to the plane. Michelle met her at the door and thanked her for the help. Tomorrow morning she would fly to Toronto before returning to Atlanta for her days off. She had barely three weeks until Christmas and her mother had called several times wanting to know what her plans were. She hadn't returned her call yet because she didn't know what to tell her. She didn't plan to take any time off for Christmas, but she wasn't sure her mother would understand that decision or even believe her.

She contemplated her decision to ditch Heidi. She knew it had been impulsive, but did it mean something more? She wasn't ready to attempt to reach Dex, but she couldn't help wondering what might happen if their paths did cross again.

* * *

Dex was in desperate need of her days off. She had flown to London and back twice in the last week. Apparently being a newbie meant taking the crappy shifts. Unfortunately on both trips, she had turn-around flights and wasn't able to do anything but sleep. Not that she would have had the strength for it anyway. She was relieved to be back in Canada. Maybe it was because she was so tired, or maybe it was only that she was getting used to her condo, but either way she was glad to be coming home.

Deidra had called several times while she was in the air so she listened to her voice mail while merging with the other travelers trying to depart the terminal. Deidra was checking to see if she would be around for dinner on Sunday so she sent a text to tell her yes. She moved toward the line of taxicabs waiting for their fares and did a double take as her eyes caught a glimpse of Lucy sliding into an open taxi door. In two decisive steps, she pulled the closing door from Lucy's hand and slid in beside her.

She gave her condo address to the driver and leaned her head against the back of the seat. She didn't plan on speaking to Lucy. She knew what Lucy would say and she didn't want to hear it. She was confident if given the chance she would be able to convince Lucy to break her own rules again. She only had to get her out of the cab once they arrived.

She felt Lucy touch her arm and she met her eyes. They were filled with questions.

"I thought we were clear."

She shrugged. What could she say? Lucy had been clear, but Dex knew what she wanted, and she was willing to risk Lucy's rejection to get it.

"I'm not getting out with you," Lucy stated.

"Why not?" she asked without lifting her head from where it rested on the seat. "We both want the same things."

Lucy chuckled. "Do we?"

"Yes, we do. Come inside. You don't have to stay if you don't want to." She knew she didn't mean it. She only needed to get Lucy inside, and then she could convince her to stay. She closed her eyes and enjoyed the feel of Lucy's hand still resting on her arm. She had almost drifted to sleep when the driver pulled to a stop outside her condominium.

She opened the door and slid out, waiting for Lucy to join her on the street. Lucy stopped at the steps leading to the condominium and folded her arms over her chest.

"Come inside." She fought to keep the begging from her voice.

"It's not going to happen. I don't—"

She stepped into Lucy's personal space and pressed her body against her. "I know it's going to happen and so do you. The sooner you follow me inside the sooner I can take your clothes off."

She tried not to shiver at the look of desire that flashed in Lucy's eyes. She grasped Lucy's hand and led her up the steps.

Inside the apartment, she dropped her bag and pushed Lucy against the wall.

"I don't do repeat performances."

"I know. And you don't do pilots," Dex answered as she moved closer.

She could feel Lucy's rapid breathing, and it made her own pulse race. She closed the remaining distance between their lips with only a slight hesitation to see if Lucy would object further. There was nothing tentative about their connection and she immediately slid both hands under Lucy's T-shirt. Her hands met the cold steel at Lucy's waist. She removed the handcuffs, dangling them in front of Lucy.

"Will I need these?" Dex asked with a grin.

Lucy took them from her, tossing them on the nearby desk with her pistol and baton before pulling her shirt over her head.

Being given the green light, Dex slid her hands around Lucy's waist again. Her skin was on fire. She cupped both of Lucy's breasts, sliding her thumbs across the cool silk of her bra. Lucy's body vibrated against her touch. She pushed her leg between Lucy's, sending a rush of blood to her center. She shrugged out of her uniform jacket and dropped it to the floor. Lucy's fingers made quick work of the buttons on Dex's shirt and then moved to the zipper of her pants. She stepped out of her pants and shoes as she guided Lucy to the bedroom. Her knees buckled as Lucy's mouth found the sensitive spot beneath her ear and she dropped onto the bed with Lucy on top of her.

Time stopped as she let her fingers trace across Lucy's back and up into her hair. This time was every bit as powerful as their first time and yet distinctly different. Lucy's touch was still as passionate as she remembered. And it was something more. Tender and loving. She could feel the bond developing between them. It wasn't that she didn't expect Lucy to be capable of it. Okay, maybe she didn't, but she certainly never imagined she would allow herself to succumb to it. And now that she had felt it, she wasn't sure she could ever live without it.

CHAPTER TWELVE

Lucy slowly straightened her legs and stretched. Her body ached in all the right places from the previous night's activities. Dex's arm was flung across her stomach and her head rested on Lucy's shoulder. The soft hair she had tried not to dream about was spread across the pillow beside her and with a slight turn of her head she buried her face in the silkiness. Dex was gorgeous and her desire to have her drove her a little crazy. She loved it and hated it at the same time.

She wasn't sure if it was good or bad that fate had brought them together once again. She couldn't have been more surprised to see Dex slide into her cab the previous night. Apparently this was somewhere Dex used as a base occasionally. It wasn't furnished enough to actually be her home. If she had known Dex worked out of Toronto, she might not have been so surprised to see her. And now that she had seen her, she wasn't sure she wanted to walk away one more time.

Which was exactly why she needed to. She needed to run, not walk, and she needed to do it now. She slid out from under

Dex's arm and quickly pulled on sweats and a T-shirt from her bag. The sun came through the curtains almost making her believe she wouldn't need a coat to go outside. Knowing that was a lie, she pulled on her coat and grabbed Dex's keys from the kitchen counter.

She stepped out on the curb and felt the cold penetrate all the way to her toes. She started to jog at a quick pace, trying to warm her body. After the first couple blocks, her lungs started to thaw and she was able to take a breath. Dodging the piles of snow that had been pushed off the sidewalks, she maneuvered around the occasional person out walking, keeping track of her location so she could make her way back to get her bag. She followed Park Road to Rosedale, making a right and winding around until Crescent Road brought her back to Park. She made the loop twice, hoping the second time would make her resistance to Dex stronger.

Thanks to the weather that had canceled her flight the previous night, she was now stranded in a city with the only woman in the world she seemed unable to resist. The only thing she wanted to do at this moment was to return to Dex's condo and join her in bed for the day. That was *not* an option. Staying for longer than she already had would give the impression she had changed her mind. But she had, hadn't she? Staying away from Dex had now become harder than staying with her. As true as that statement was, she knew she didn't know how to be in a relationship. Even attempting it would be devastating for both of them. She had to find a way to get away from her. Making an escape before she woke up was her only choice.

As she climbed the exterior stairs into Dex's Park Road condominium complex, her eyes caught the entrance to the underground mall. She hadn't noticed it yesterday when she arrived with Dex, but it wasn't surprising she had missed everything around her after the way Dex had spoken to her on the street. She hadn't been able to think about anything but getting her hands on Dex's body. Truth was she had already been thinking about that from the second Dex had climbed into the taxicab.

She checked the directory when she reached the landing and followed the signs to the Hertz rental car counter.

"Would you like to rent a car?" the young woman at the counter asked. She was overly thin with a narrow nose and high cheekbones. She smacked her lips together loudly as she chewed the gum in her mouth.

"I would," she said as she laid her driver's license and credit card on the counter.

"Headed to the falls?"

Lucy shrugged. "Sure." She had always wanted to see Niagara Falls and now would be a perfect time. "Can you give me directions?"

"Yep. I have a map. It'll take you a couple hours, but it's worth the drive. I can make you hotel reservations too. If you want."

"That would be great."

"Days Inn or would you like the Hilton?"

"I'd like a room with a view of the falls, please. Whichever hotel offers that."

"Hilton it is then."

As young and inexperienced as the young woman had looked, she proved to be capable of the tasks requested. Within a few minutes, Lucy was returning to Dex's apartment to get her bag. Her clothes were chilly from sweating, but a shower was out of the question. She knew she couldn't remain in the room with Dex any longer than necessary and certainly not if she was naked. She unlocked the door and was surprised to find Dex standing in the kitchen. Her hair hung loose and she wore nothing but a T-shirt that ended too far above her knees for Lucy to look longer than a second. She leaned against the counter with both hands wrapped around a coffee mug.

"Nice run?" Dex asked.

"Yeah."

She hurried to the bedroom and gathered her clothes, tossing them into her bag. If it was possible, Dex looked even more beautiful than she had the night before. She had to get out of this apartment before she did something she would regret.

She had already spent one night longer with Dex than she should have. Forgetting her the first time had been harder than expected. This time she already knew it might be impossible.

* * *

Dex's throat tightened as she struggled with her desire to block Lucy's path. She could tell by the way Lucy looked at her that she could coax her into staying again, but she didn't want her company that way. She wanted Lucy to want to stay with her and to be brave enough to make the decision to do that. She could see Lucy moving around the bedroom as she gathered the clothing that had been so hastily discarded the night before. She couldn't shake the feeling of Lucy's touch as she surrendered to her.

She met Lucy's eyes as she came back into the kitchen. The pain she saw there showed Lucy's internal struggle. How was it possible she could even read this woman that she hadn't even had a conversation with? Their time together had been so short and she wanted so much more. But she didn't want to want a woman who wasn't obtainable. She wanted someone who wanted her too. Even though she knew Lucy did want her, at least sexually, she also could see the demons Lucy was fighting. Clearly she had been hurt before and for whatever the reason, the experience had left her scared to death of relationships. Even though her heart raced at the thought, Dex knew that wasn't the basis she wanted to start anything on.

So she took a deep breath and watched Lucy walk out. Again. As the door closed behind her, she walked to the window. Where was Lucy going to go? Maybe she had to work today. They hadn't talked at all last night so there'd been no way for her to even ask. Lucy emerged from the building and crossed the sidewalk to meet a woman standing beside a blue SUV. Dex moved to the other window to get a better view of the scene below her.

At first she was angry. How could Lucy leave her to meet someone else? The woman looked so young. Clearly, it was someone that would let Lucy continue her string of one-night stands. After a few minutes, Lucy slid behind the wheel and the woman returned to the building. As the SUV pulled away from the curb, heading out of the district of Yorkville, Dex saw the Hertz sticker on the bumper. *It was a rental!*

She quickly pulled on shorts and bolted out the door, stopping only long enough to grab her keys and the wallet they were sitting on. She wanted to know where Lucy was going. She didn't pause long enough to wonder why she wanted to know. It wasn't like she was going to follow her. Was she? Was she really that desperate?

She approached the counter at the Hertz office and the man behind it looked up at her. He didn't offer a greeting, but his smile told her all she needed to know. His large bulk filled the length of the short counter, making him the only thing she could see in the small office. She surged forward before she could let herself change her mind.

"I'm not sure if you can help me or not, but I believe you just rented an SUV to a woman with short, dark hair. She was wearing a Toronto Blue Jays T-shirt. Could you tell me when she's scheduled to return it?" Hearing her words out loud made her cringe. What was she doing? She felt and probably sounded like a stalker.

"I'm not aware of any rentals today, but we have plenty of SUVs if you'd like to rent one?"

"No, no. That's okay."

She turned to leave. This was crazy. If Lucy wanted to be with her then she wouldn't have left.

"Sunday evening," a female voice said.

Dex turned back to the counter. The man had stepped to the side and she saw a woman sitting at the desk behind him. It was the same woman she had seen outside with Lucy.

"She's going to return it Sunday evening."

Dex nodded. "Thank you."

"Do you want to know where she went?" The chewing gum popped as the young woman stood and approached the counter.

"No." Dex shook her head. "No."

She hurried out of the office and back to the staircase that led to the condominium above. Lucy would be back Sunday evening, which probably meant she had to work Monday morning. The young woman had seemed eager to share Lucy's destination. She could leave a note for Lucy with her. Or she could follow her? What if Lucy was going to meet someone else? At least she could find out where Lucy was headed and then she would decide what to do.

She returned to the Hertz counter and smiled sheepishly at the man. "I changed my mind. I'd like to know where she's headed."

He looked at the woman seated behind him. She jumped to her feet, pulling maps and brochures from a stack behind the counter.

"Niagara Falls." She used a highlighter to show on the map which roads led to the famous resort. Dex had been there many times as a child and knew the way well, but she didn't stop the woman from talking.

"And then turn right and you're there. Do you need to rent a car?"

"Yes." The words sprang from her mouth. "No. I mean no." She wasn't going to follow Lucy. Besides Niagara Falls was a big place and the odds of finding her wasn't likely.

"I can book you a room at the Hilton too," the woman pushed.

"You booked her room?"

"Yep. Falls view. Just like she asked."

Dex dropped her driver's license and credit card on the counter, glancing at the man. "I'd like that SUV you offered."

He quickly began filling out the paperwork. Maybe he thought Dex would change her mind again.

"Do you want a view too?"

"No, a regular room is fine."

When the paperwork was completed, she hurried back to her apartment and packed a small bag. She met the gum-chewing woman in front of her building with a red SUV.

"I hope she's happy to see you. She seemed sad to be leaving."

Dex gave her a half smile. She hoped Lucy was glad to see her too. As she maneuvered the SUV through the streets of Toronto toward the Queen Elizabeth Way, she forced herself to be logical. Not that anything she had done in the last twenty-four hours had been logical. She didn't know how Lucy would react to seeing her there. She might even be angry. Preparing herself for the unknown was what she had done her entire military career and even now in commercial flying. But this was different.

She didn't want to feel the things she did for Lucy. The uncertainty of dealing with someone else's emotions wasn't in her wheelhouse. She liked to be in charge. To make a plan. To call all the shots. But with Lucy she was at a loss. Convincing Lucy to spend the night with her had been easy, and she had been confident when she made the decision to do it. Now she felt all messed up inside. She wanted Lucy to want the same things she did.

CHAPTER THIRTEEN

Lucy stood at the window watching water gush over the frozen ice sculptures spread throughout the river. It was possibly the most exquisite sight she had ever seen. Even as cold as the temperature was outside, tourists still lined the Niagara Falls overlook on the Canadian and US sides. She was grateful she had booked a room with a view, thinking she would skip the frigid up close and personal view from below.

One look at the Christmas decorations when she had arrived helped her decide how to spend her weekend. There was an animated Christmas light display that stretched for three miles and she planned to walk the entire thing. The brochure recommended visitors come by car and only walk the portions that interested them, but she didn't want to drive any of it.

She followed the pedestrian bridge to the Fallsview Casino Resort and through the Galleria of shops and restaurants. As she got closer to the end of the strip of shops she could see through the glass doors to the patio beyond. It was covered in a dense fog that made her think of a rock concert she had attended in college. A small silver placard at the door read "Caution: Falling Ice" and made her think twice about stepping outside. Not that she had even considered it.

The red leaf trademark for the Canadian coffee shop lured her to the left, where she stepped inside a small food court. Making a straight path to the legendary shop, she ordered a strawberry-and-cream-filled doughnut and a large coffee with cream. She wanted to immediately take a sip as she made her way to an empty table, but the steam escaping through the open hole told her what a bad idea that would be. The doughnut was soft, and gooey filling spilled out as she tried to squish it flat enough to fit in her mouth. She managed to take a few sips of the hot coffee as she devoured the doughnut in only a few bites.

She took her coffee and wandered back through the mall of shops to the entrance of the casino. She wasn't a gambler and hadn't planned to visit this part of the attractions. Standing at the entrance in the semi-quiet of the open mall, she could feel the level of excitement inside the room. The ringing bells and constant music blended with the voices of the tourists already inside. Sipping her coffee, she slowly wandered through the rows of machines, watching the bars on the screens flip at each spin.

One machine caught her attention and she dropped into the chair in front of it. Her eyes scanned the list of payouts should she be lucky enough to match any of the displayed patterns. She fed a few bills into the slot and waited for the money to register on the screen. The cost of one spin was so far below a dollar that she hit the button to max her bet. On her third spin, she felt her heart race as the identical kittens lined up across the screen to double her money.

The adrenaline rush she felt at her job when she had to step into a potentially dangerous situation was different from this flow of endorphins. She could easily see how someone could get addicted to the thrill of winning. It almost didn't matter how much a win paid out. It was the sound of the winning music combined with watching the characters dance across the screen that made her want to see it again and again.

After an hour or so and the loss of the original donation to the interactive machine, she finally stood and pocketed the money she had won. She walked through the rest of the rooms but didn't see a machine that attracted her like the first one had. As she prepared to leave, she saw a tall woman with a dark ponytail at the entrance. From behind the comparisons to Dex were unmistakable. Her mind was playing tricks on her, she decided. It had to be.

After the way she had left Dex that morning, she was confident she would never see her again. How many times had she said that? Too many, for sure. But that was what she had wanted, right? To convince Dex that she only had one-night stands no matter what had happened between them. She knew she should never have spent the previous night with her, but she had no regrets. When it came to women, she had rules.

But…she also did what she wanted. And she had wanted to be with Dex. Truth was she still did.

She also knew the natural progression of spending time with one person would likely lead to something she couldn't give. Which meant disappointing Dex. That thought made it easy to accept she couldn't see her again. Well, maybe not easy, but at least understandable.

* * *

Dex looked around the crowded room, wondering if she should go in and forget about her reason for being here. Finding Lucy in this crowded tourist trap didn't seem possible, even if they were in the same hotel. Yes, she had thought about having the front desk transfer her call to Lucy's room. In fact, she had even picked up the phone in her room twice before deciding against that option. Lucy had made it clear she was finished with her.

So, why was she even here? Deidra had been disappointed with her when she called and told her she wouldn't be around for dinner on Sunday. Maybe she should return to Toronto and forget about Lucy. Clearly Lucy had forgotten about her.

She walked toward the exit but turned at the feeling she was being watched. Lucy's dark eyes met hers, and Dex was powerless to turn away. She tried to read the emotions in Lucy's face as she watched her walk toward her, dodging the tourists in her path. She stopped inches from Dex, her arms folded across her chest.

"Coincidence?" Lucy asked.

Dex shrugged. What could she say? I bribed the rental car people and followed you? She was pitiful. Never in her life had she pursued a woman like this. And certainly never one who didn't want her.

Lucy turned toward the exit and she followed. When they reached the quietness of the shopping mall, with the roar of the casino crowd left behind them, Dex touched Lucy's arm.

"Wait."

Lucy stopped, but she didn't face her. Dex couldn't tell if she was angry, but she knew she only had a few seconds to say what she wanted to say and then Lucy would be gone again. And she might never have this chance again.

"I did follow you. I didn't like the way we left things and I wanted to talk."

"So talk."

Lucy remained facing away from her and laced her arms across her chest again. All of her body language said, "leave me alone," but Dex needed to see her eyes.

"Look at me. Please?"

When Lucy didn't move, Dex stepped around her, moving directly into her path. Lucy's eyes were dark and unreadable. She took a chance and blurted out the honesty of what she felt.

"I want more. More of you."

"I don't have anything to give. I'm not that kind of person."

"You mean you choose not to be that kind of person."

"No," Lucy said with conviction. "This is who I am. I can't give you what you want."

Lucy moved around her and began walking again. After her words, Dex knew she should let her go and try to move on, but there had been something in Lucy's face. Something sad. Something that said maybe this wasn't who she wanted to be. And that little inch of doubt opened the door for Dex; she decided she couldn't let the moment pass.

"Lucy, wait."

Lucy stopped again, but Dex could tell she would flee at any moment. "Have dinner with me. Nothing more. If after that you still want me to disappear, I'll honor your request."

She would have bet Lucy was going to say no, but she waited, hoping she would prove her wrong. After what seemed like forever, Lucy started walking away again. Dex sighed. She knew she had given it her best effort, but to say she was disappointed was an understatement.

"Fine," Lucy called over her shoulder. "I'll be at the steak house at six."

Dex's heart leapt. She wanted to run in circles and scream. It was a small success, but it seemed larger to her. She walked in the opposite direction of Lucy and the hotel, barely looking at the stores on either side of her. When she reached the glass doors at the end, she pulled them open, allowing a huge gust of wind to suck her outside. The cold felt good on her face, but the constant mist from the falls was chilling, so she walked forward until it was partially blocked by a row of trees lining the path. She turned and looked through the glass to the building she had just left.

Niagara Falls was a winsome place any time of year, but in the winter it became a kind of a wonderland. Icicles hung from every available spot on the building and trees, glittering in the stray rays of sunlight. She knew from past visits that after dark the Christmas lights would come on and the entire town would be bathed in the glow. It was magical and the thrill she felt at being able to see it again was second only to the anticipation she felt about her dinner date.

Her body was numb from the cold and she hurried back inside, grabbing a cup of coffee from the food court. She wandered through the stores, including the tourist shops, trying to kill time. After a short time, her eyes burning from lack of sleep, she decided a nap might be a better way to pass the afternoon. As she passed the steak house, she stopped to make reservations and discovered Lucy already had. Did dinner reservations signify a date? It did to her, but something told her Lucy wouldn't see it the same way.

In her room, she stripped and crawled between the sheets. Setting her alarm to make sure she would have time to prepare for dinner, she allowed her mind to play images of Lucy while she drifted off.

It felt like she had barely fallen asleep when the alarm woke her. She jumped in the shower and tried not to agonize over what to wear. The few items she had brought with her weren't what she would normally wear on a date. Her favorite dark blue shirt with six mini buttons at the top would have to do with jeans and running shoes. As she passed the mirror on her way out, she stopped for a final look. She opened the remaining buttons on her shirt. A hint of cleavage beneath the cotton shirt might not be a bad thing.

She arrived at the restaurant ten minutes early and was shown to their table. She ordered a bottle of wine, hoping Lucy would help her drink it. It was a bit presumptuous, she knew, but maybe it would help them relax and open up. Lucy arrived at exactly six and walked to the table without the help of the hostess. She was dressed in her usual jeans and a T-shirt, but without a sports team logo for a change. This one had a Canadian maple leaf in the center built from a patchwork of patterned fabric.

Dex poured her some wine and then refilled her own glass. "I'm glad you agreed to this."

"It's only dinner."

Lucy's arms weren't folded like during their earlier conversation, but her tone hadn't changed. Dex was content to let it ride. She was hopeful Lucy's attitude would change as the evening progressed. The waiter arrived and took their orders, quickly disappearing in the darkened room. A small candle in a glass globe sat between them, casting a glow across Lucy's face.

"Rather than painfully pulling words from you, I'll start," Dex said with a smile. "I was born in the US, but my father is

Canadian. We traveled back and forth between the two countries a lot while I was growing up. College sucked or maybe it was my psychology major. Either way, I wanted more. I joined ROTC and liked it. It took me eight years on active duty to figure out it wasn't what I'd hoped." She spoke briefly of her military career, skipping over the harder assignments, and went straight to her civilian job. She could see Lucy starting to relax as she spoke about airline travel and dealing with the public on a daily basis.

"Don't you get sick of being crammed on a plane like a sardine? At least I can escape to my own compartment," she asked, trying to pull Lucy into the conversation.

"I only mind when I get stuck by a sweaty, smelly guy."

"I bet those end-of-day flights are the worst."

"No, actually it's the early morning flights. Men smell funky in the morning."

"And women?"

The first smile of the evening stretched across Lucy's face, and it warmed Dex all the way to her toes.

"Women can stink too." Lucy laughed.

"Trust me. I've seen the worst of it. Or smelled rather. Hot desert climate brings out the worst in everyone."

"Were you in Iraq or Afghanistan?"

Thankfully before she could answer, the waiter arrived with their dinner. Steak and shrimp for both of them. She couldn't believe they had almost finished the first bottle of wine and she quickly shook her head at the waiter's offer of a new bottle. She wasn't trying to get either of them drunk, and a second bottle would certainly do that. Lucy agreed and they each asked for bottled water instead.

"When did you become an air marshal?" Dex asked, hoping Lucy had forgotten her earlier question.

The look Lucy gave her dispelled that hope, but she was relieved when Lucy answered instead of pushing back at her.

"As soon as I graduated from college. It was post-9/11 and they were hiring like crazy."

"And that makes how many years?"

Lucy smiled again. "Are you asking how old I am?"

"Maybe. And?"

"I'm almost forty," Lucy said disgustedly, making Dex laugh.

"Wow, you make that sound repulsive."

"It is. How old are you?"

"I'll be thirty-five next month," she held up a hand. "But I'm not afraid of forty."

"Puh-lease." Lucy drug the word into several syllables. "You still have five years, so you can't say that yet."

She laughed again. "I'm really not. It's just a number. It doesn't mean anything to me personally. It's not going to change the way I live."

"Even though you have to realize that your life is almost half over."

"My life could end today. Or next week."

"I hope I'm not on the plane you're flying."

"Odds are I won't die flying. I've come through many situations that I shouldn't have and I'm thankful for each one."

Yes, there was more than one occasion for her to be thankful for. The flickering candlelight in the red globe on the table merged in her mind with the red emergency lights of the cockpit and alarms sounded faintly in her head. She could hear the ping of intermittent single rounds hitting the outside of the Blackhawk as she fought the decreased power and loss of thrust. She looked away from the globe and steadied her breathing, her eyes following the fluid movement of the wait staff as they tended to the tables around her. She focused for a moment on outlining for herself the safety procedures that had kept them in the air until they could land at the nearest safe landing zone rather than on top of enemy fighters on the ground.

Lucy's expression had softened as the conversation progressed, and Dex knew they were getting close to more personal questions. Lucy didn't prove her wrong.

"Why flying?"

"The view is amazing once you're in the air. It's like a solitary escape from this world. It puts things in perspective." She took her last sip of wine, tipping her glass at Lucy. "Why an air marshal?"

Silence stretched while Lucy's fork played with the last few bites on her plate. She had almost given up on hearing the answer to her question, when Lucy finally spoke. Her voice was hoarse and filled with emotion.

"My dad was on one of the planes that hit the World Trade Center."

Her heart sank at the sadness in Lucy's eyes. She searched for the proper words, but nothing would come to her. Given the illness her father had, death was an ever-present part of her life, and she felt Lucy's pain. She reached her hand across the table and covered Lucy's. Their eyes met and held. Lucy's filled with tears as she pulled her hand away and wiped her eyes with her napkin.

"That doesn't normally happen," Lucy said gruffly.

"I don't think the death of someone you care about ever gets easier."

Lucy took a deep breath. "He was mine and my mother's world. Things kind of fell apart after that, and I needed to feel like I was doing something worthwhile."

"And then you discovered you liked the job," Dex said, more a statement than a question.

"True. What's not to love? I wear my own clothes and I get to carry a gun."

"What *pistol* do you carry?" Dex asked, chuckling at the grin Lucy gave her in response. She hadn't been sure if Lucy would be familiar with the age-old army saying. The men in her unit were known for grabbing their crotches and reminding anyone who would listen that their gun was for fun and their pistol was for protection.

"My *pistol* is a Sig Sauer P229. You carried a Beretta in the army, right?"

"Actually we switched to the Sig 320 a couple of years ago."

"It's about time. The Beretta is big and clunky. I like how compact the Sigs are and the 229 fits my hand perfectly. It's easy to conceal too."

Dex was glad the conversation had moved onto an easier topic for Lucy and her smile had returned.

"And what's with your clothes, anyway?"

It was Lucy's turn to chuckle. "It started my first year flying with the Air Marshals. I would buy souvenir T-shirts everywhere I went." She motioned at her current T-shirt. "Like this one. My coworkers started teasing me and I realized I looked like a tourist. Which goes against our lay-low policy. So I switched to major league baseball teams."

"So who's your favorite team?"

"I don't even watch baseball."

"That's crazy. How do you carry on a conversation when someone comments on your shirt?"

Lucy frowned. "Travelers aren't really looking to have a deep conversation. I just say something like—'season's not over yet.' Or 'next year we get a clean slate.' Baseball junkies totally fall for that one, especially if they're cheering for a losing team."

"It seems to me that being an air marshal is a lot like acting."

"Yeah, it is."

The waiter arrived with dessert menus, and she was surprised when Lucy ordered the hot fudge sundae. That was what she wanted, and she felt silly ordering the same thing again so she picked the hot fudge cake instead. When the desserts arrived, Lucy pushed hers into the middle of the table so they could share and Dex did the same with her cake. The hot fudge was thick and sweet and she savored each bite. The blissful expression on Lucy's face said she was doing the same thing.

The evening had been pleasant and she was sad to see it come to an end. She knew Lucy would never follow her back to her room. Even though that's what she wanted. Her crazy one-night stand policy was so annoying, and Dex wanted to know the reason behind it. Logic told her Lucy had been burned in the past, but she wanted to hear her say it. Maybe if she could get her to talk about it, then she might be able to move them past it.

"Have you ever been in love?" she asked.

Lucy's hand froze halfway to her mouth and she dropped the spoon back in the dish. "No, I haven't. I thought I'd made myself clear how I feel about relationships."

Lucy's face was stolid, and Dex was so disappointed that she had pushed the wall back in place between them. But now it was there, so she figured she should keep pushing and see where it got her.

"Oh, you've been perfectly clear. I only want to know why."

"Why what?"

She rolled her eyes. Lucy knew what she was asking, but she was stalling. "Why only one-night stands. Why won't you date me?"

"Love means depending on someone and people aren't dependable." Lucy stood and tossed several large bills on the table before walking out.

Shadows from the flickering candle danced on the empty chair across from her while she waited for the waiter to return with their check. She should have been discouraged by the way the evening had turned out, but she wasn't. Lucy had given her an opening. All she had to do now was prove that she was dependable.

CHAPTER FOURTEEN

Lucy tossed and turned under the fluffy white comforter all night. It was hard to not be disappointed when Dex didn't follow her out of the restaurant. Dinner had been enjoyable and she hated to see the evening end. And then there was Dex. Engaging and intriguing. And so lovely in the candlelight. It had taken all of her strength not to invite her back to her room as soon as she saw her. The small display of cleavage had distracted her throughout most of the dinner. That is until Dex had reminded her that she knew the truth about people. In the end, no one was trustworthy when it came to relationships.

In the back of her mind, she knew she didn't actually blame her father for leaving her mother. It wasn't his fault he had to work or that the terrorists had chosen his plane. Her twenty-year-old memory still blamed him though for choosing to attend the sales conference preparation meetings with his boss in Boston before heading on to the conference in Los Angeles. And the outcome had been the same. Her mother was still left alone, clinging to a love she thought would last forever. And when she was unable to face the future, she left Lucy to cope and grieve on her own. The fact she hadn't been there for her mother either didn't escape her notice. Not only did love never last, but people weren't dependable either. And she put herself at the top of that list. The guilt at not returning her mother's phone calls weighed heavy on her.

Sighing, she placed the lid back on her partially eaten breakfast. She didn't feel hungry anymore. Her stomach was in knots. Her mind knew the facts, but the rest of her was having trouble saying no to Dex. She wasn't happy with the way dinner had turned out, but at least it was over. She had probably blown her last chance with her, and she didn't anticipate hearing from her again. Deep down she knew that was for the best anyway. She could never be what Dex needed her to be. Dependable.

Craving a coffee that didn't come from room service, she showered quickly and made her way through the covered hallways. Even at this early hour, the sound of tinkling slot machines poured from the open entrance of the casino. She quickly walked past. She had other things she wanted to do today; getting sucked back into sitting in front of a spinning machine would only make her feel more depressed.

The line at Tim Hortons was long, but the staff was expeditious. Within a few minutes, she was looking for an empty table. She chose the one farthest from the crowd. As she sat down in front of the huge floor-to-ceiling window overlooking the patio, she noticed the abundance of icicles covering everything. Hanging from the tables, chairs, trees, and roof of the building, the icicles played with the morning light making it dance across them. This trip had turned into every bit the winter wonderland she had expected. She slowly let her teeth sink into the strawberry-and-cream doughnut she had ordered and almost groaned at the explosion of sweetness in her mouth. It was even better than the one she had yesterday.

"That's a look of ecstasy if I've ever saw one," Dex flirted as she stepped in front of Lucy's gaze.

She glanced up meeting Dex's eyes. She had been sure Dex would be on her way back to Toronto. Her heart leapt at the thought that Dex had not only stayed but had searched her out again. She gave her a lopsided grin as she swallowed the bite. "I highly recommend the strawberry and cream."

Dex lifted her coffee cup. "I'll take your word for it, but I'm sticking with the hard stuff."

Lucy motioned to the chair across from her, and Dex sat, removing the lid from her coffee and letting the steam escape. She hated to admit it, but she was glad to see her. Maybe she could make up for the way she had left things at dinner. *What am I thinking? Wasn't I just telling myself all the reasons why I need to avoid spending time with Dex?* Her mouth blurted out the invitation before she could remind herself again.

"Would you like to see the Christmas lights with me tonight?"

She watched Dex's eyes sparkle as she weighed her words. She was pretty confident Dex still wanted to spend time with her. After all, she had shown up this morning. Or was it only another coincidence?

"Or did you plan to leave today?" She couldn't stop herself from asking and giving Dex a way out. After last night's dinner, she certainly wouldn't blame her.

"I was thinking about it, but your offer sounds better."

She stood, tossing her doughnut wrapper in a nearby can. "I'll see you tonight about six in the lobby then."

Dex nodded and stood too. They walked together to the escalator, but at the last minute she stepped to the side. With Dex hanging around, she had almost forgotten the other reason she had walked to this end of the Galleria. She had decided this morning she couldn't come to Niagara Falls and not visit the falls. No matter how cold it was.

"I think I should go see the falls," she said.

"I wouldn't recommend it. It can't be over twenty degrees outside, not to mention the freezing mist floating around."

She frowned. "But I drove all the way here. It seems wrong not to see it."

"Didn't you book a room with a view?"

How did Dex know what room she was in? "I did, but it doesn't come with sound. I want to hear the roar of the water too."

"It's not much of a roar in the winter. Everything's frozen. Including the people looking at it."

She shrugged. She wanted to see the falls and she was going to. She didn't need Dex's permission or approval. She started toward the exterior doors.

"Wait, Lucy. Seriously, let's wait a few more hours. I'm sure it'll be a little better in the heat of the day."

Dex's suggestion implied they would go together. All right, she would wait. It appeared Dex intended to wait with her. She decided to find out for sure. And she wasn't disappointed. When she turned back toward the escalator, a large souvenir store caught her eye.

"Okay, let's go shop then," she suggested.

She was sure she heard Dex groan, but she followed behind her anyway. The shop on the first floor was filled with anything and everything a tourist visiting Niagara Falls in Canada would want. From T-shirts to shot glasses and every item in between. When she was a child, her father had always purchased her a stuffed animal from every place he visited. She hadn't opened it in years, but the plastic box of ragged stuffed cloth still traveled with her whenever she moved.

She couldn't remember the last time she had indulged in buying something for herself that wasn't clothing. Aside from her baseball T-shirts, which counted more as necessities than treasures, frivolous items weren't on her budget list. Tossing all logical thought from her mind, she went straight for the rack of stuffed animals. There were bears in every shape and size, along with almost every other animal you could think of. Most of them wore little T-shirts with Canada or Niagara Falls written on them.

Slightly overwhelmed by the number and variety of animals, she took a step back to allow for a broader view of the entire rack. Sitting on the top shelf was a large brown moose. His antlers were so large they covered the faces of the bears on either side of him. On the left side of his chest was a bright red Canadian Maple Leaf. He was larger than she had planned to indulge in, but she immediately pulled him down. His floppy arms fell around her neck as she hugged him to her chest. Childlike enthusiasm coursing through her, she knew this was the one she wanted.

She settled the moose's back against her chest, hugging him tight to her body. His long dangling limbs swayed and bounced against her legs as she walked. She heard Dex's laughter when they passed each other in the coffee cup aisle, but she didn't make eye contact with her. She couldn't explain how attached she already felt to this stuffed animal. Besides she was here to be a tourist and she didn't care what anyone else thought.

She wandered the store looking at everything, selecting some refrigerator magnets for Karen and Sheila. It was a weird experience for her since she had never bought souvenirs for anyone before. She knew at first glance, though, that they would like the playful bears posed in various positions around a red maple leaf. Twice as she passed through the store she stumbled on Dex standing in front of the snow globes. The second time she remained at a distance, trying to see which one she was admiring the most. When Dex stepped away, she quickly grasped the glass ball that contained a miniature version of the falls. Sneaking over to the checkout counter, she paid for her items, watching over her shoulder to make sure Dex didn't see her purchasing the globe.

She wasn't sure when she would give it to her or if she even would. What would Dex think of getting this gift? She wasn't sure what she thought about buying a gift for Dex. Truth was, she didn't want to think about it. The globe had made Dex smile and what was the harm in that? She only hoped to accomplish the same thing by giving it to her. She wasn't ready to read anything else into the situation and she certainly was not going to dwell on it at this moment.

"I'm starving," Dex said, pulling Lucy from her thoughts.

She glanced at her watch, surprised to find it almost noon. "Wow. I can't believe we shopped that long."

Dex stared at the bundle of shopping bags in Lucy's hands and then at her own empty hands. "I think you should refrain from including me in that statement."

She bumped Dex's shoulder. "Admit it. You had fun."

"I had fun watching you act like a tourist. With all the places you travel, do you always do this?"

"Do what? Have fun? I try to." She shrugged. "I don't normally buy stuff, though." The smell of fresh baked dough and melting cheese engulfed her as they stepped off the escalator. On the right, a set of wooden doors stood open, inviting guests into the darkness of the restaurant. The windows on both sides were also dark, but bright red writing announced deep dish pizza.

"How about pizza?" she asked, assuming Dex would be joining her for lunch. It wasn't that much of a stretch considering Dex had stayed with her for hours and had left the tourist shop empty-handed.

Dex's answer was to lead the way into the dimly lit restaurant. The scent of Italian spices permeated the air around them and her stomach came roaring to life. The waitress seated them in a corner away from the only other occupants, a family of four. Both children were coloring pictures on their placemats while the parents talked. It was a comforting sight until the older boy grabbed a specific crayon and the girl began to screech. She quickly looked away while the parents attempted to handle the dispute.

Being an only child, she had never had to fight for anything growing up. There wasn't any arguing in her life. Any disagreements her parents had were always behind closed doors and never within their daughter's earshot. As an adult, it was one of the many ways she had excelled at being a marshal. She didn't fight with anyone. She would negotiate for a peaceful resolution, but when it was time to use force she quickly took charge and squashed any dispute.

"So what did you purchase?" Dex asked.

She began pulling things from the bags, starting with the moose.

"Is that for a niece or nephew?"

"Uh. No."

"Don't tell me you have a kid?" Dex teased.

"Absolutely not," Lucy said, stuffing the moose back in the bag. "It's for me."

Dex grabbed the bag from her and pulled the moose back out, sitting it on the table between them. Its arms, legs, and antlers were limp with minimal stuffing and they flopped in all directions. A stitched black smile stretched from one side of its large nose to the other and she could see the corners of Dex's mouth starting to turn up. She knew the moose was talking to Dex too. Her purchase didn't feel so impulsive anymore. She almost wished she had bought one for Dex as well.

She smiled. "I know it's ridiculous, but I wanted it."

"It's very cute. What else did you get?"

She showed the magnets first, saving the globe for last. If their food arrived, she would hold on to it for a while longer. She put the gifts for Karen and Sheila away and set the moose on top of the bags on the chair.

"What's in the other bag?" Dex asked.

"An impulse buy."

"More impulsive than the moose. I have to see what it is."

She picked up the bag and removed the snow globe, setting it on the table in front of Dex. She watched Dex stare at it and then twist the key to make it spin. She was surprised when the miniature falls began to flow and multicolored lights twinkled under the water.

"I didn't know it did that," she gushed as she twisted the metal key to keep it moving.

"Yeah. I liked this one the most."

"I noticed. That's why I bought it for you."

Dex's head swung up and her eyes locked with Lucy's. "You bought this for me?"

She nodded.

"That was really sweet."

"Don't look so surprised."

Dex chuckled. "Why not? You constantly surprise me."

* * *

Dex leaned back in the chair, her gaze locked on Lucy. She had barely started to think she understood this woman and now this. Lucy didn't seem like the type to do anything on impulse, and yet more than once in the last twenty-four hours she had proven her wrong. First the trip to Niagara, the moose, and now an unexpected gift. Not just a gift, but a carefully picked gift.

"You can stop staring at me now," Lucy stated.

"I'm just trying to figure you out."

"No chance of that."

She glanced up as their waiter arrived, setting two slices of pizza in front of each of them. Grease from the pepperoni covered the cheese, giving each slice a shiny glow in the shimmering candlelight. Normally she would be inclined to avoid a meal like this, but the smell already had her mouth watering. Italian spices mixed with melted cheese, cooked pepperoni, and baked dough was not something she could refuse.

"Hot, hot," Lucy chanted around her first bite, grabbing her water glass.

Ignoring Lucy's warning, she bit into the thick crust. Her eyes watered at the first steaming bite. The gooey cheese spread across her tongue and she pushed it from side to side in an attempt to cool it enough to chew. When she finally swallowed the bite, she took a drink before meeting Lucy's eyes.

"You didn't believe me?" Lucy laughed.

"I did, but it smelled so good. I couldn't wait."

"It's definitely good."

She echoed her agreement, carefully taking another, much smaller bite. She savored the taste as all conversation came to a halt. Neither paused when their first slice was gone, moving straight to the second slice. Tossing her napkin on the table, Dex sat back in her chair.

"Tell me I can't order another slice."

"Oh, but you can," Lucy teased.

She studied Lucy's face. It was relaxed and without the usual professional screen in place or the brick wall she had seen the previous night. She felt like she might be seeing the real Lucy for the first time.

"You must like being an air marshal, right?" she asked.

"I do. Why?"

"You're always pretending to be someone you're not. I guess that must be hard."

"In some ways it's easier than a regular job. When I go to work, I can put on my mask and be anyone I want to be."

"Easier—because it keeps people at a distance, I'm guessing. They never know the real you."

Lucy shrugged.

As the relaxed look on Lucy's face began to fade, she knew the conversation had reached its limits. She wasn't sorry she had pushed, but she wished she could bring the good feeling back again. Her desire to know Lucy better wasn't diminished, though. She stood, motioning Lucy to stand.

"Let's go check out those falls," she suggested.

"Oh yeah. I'd almost forgotten."

"Distracted by the pizza or me?" she asked without thinking.

Lucy studied her for a second, and then without answering, she made her way between the tables toward the restaurant exit. She sighed and followed her. She wasn't able to identify the look that had crossed Lucy's face. She was positive she had seen desire, but there was something more. Maybe…insecurity? Still, she felt like she was starting to break through the hard exterior Lucy worked so diligently to display. She liked the tough side, the one that suggested she could tackle whatever her job might throw at her, but she liked the softer side even more. Lucy was complex, but she was more than eager to convince her they could fit together. They had already proven that they fit together pretty well sexually. That wasn't the problem. Stopping Lucy from running from anything that hinted at more than a one-night stand was her challenge.

She was a bit surprised when Lucy waited for her at the top of the escalator. She hadn't been sure if their day would continue or not. They rode down together in silence, and Lucy moved right out the door when they reached the bottom. She paused, taking a deep breath before pulling her jacket tighter around her body. The cold hit her square in the face as soon as the door opened. The wind swirled around the patio as it made contact with the building behind them, whipping her hair around her face. She quickly pulled it into a ponytail and stuck it in the back of her jacket. Lucy pulled up her hood, making Dex laugh as she tightened the string around her face, leaving a small opening for her eyes.

"The woman at the desk said the incline cars run year round," Lucy explained as she practically ran up the sidewalk to the Falls Incline Railway. Dex didn't argue as Lucy purchased both of their tickets. She was eager to be inside the car and out of the wind. When the attendant motioned them to board, she didn't wait to see if Lucy was following. Her face was numb and she wondered if they would be able to stand the wind once they got to the overlook.

She hoped so. Though she had been to Niagara Falls many times in her life she had never been here with someone who had never seen them. She was looking forward to seeing the falls through Lucy's eyes. Her uninhibited enthusiasm was endearing and provided a surprising contrast to the normal seriousness she displayed. She remained standing, holding on to one of the handles hanging from the ceiling of the car as they began to move. She could see the top of the falls; all but the center of the river appeared to be frozen. Frozen stalagmites stretched toward the sky, making little miniature cities at the edges of the river. There had been a light dusting of snow the night before and now it too was frozen.

She led the way through the observation building and out the other side. A huge mist rose up from the base of the falls, and although she could see it moving extremely slow it never moved away from the hole in front of them. She approached the edge, being careful to avoid touching the ice-covered stone railing separating them from the cliff below. Chunks of ice in varying sizes floated into the moving waters as the force of the river pried them away from stationary pieces closer to the edge. She heard Lucy draw in a breath as she approached the edge, getting her first unobstructed view.

"That's amazing."

She nodded, her attention on Lucy as her eyes took in the millions of icicles and ice sculptures formed as the water met air at the crest of the falls. Exactly as she would expect a full-time observer to do, Lucy took in every inch in each direction before turning to face Dex. The small amount of Lucy's face she could see was flushed with excitement and cold. Moving without thought, she reached out and cupped Lucy's cheek, sliding her fingers into Lucy's hood and threading them through her hair. Before she could stop her actions, she pulled Lucy toward her and their lips met.

She didn't think her frozen lips would feel anything, but when they connected with Lucy's, she felt their warmth burn through her. The sound of children's laughter brought her back to reality and she slowly took a step back. The cold instantly enveloped her again, and she shivered. As Lucy's dark eyes searched her face, Dex hoped she was seeing the truth of what she felt. Because she wasn't ready to put anything into words, and she knew Lucy would run screaming if she even tried.

"Let's head back inside," she said, her voice hoarse from arousal as much as from the numbing cold.

Lucy nodded. They walked through the tourist shop, seeing many of the same items the earlier store had carried. The last shop on the end was filled with photographs in varying sizes. She stepped inside and purchased two identical postcard-sized pictures in black and white. The frozen ice clearly displayed in white as it would have been in a color photo stood out in contrast to the black of the surrounding area.

She didn't need a reminder of the feelings that Lucy invoked in her, but she wanted the photo anyway. Lucy had left an imprint on her heart in ways no one ever had before, and she wasn't through trying to reach her. It was no doubt that Lucy was a mystery at times, but giving up wasn't an option. With each chance Lucy took for them to be close, she showed she was waiting and maybe hoping Dex would be more than she expected.

Lucy didn't ask what she had bought so she waited until they were back inside the main building and riding the escalator before handing her one of the copies.

"To remember your trip," she said as she passed her the photo.

Lucy studied it with such an intensity that Dex placed a hand in the small of her back, guiding her off the escalator and away from the flow of people.

"Do you like it?" she asked. "I thought the black and white brought out the view better than the color photos."

Lucy nodded as she looked up at Dex. To distract herself from the burning desire to kiss Lucy again, Dex took a moment to untie the string holding Lucy's hood closed. Lucy's crooked grin was in full display as Dex pushed the hood off her head. The mischievous glint in her eye was back and Dex took a step back to put an appropriate amount of space between them.

Lucy glanced around at all the people and gave a sigh. "I thought you were going to kiss me again."

"You say it like it's a bad thing," she teased.

"I know Canada is more liberal than most of the US, but it still would be awkward making out in the middle of the mall."

Hearing Lucy say the words sent a chill through her body. She lowered her voice. "If that's the problem, then I know somewhere we can go where no one will see us."

Lucy chuckled. "Not so fast, Captain. I haven't been in all the shops yet. Besides—"

"I know. You don't sleep with pilots."

Lucy put her arm around Dex's waist, guiding her toward a shop with Christmas ornaments and decorations filling the display window. "I was going to say I've been dying to go into this store."

"Right. That's what you were going to say."

She felt Lucy's laughter without turning around. And just like that Lucy's relaxed demeanor was back. Lucy was having fun and she liked that she was kind of the cause of it. She also liked the heated frozen kiss they had shared by the falls. Could she penetrate Lucy's resistance for a shared room tonight? One more night. To touch her and hold her. Would it be enough?

CHAPTER FIFTEEN

Lucy finally pulled herself away from the shops but not before she had purchased several T-shirts and a pair of sweats from the Roots store. They were probably the softest pieces of clothing she had ever owned and they all sported a cute little black beaver, the store logo. Dex had tried on a few things, but her purchases numbered many fewer than Lucy's. It was clear Dex was hanging out with her for the company and not for the shopping experience.

Everything about that statement scared the crap out of her. Being with Dex was like the high she got from running. Everything around her was clearer. Kissing Dex beside the falls with the roar of the water in her ears had blocked out the rest of the world. And made her feel things she didn't want to feel. Things she swore she would never feel. In the past her desire to see a woman again, even if she resisted, was always based on the good sex. Now, Dex felt like a drug she couldn't live without. Dex made her laugh. She made her feel like she could relax and be herself without the fear of being caught in a position she didn't want to be in.

Even if she didn't want to admit it, she knew she had revealed too much of herself already. The purchase of the stuffed moose had opened a window to her softer side and a door between her and Dex. Without even knowing her reason for making the purchase, Dex hadn't questioned her impulsiveness. This evening's walk through the Christmas lights would be magical too, she knew, and it would take everything in her power to resist holding Dex's hand. That would be her first challenge and when they returned she would battle the temptation of spending the night with Dex again.

"Did you spend every penny you have?" Dex asked as they walked over the enclosed bridge back to their hotel.

"Probably." She smiled. "But it was worth it."

As they entered the glass passageway that hung over the street below, she saw the sun had set and the last rays of light were beginning to fade. Christmas lights were already glowing up and down the street. On every building and street sign. As they passed through the hotel lobby, a rack of brochures for local attractions caught her eye. She pulled one that showed several lighted animals on the cover. While they waited for the elevator, she began to read the pamphlet out loud to Dex.

"The Ontario Power Generation Winter Festival of Lights is proud to celebrate thirty-five years of making Christmas memories, transforming Niagara Falls into a palette of breathtaking color with millions of sparkling lights and animated displays, located within Niagara Parks, Dufferin Islands and the surrounding tourist districts."

"Did you say millions?"

"Yep. Three million to be exact."

Dex leaned closer to look over her shoulder and Lucy smelled a spicy scent of citrus with a hint of something else. Maybe lavender. It flooded her senses, making it hard to breathe. She stepped into the elevator as soon as the doors opened, putting space between them. She felt Dex's eyes follow her escape, but she didn't care. Resisting the pull Dex had on her meant keeping her at arm's length. She tucked the brochure into her back pocket to prevent Dex from stepping close to see it again.

"Should we meet back in the lobby after we drop our shopping bags?" Lucy asked.

"I'll just follow you to your room and then we can go to mine. Since it appears we're on the same floor."

Did she hear something more in Dex's voice or was that her imagination? Or maybe her own longing? She stepped out of the elevator and made a beeline for her door, determined to drop her bags inside the door without letting Dex cross the threshold. Her attempt almost worked, but when she spun to leave her body crashed into Dex's. That spicy scent attacked her again, and she staggered to the side, catching herself with a hand on the wall.

"Hey," Dex said, placing a hand on her shoulder to steady her. "Are you okay?"

"I'm fine. I'm starving so I want to get going. I heard there were food vendors along the light path."

Dex stood for a few moments longer, and Lucy could feel her studying her face. She avoided eye contact, looking beyond Dex and into the hallway. "What's your room number?"

Dex took a step back into the hallway and led the way to her room, which was a few doors down. When Dex entered, she pushed the door completely open, ensuring there was enough time for both of them to get inside the room before it automatically fell shut again. Lucy chose to remain outside the door, but she almost wished she hadn't when she saw the look of teasing on Dex's face when she returned.

She didn't give Dex a chance to say anything, though. Pulling the brochure from her back pocket, she appeared to study it. "I think we should take my car. I'd thought about walking since it's only about three miles, but it's not recommended. We can enjoy a little of the downtown scene if you don't mind walking to the Misty Dog first, though."

"Seriously, the Misty Dog. That's the best place you can find to eat?"

Dex appeared serious, but the hint of a smile that played on the edges of her lips gave her away.

"They have sweet potato fries."

She didn't wait to see if Dex would follow as she returned to the elevator. As soon as the doors closed, she rested her back against the wall and began reading aloud from the brochure again. "The decorations are located over a three-mile area." She glanced at Dex to see if she was listening. "We can drive through most of it. We have to see the three-dimensional Canadian wildlife display on Murray Hill plus the road is lined with Christmas snowflakes. I'd like to walk through Dufferin Hill, though. There are more than fifty trees wrapped in lights."

"That's fine. I'm following you."

"Okay then. We'll start downtown so we can grab some dinner," she said as she stepped through the door Dex held open for her. She quickly wrapped her scarf tighter around her neck. The air was frigid, but at least the buildings blocked the breeze blowing off the water. "Okay, now I'm glad I'm not walking the entire course. It's freakin' freezing out here."

"You'd planned to walk the entire thing?" Dex asked, falling into step beside her.

"I thought about it."

"But changed your mind when I decided to join you?"

She glanced at her to see if she was teasing or really offended. Dex's face sported a half grin so Lucy shrugged.

"You think I'm not capable of making a three-mile walk?" Dex asked.

"You said it, not me."

Dex nudged her shoulder. "You're lucky I don't take offense easily, but I can assure you that I'm fit enough to walk three miles."

"I'm well aware of how fit you are," she said softly. Her words were surprising even to her, but they were honest. Dex had an amazing body. For a short moment she considered skipping the lights in favor of returning to the hotel with her. A door to one of the many restaurants along the street opened and the scent of cheese and spices drifted past her. She remembered how hungry she had been two minutes ago. Taking Dex back to the hotel wasn't a good idea anyway—for too many reasons to count. She was only slightly relieved when the Misty Dog came into view.

Tracer lights raced around the outer edges of the neon sign, inviting patrons inside. She eagerly pushed open the door into the brightly lit restaurant.

* * *

"Great pick," Dex said, casually placing her hand on Lucy's waist as she guided her toward the line waiting to order. Along with a variety of fried foods and hot dogs, the restaurant offered a bountiful supply of soups.

She listened while Lucy changed her order of sweet potato fries to baked potato soup with cheese and bacon. Then she placed her own order for butternut squash soup garnished with bread crumbs. It didn't take long for their order to be prepared and they carried their disposable bowls back outside to get away from the crowd.

They circled the block and headed back toward the hotel while they ate. The chill around them was warmed by their bowls of soup, and Dex felt no need to force any conversation as they walked through the streets filled with Christmas lights. She stood beside Lucy when she stopped to watch a video display cast onto a hotel in the distance. Stretching the width of the hotel, it covered the top fifteen or twenty floors.

"What was that all about?" Lucy asked as they started walking again.

"I'm sure it told a story, but I think we caught the end of it. I'm not sure which one it was."

"The dragon was cool. Especially the way it moved up and down the building." Lucy nudged her. "Need to brush up on your Canadian history."

"Funny, but no, I don't," she said, pretending to be offended again. "I know plenty of Canadian stories from the past."

"Really? Tell me one," Lucy suggested as she dropped her dinner trash into a nearby can and held the flap open for Dex to do the same.

"Okay. How about the story of the falls?"

"Excellent," Lucy said, sliding her arm through Dex's and pulling her closer.

Her breath caught at the unexpected touch, and she took a moment to gather her thoughts. "Once upon a time—"

"Really?"

"Do you want to hear the story or not?"

She could barely see Lucy's grin in the glow from the Christmas lights that were strung nearby. A pleasant warmth flooded through her at the closeness of Lucy's body and she tightened her arm where Lucy held it.

"Once upon a time there was a Seneca Indian tribe that lived along the Niagara River. Their chief had a daughter named Lela-Wala—"

"Lela-Wala?"

"Honestly, can you be quiet for more than a minute?"

This time she could feel Lucy's chuckle. It made their shoulders bump together and she felt Lucy's grip loosen a little. She wanted nothing more than to hold on to this second. Tightening her arm to keep them close, she reveled in how good it felt to joke and play. Her feet were no longer touching the ground. She was floating on the joy that filled her. She wished she could share these feelings with Lucy and hear her agree. But Lucy had been completely honest about the way she felt. She had never imagined feeling this way. Maybe Lucy's beliefs were changing too. She hoped so.

"Lela-Wala's husband had died and she was inconsolable. One day she was paddling her canoe on the river without thinking and she found herself caught in the current. Soon the rough waters pushed her over the falls. Heno, the God of Thunder, lived behind the falls, and he caught her in his hands and took her back to his quiet cave. He and his sons tended to her and soon her broken heart healed, allowing her to fall in love with one of Heno's sons. She was finally happy again, but she never forgot her people."

"That was very sweet."

"The story isn't finished."

"Then continue." Lucy chuckled again as she pointed down a street lined with lighted snowflakes. "Let's walk that way."

"One day a mighty serpent came down the river and poisoned it. Lela-Wala begged Heno to let her return home and warn her people. So he lifted her out of the falls and she appeared to her people as a mist. She told them about the serpent and told them to move to a new location. They saw she was their daughter and immediately began packing their canoes with everything they would need to start a new village. When the serpent returned the next day to eat everyone who had died from his poison, he was very angry to find the village empty. He started to follow them upstream, but Heno threw a great thunderbolt at him. The Seneca tribe heard the crack and saw the serpent shrieking in distress. It whipped its tail around, thrashing in the water and then it was still. Its body floated downstream and lodged above the home of the gods, creating the horseshoe above the falls. It diverted the river and poured water into the home of the gods. Heno quickly grabbed his family and moved them into the sky where today, along with the Maiden of the Mist, they watch over the people of Earth." She leaned closer to Lucy. "If you listen closely you can hear Heno's voice in the roar of the falls and you might even see the maiden in the mist of the water disappearing into the sky."

Lucy squeezed her eyes shut. "I love it. Maybe the dragon on the building was actually a serpent."

She nodded. "It might have been. Do you want to walk back over there and see if we can catch it from the beginning?"

"No, I liked your telling of the story better. Let's get the car and check out the lights on Dufferin Island."

Dex pulled her keys from her pocket and offered to drive the short distance. She had a pretty good idea where the best place to park would be so they could walk through the tree-strung lights. She was surprised when Lucy didn't argue and easily slid into her rental. The drive took them almost ten minutes with all the traffic, but Dex quickly found a parking spot and they walked toward the flow of people moving along the path.

The transformation in Lucy as she took in all the lights was amazing, and Dex embraced her enthusiasm. A few times she even took her hand to guide her closer to something she wanted her to see. The three-dimensional moose was clearly Lucy's favorite and she allowed Dex to snap a picture of her standing near it. The picture was too dark to see Lucy's features, but Dex knew she would treasure the photo anyway. When they reached the end of the display, they turned and began to walk back toward the car.

Lucy placed a hand on her arm, stopping her next step. "Wait here."

Lucy bolted into the darkness toward a lit vendor display that Dex could barely see between the trees. She leaned against a large boulder and watched children running and playing through the trees. They had multiple glowing necklaces and bracelets of different colors wrapped around their bodies. Their screams pierced the stillness of the cold evening, making Dex shiver involuntarily. She jumped slightly when Lucy leapt onto the boulder she was leaning against.

"On guard," Lucy said, tossing a multicolored light sword to Dex and then taking up a fighting position.

Dex couldn't help but laugh. Seeing the childlike excitement flashing in Lucy's eyes, she quickly took up her own fighting position. Lucy did a forward flip off the boulder and landed a few feet from Dex, resuming her fighting position. Dex stared at her. She knew her mouth was probably open, but she couldn't seem to close it.

"What?" Lucy asked innocently.

"I can't believe you just did that. How old did you say you are?"

"Oh, so buying the light swords isn't what made you ask? You can't believe I have the dexterity to perform acrobatics."

"That was impressive. I—"

A loud explosion echoed around them, and Dex steadied herself against the boulder. She could see the flash of lights across the sky as the fireworks exploded above them, but she couldn't stop her body from wanting to seek cover. *Fireworks,*

fireworks, fireworks. No missile. Just fireworks. Drawing on months and months of repetitive practice, she forced herself to walk, not run, toward the closest building, a restroom facility. She fleetingly thought to protect Lucy, but then her mind reminded her there was no threat. Not really. They'd be okay. She only needed to remove herself from the situation until she could gain control again.

Breathing deeply, she stepped into the bathroom stall and placed her head against the cold wall. Everything around her told her she was overreacting and she fought hard to stop her racing heartbeat. She heard the bathroom door open and then close. She squeezed her eyes shut. How could she explain this to Lucy without looking like an idiot?

* * *

There was absolutely no doubt in Lucy's mind what had happened. She had never been in combat, but she had seen plenty of post-traumatic stress syndrome reactions. Clearly Dex had a past she hadn't shared yet. Of course, on today's battlefield all soldiers were forced to endure things she could only imagine. PTSD displayed itself in so many different ways. She had seen survivors of 9/11 have irrational reactions to the simplest of daily noises. She wasn't sure how to help or even if she could, but she hesitated only a second before following behind Dex. The bathroom door slammed shut in her face, and she slowly pushed it open. Following Dex might not be the right thing to do, but she followed her instinct. She needed to be close to her. Maybe Dex would want her to be close too.

She passed each empty stall and paused at the closed door of the last one. She could remain outside and try to talk with her, but she couldn't think of any words that seemed appropriate. All the consoling words that came to mind only sounded trite and would probably come across as belittling. Saying everything would be okay only worked when the logical mind was working. Dex's reaction had been instinctual, so telling her the sound had only been fireworks wouldn't make everything right again. The last thing she wanted was for Dex to think she was minimalizing her trauma or her response. She opened the door and stepped inside the stall, wrapping her arms around Dex's body. She pressed her chest against Dex's back and rested her head against her shoulder.

"I'm here," she whispered into Dex's ear over and over until she felt Dex begin to relax into her embrace.

CHAPTER SIXTEEN

Lucy squeezed Dex's hand as they strolled a jagged path through the trees strung with multicolored lights. The crowd had dissipated and the emptiness was comforting. She didn't feel conversation was necessary, but she wanted to give Dex whatever she needed. Talking about her emotions didn't come easy to her, and she was reasonably sure Dex felt the same way. She'd undergone therapy for a while after her father died, but she didn't really have anyone in her life to share her feelings with now. Not that she wanted to, of course. Dex on the other hand had experienced her trauma as an adult. She didn't know how the military treated therapy, but she knew there had to be a lot of soldiers who needed it. Even though it was so long ago, she could still remember the words of her therapist. "Keep talking." "Never let anything sit inside you." Nothing in her life had ever been important enough for her to follow that guidance. Until now.

"Would you like to talk about what happened back there?" she asked.

"Not really."

"But should you?" She glanced at Dex's face and was surprised to see the grim look. In their short time together, Dex had been the one doing most of the pushing for them to spend time together. She had always seemed positive and upbeat. But now Lucy could see the demons dancing in the depths of her eyes.

This was a turning point for them, she knew. She could only hope that so far she had done the right thing. Pressing Dex to confront her past before she was ready could drive a wedge between them. She certainly wouldn't admit it, but she was growing fond of Dex and she didn't want to drive her away. She wasn't qualified to offer advice, of course, but she could listen. She shrugged. "Never mind. Just know that if you want to share I'm here."

The only sounds were the crunch of their shoes on spots of softened snow and the occasional child's laughter in the distance. She squeezed Dex's hand tighter, hoping to offer support for whatever she was feeling. Dex was silent for so long that her voice almost surprised Lucy when she finally spoke.

"A professional would probably say I should talk about it. Over and over and, oh yeah, over again." She gave a nervous chuckle. "I'd rather talk about why you didn't run screaming in the opposite direction."

Lucy shrugged again. She couldn't put into words the protective way she had felt about Dex. Or how she would have given anything to take away her fear. Saying any of that would totally give the wrong impression about their relationship. So she went with the most obvious reason. "My mom and I attended a lot of public events after 9/11 so we spent a fair amount of time around Ground Zero survivors. Everyone handles the trauma differently, but you can usually see it in their eyes. PTSD is also fairly common with all types of law enforcement as well as prior military, and those are the people I work with."

"I've watched plenty of fireworks without a problem. Had I known they were about to go off it would've been fine. Being surprised is what sucks."

"Yeah, you're submerged before you have a chance to think logically."

"The logical part of my mind is talking reality, but the rest of my body ignores it." Dex was quiet again. Her voice was even softer when she spoke this time. "War really is hell. No matter what kind of spin is put on it. I didn't see any real combat, but I saw enough to wonder how our soldiers ever forget."

"They don't. They just learn to live with it."

When it was clear Dex had said all she was going to about the situation, Lucy turned their conversation to the animated three-dimensional animal displays they were passing. She was pleased to hear Dex's voice begin to return to normal, glad they could end the evening on a more enjoyable note. She knew Dex was more than slightly embarrassed by her reaction and she wasn't sure anything she could say would ease her mind.

The ride back to the hotel was quiet. She enjoyed being close to Dex. She was a bit surprised at how comfortable the silence between them was, and she was hesitant to disturb it. Dex rested one hand on the center console, casually steering with the other. She wanted Dex to stay with her tonight. She wanted to hold her and reinforce that everything was okay. Words would never be enough to convince her she didn't think any different of her. Actually, if anything she had even more respect for her.

After her father's death, a friend of his had pressured her into seeing a wonderful lady who specialized in children's therapy. She had been almost twenty and not really a child, but due to the circumstances the woman had agreed to see her anyway. It had made the loss of her father more bearable for her. She hadn't planned on continuing therapy when she returned to college. She was perfectly aware of the stigma that followed psychiatric care, especially for future law enforcement personnel. Fortunately for her the college guidance counselor had tracked her down and practically forced her to talk. She had never met him in his office but always at different spots around campus. She would step out of a class and there he would be. They would walk and talk until Lucy reached her next class. She never felt like she was seeing a psychiatrist, but looking back on it she could see how much she needed to talk and hear the words he said to her.

The change she was seeing in her mother was clearly due to therapy too. She had more voice messages from her in the last couple weeks than she had in years. She was glad her mother had found a reason to live again, but she wasn't sure how to start over with her. And there was always that nagging feeling of what happens when the good feeling is gone and the new happy mother leaves. She didn't have the strength or desire to face the feelings of that kind of loss again. The easiest way to avoid all of that was to continue the way she had learned to live without everyone. Depend only on yourself.

She waited beside the doors into the hotel as Dex passed her keys to the valet and received her parking ticket. They joined several other people, stepping into the first open elevator. When it stopped on their floor, she walked to her door without looking back at Dex. She hesitated for a second before pushing inside. She leaned her back against the closed door and berated herself for not asking Dex to stay with her. Was she crazy? She wasn't looking for sex, although the thought of Dex's naked body in her bed sent her body into overdrive. She simply felt a need to be close to Dex. To make sure she was okay.

She locked her door and flipped on the lamp by the bed. Pushing aside crazy thoughts of going to Dex's room, she prepared for bed. When she crawled under the covers, she reminded herself for the one hundredth time that she wasn't a relationship person. She knew once she returned to work and was no longer sharing a space with Dex that she would be able to easily push aside the feelings she was having. And for her that couldn't happen fast enough. She would get up early in the morning and head back. Her flight wasn't until late tomorrow evening, but she could find something to do at the airport while she waited.

She flipped off the lamp and was burrowing into the fluffy white comforter when a knock on the door pushed her to her feet. She crossed the room to check the peephole. Dex was standing in the hallway in shorts and a T-shirt. Lucy pulled open the door and stepped aside to allow her to enter. She watched Dex crawl into her bed as the door closed, blocking the light from the hallway. She walked around the bed and pulled back the covers on the other side. As soon as she was settled, Dex snuggled into her side, laying her head on Lucy's chest. Lucy wrapped her up in her arms, holding her tight. She took a deep breath, inhaling the scent of Dex's hair. Sweet. And spicy. Trying to identify the wonderful smell was the last thing she remembered.

* * *

Dex stretched and groaned as her body rejected her mind's desire to move. She ran a hand over the bed beside her and quickly opened her eyes when she felt the cool, empty sheets. Lucy stood at the foot of the bed, her back to Dex, watching a muted television.

"You can turn that up," Dex mumbled.

Lucy spun around to look at her as she stuffed the last bite of toast in her mouth. "No need. They aren't saying anything important. There's food if you want something."

"Coffee?"

"Yep."

Dex sat up slowly, the pull of the bathroom forcing her to her feet faster than she would have liked. She knew she should feel awkward after showing up at Lucy's door last night, but she didn't. She could feel Lucy's eyes on her as she walked the short distance to the bathroom and closed the door behind her. Lucy's eyes briefly passed over her when she returned to the room, then returned to the television.

Dex poured herself a cup of coffee and sat down on the bed. The morning news show host was annoying to her even at the low volume. She didn't have to be at work until tomorrow morning, but she wanted to get back today. She hadn't done anything with her uniforms when she arrived home on Thursday, but the mall under her condo had a dry cleaner that was open twenty-four hours.

"Are you headed back today?" Dex interrupted Lucy's focus on the television.

Lucy nodded, flipped off the TV, and poured herself a cup of coffee. When she turned to face Dex, her face held no emotion, and Dex wasn't sure what she was thinking.

"I think you should return your car here and ride back with me then," Dex suggested.

"Okay." Lucy's quick response surprised her.

"Are you ready to go now or is there anything else you want to do before we leave?"

"One more cup of real coffee and a shower, I guess."

Dex stood, placing her cup on the tray. "Then I'll stop drinking this sludge." She smiled. "I'll come back for you after I shower. About thirty minutes?"

"That'll be fine."

Dex let herself out of the room and walked down the hall. The room felt as empty as it had last night when they returned from seeing the lights. She hadn't been sure what kind of reception she would get from Lucy when she arrived at her door, but after standing there for a few minutes in the coldness of her own room, she had been willing to take the risk.

Her PTSD had rarely reared its ugly head since she had left the military. She felt in control when she was in the cockpit. Outside of the cockpit, however, a loud muffler or the smell of gasoline could throw her around the world in half a second.

Not all flashbacks were bad, actually. The smell of toast brought back memories of early morning mess hall meals and powdered eggs. Okay, maybe that was bad. But not a trauma memory that took a while to dissipate. When Lucy had wrapped her arms around her in the stall last night, she had felt at peace, and when she returned to her empty room last night, she only wanted that feeling again. The blanket of comfort and strength Lucy had provided was exactly what she needed.

She quickly showered and threw her clothes back into her bag, then forced herself to sit patiently on the bed until the thirty minutes she had allotted Lucy had passed. She wished she knew how Lucy felt about what was happening between them.

She hadn't forgotten everything Lucy had said so clearly when they met, but she had to believe at this point she was feeling something different. Unfortunately, she knew she might not be able to get her to admit those feelings.

After stopping in Lucy's room, she carried their bags to her car. Lucy made the coffee run, returning with doughnuts as well. She gave an embarrassed grin as she passed their drinks and the sweets through the car window to Dex.

"I had to have one last doughnut. Strawberry and cream filling together is heavenly."

"I remember from yesterday. Did you get one for me too?"

"I did, but you should eat it now. It might be hard to enjoy while you're driving."

Dex pulled the doughnut partially from the bag and bit into it. Lucy was right; it was heavenly. She didn't normally eat sweet things and certainly not doughnuts, but she was stuffing the last bite into her mouth when Lucy pulled up beside her.

Rolling down the window, Lucy called to her, "I got directions from the valet so follow me."

She didn't give Dex a chance to respond, not that she could have with her mouth still full of doughnut. She followed Lucy out of the parking garage and down the main street. The rental car office was a small glass building hidden behind a brick five-story building that fronted the main street. Luckily they had a sign on the street or maybe the valet had explained to Lucy how to find them. A few minutes later, Lucy slid into the passenger seat beside her.

"That was easy enough," Lucy said as she buckled her seat belt.

"Good. Sometimes they can give you a fit about returning somewhere other than where you rented."

"He said normally people do one way from here to the airport so they lose a lot of their vehicles. He seemed happy that I was leaving mine." She paused for a second. "So what did you fly in the military?"

Dex took a deep breath to settle her own nerves before answering. This wasn't the conversation she had planned for their drive back. Talking about her past wouldn't make for a relaxing time for her. If she could keep it to general answers, though, she wouldn't have to share the worst of it. "I started with helicopters and then moved to fixed wing."

"Army, right?" She continued when Dex nodded. "I didn't think they had anything but choppers."

"That's what army pilots are trained to fly, but they have a few fixed wing for moving supplies and troops."

"Tell me a funny army story."

Dex's mind raced. Did she have a funny story? There had been so much death and dying sometimes she couldn't see past it. She had laughed during her tours, but army humor wasn't necessarily something a civilian would find funny. Soldiers found humor in things others wouldn't. Like the time she slept outside. It was supposed to be a short-term prank to lock her out of her sleeping compartment, but then her friends were called away on an urgent mission. She could have asked to borrow someone else's bed, but it was easier to find a shady spot and wait it out. No one on the outside would find that story funny. They would only feel sorry for her. Sometimes pranks were the only thing that broke up the monotony of war.

Lucy glanced at her. "Come on. You have to have at least one funny story."

"Okay." Dex sighed, wishing she could think of something that was funnier than this story. "My first week in Afghanistan I was sent to pick up soldiers at an FOB. That's a forward operating base. Pilots seldom fly by landmarks. Especially in new terrain. They rely on their instruments for direction, so I was surprised when another pilot told me to make a right after the first mountain. I didn't, of course. I followed my navigation system. As a result, I ended up touching down outside a small Afghan village instead of the FOB. It took about two seconds for all the kids to come running. My co-pilot thought it was hilarious since all new pilots were given the same initiation."

"So the village was safe?" Lucy asked.

"Oh yeah. Our security patrols made regular checks since we had relocated an orphanage there. The kids knew the sound of the chopper meant snacks and fun stuff."

"Fun stuff?"

"Little pocket flashlights were the best. It was one of those items that everyone carries and care packages from home usually contain a couple. My co-pilot had stashed a box of goodies for the kids before we made the flight."

"So why the navigational screwup?"

"I'm not really sure. Some guess there's a magnetic field or something like that, but it could be the high elevation or the terrain. If you make the right turn at the first mountain then your nav system will lead you straight into the FOB. We never lost a chopper because of it, so no effort was spent on trying to figure out why."

Lucy nodded. "That's kind of a sweet story. The kids probably didn't have a lot to look forward to and you guys were like Santa for them."

Dex sighed. "I know that wasn't the best funny story. Military humor doesn't always translate back to civilian life."

"I know what you mean. Every job has its own language."

"So tell me your funny story."

Lucy groaned. "We aren't funny in the Federal Air Marshal Service."

"That's funny." Dex laughed. "Okay then, tell me your initiation story."

"Probably the best story is from passenger rescue. The training is mostly serious, but everyone is a little pissy after the first day at the pistol range. Too many egos. So the instructors started doing the chemical training then too. 'Let's make everyone a little more miserable.'" Lucy shrugged. "So the mission was to find the protective mask and then rescue the passenger. Sounds easy, right?"

She nodded to let Lucy know she was listening. It was possible these were the most words she had heard Lucy say at one time. She wasn't going to ruin it by mentioning that, though.

Lucy continued, "The trainees started adding a practical joke to the training—leaving the trainee with the highest pistol range score to carry out the passenger on their own. Of course, they added a few more ten-pound weights to his body for me."

She laughed. "So, you had the highest score at the pistol range?"

"Apparently. I didn't really think about it until after the practical joke. I didn't care about being the best in the class. Only the best I could be."

Lucy's words rang in her head. *Only the best I could be.* She tried to imagine a younger Lucy struggling with the loss of her father and finding purpose in a lifelong career. Getting Lucy to talk about her life was like pulling teeth. Unfortunately, for now, she could tell Lucy was finished talking. Her head was resting against the back of the seat and her eyes were closed.

She knew she was in for some teasing from Deidra when she admitted to where she had been and who she was with. She knew she also should have called her to explain why she wouldn't be around for dinner today. She certainly didn't want to call her in front of Lucy, though. Deidra would push and push until she told her everything.

Deidra would be disappointed that she wasn't there, even though there was a good chance their father wouldn't be able to attend dinner today either. She would have to make an effort to make it up to her. Deidra had gotten used to Sunday afternoon visits with their dad and it would be hard for her when he was gone. It would be hard on the whole family. She wasn't sure she could throw herself into work like she had when her mother passed. At least she wasn't alone. She had Deidra and her family.

* * *

"I could use a bathroom break, if you know of anywhere to stop," Lucy suggested, straightening in her seat. "And a stretch."

She hadn't meant to fall asleep, but she had closed her eyes for too long and it just happened. Sometime during the drive, Dex had turned on the radio and soft music was streaming from the speakers. Maybe James Taylor. She wasn't really sure. It didn't matter. It was soothing.

"There's a rest stop not too much farther," Dex said, interrupting her thoughts. "It's a great place for a snack too."

"Sounds good to me."

She hadn't thought about food, but now the mention of it made her hungry. She rested her head against the back of the seat again. She appreciated that Dex didn't feel the need to force conversation. She could imagine them traveling to other places together. Without any stress or anxiety.

Her head was a jumble of thoughts. She was surprised, but glad Dex had shown up at her door last night. She couldn't identify the feelings she was having. Were they dating now? How was she supposed to behave in a relationship? Was she supposed to put her hand on Dex's thigh while she drove? She liked that idea, but what would Dex think?

Before she had time to consider moving her hand to Dex's thigh, Dex was pulling off the QEW and into a parking lot. There was one tan building built almost in a circle with blue and white trim awnings and a matching roof. A center peak with glass windows gave it a slight lighthouse look, though it was certainly not as high as a lighthouse would be. A small blue sign at the entrance said Gateway to Niagara.

She followed Dex inside to a mini food court. Dex stopped there and pointed toward the restrooms. As she scurried toward the women's room, she hoped Dex would order some of whatever she was buying for her too. She hadn't realized how hungry she really was until she smelled the food.

When she returned, she was pleased to find Dex holding two containers full of what she initially decided were french fries. Looking closer, she saw some sort of concoction covering the fries. She frowned.

"What is this?"

"Poutine."

She pushed the container back toward Dex. "Can I get plain fries, please?"

Dex laughed. "Okay, but at least try it first."

Try it? She wasn't a child. She didn't have to try everything. She looked at Dex's expectant face and felt her resistance fade. For Dex, she was willing to try it. She lifted the fork and dug out the fry that was covered the least. The gravy was light and creamy, not at all heavy like you would find on a pot roast. Or maybe that was the melting cheese. Either way, it was delicious.

Dex laughed when she took the dish back and dug her fork in again.

"Better than it looks?"

She grunted a response in Dex's direction without losing focus on the small dish. Her second bite had more gravy and cheese on the fry. She could taste the melting cheese and the meaty taste of the gravy. Dex steered her toward the car as they continued to eat. It didn't take her long to devour the entire dish, and she glanced longingly at what was left of Dex's container. As Dex slid behind the wheel, she handed her the dish.

"Go ahead and finish it."

"Thanks," she said with her mouth already full. She tried to savor the last bites, but it was gone so fast. She stacked the dishes together and set them on the floor of the car before glancing at Dex. "Okay, tell me what I just ate."

"Does it matter? It was good, right?"

"Oh, man, it was something disgusting, wasn't it? Am I going to puke?"

"Like I said, it's called poutine. Homemade french fries covered with cheese curds and a vegetarian gravy. It's nothing repulsive."

Lucy looked at the containers on the floor and read the writing on the side aloud. "NYF?"

"New York Fries. They make the best poutine in Canada. Other restaurants make an expensive version, but this is a fast food version. Fresh Quebec cheese curds and a trans-fat free gravy. See? It's almost healthy."

Lucy picked up her phone, opening an Internet search engine, and searched for New York Fries. "Okay, but I think healthy is a stretch. I won't complain, though, after the doughnut I fed you this morning. Wait...New York Fries is not in New York or even in the United States. That seems so wrong."

"They're only in Canada, I think."

"No, there's some in China, Egypt, Turkey, and a bunch in Saudi Arabia, but not a single one in the US."

Dex's phone rang and she looked apologetically at Lucy before swiping to take the call.

"Hello…I'm sorry, I saw you called but haven't had a chance to call you back…I'm not in Toronto…Can I call you later?"

Lucy waited silently, trying not to listen to Dex's side of the conversation. It sounded like an upset girlfriend, but surely Dex wouldn't have answered the call in front of her if that was the case.

"Okay…I'll call you in a few hours…Love you too."

She glanced at the now silent phone lying in the middle console and then at Dex. "Girlfriend?"

Dex's head whipped toward her and then back to the road. "No! Absolutely not. Family."

"Oh, same demands sometimes."

"Sometimes worse. My sister has perfected her ability to make me feel guilty. Been working on it for years."

Lucy wanted to ask more, but she wasn't sure she wanted to know either. Learning about each other's families would bring them even closer, and she was already second-guessing her feelings from earlier. They had left the resort and were now back in the real world. She needed to gain her resistance back. Dex was a pilot and she didn't stay in one place either. Having a relationship with each of them traveling as much as they did wouldn't be healthy. She had enjoyed a great weekend, and she told Dex that as she climbed from the car at the Toronto Pearson airport, but Lucy could tell something had shifted between them even though Dex had agreed. She wasn't sure what it was.

CHAPTER SEVENTEEN

Dropping Lucy at the airport hadn't been Dex's idea. She had hoped they would go back to her condo for a while. Lucy had been carefully vague about when her flight departed that evening, however, and had insisted she needed to go straight to the airport.

She was sad to see their time together end. The drive back had been pleasant, and she wasn't sure if or when she would see Lucy again. She had said she would call or text, but Dex wasn't feeling very confident about that.

She wanted to spend more time replaying the weekend, but her personal responsibilities were calling. As she left the airport, she dialed Deidra and prepared to face the inquisition.

"Where have you been?" Deidra blurted as soon as she answered.

"I went to Niagara Falls. I needed to get away." She almost said by herself but knew she couldn't pull off that lie to Deidra. It would eventually come out that she hadn't been alone anyway.

"Niagara Falls? Why?"

"A friend from the US wanted to go so I went with her."

"Wait. You went away for the weekend with a woman?"

"It wasn't like that."

"Oh my. Is this the woman you mentioned to me before? It is, isn't it? You ran into her again. I'm so excited for you."

"It's not like that, Deidra."

"Tell me then. What's it like?"

"We're only friends. We even had separate rooms." Dex wouldn't mention that she had slept in Lucy's arms last night. It was all too new. She didn't want to hash it all out with Deidra when she hadn't even had a chance to process it herself. She pulled to a stop in front of her building. "I have to go. I need to turn in the rental car."

"I want to hear all the details. She's not with you now, is she?"

"No, I just dropped her at the airport. I'll call you later."

She knew as she said it that she wasn't going to. She was tired and wanted nothing more than to crawl into bed. And maybe to savor the weekend. There were a lot of moments she wanted to remember and replay. From the first night in her condo to the gentleness of Lucy's arms as she held her last night. She had seen the change in Lucy as they traveled back to the airport, though. It was almost like their days together had been a fantasy and then they had returned to the real world. A world where Lucy didn't want to be with anyone.

She took a deep breath and gathered her uniforms to take to the dry cleaners. As she rode the elevator, she had the sinking feeling she would never see Lucy again. How could she convince a woman to take a chance on her when she was so against risking her heart to anyone? She didn't have the answers and even if she did she wasn't sure she was willing to take the chance. Risking her own heart with someone like Lucy was sounding less and less like a chance she wanted to take. Maybe it was time for her to forget the woman who wanted to be forgotten.

* * *

Lucy cleared security and then found a quiet spot to email her findings to Deputy Avila. One of the many responsibilities of an air marshal was to test the security checkpoints. Often they were asked to attempt to slip items through to test the process of security agents. It was probably the task she hated the most. It always made her feel a little underhanded. At least this time she could report that all security protocols were being followed and she hadn't observed anything negative to report.

She had received her schedule for this week of travel and knew she would be exhausted by the end of a week. She would be flying from Miami to Los Angeles and then to Boston before heading back to Atlanta. She was looking forward to getting back to her cabin at the end of it all and having a few days of peace and quiet. Even though she had a wonderful time with Dex, she needed her alone time. Didn't she?

Her phone buzzed with a text message. *Dex.* She felt her pulse race as she swiped through the screens to read the message.

Had a wonderful weekend. Maybe again sometime?

She almost typed yes without even thinking. Where had all her resolve gone? She knew the dangerous path of relationships. She had seen plenty of coworkers slip off the grid when they started dating or got married. No more dedication to their job. Never willing to work extra shifts or holidays. That wasn't her. She wouldn't allow her life to stop being her own. She didn't need that kind of pressure—even if she did like Dex.

Maybe.

Oh, that was nice and vague. Did she want Dex to move on? Or didn't she? She needed to decide what she wanted from her and stop giving mixed messages.

Her phone vibrated with Dex's response. *Soon?*

Crap. How was she supposed to respond to that? She needed a few days at her cabin to think things through. This was not something to decide while sitting in a busy airport terminal. But she also needed to respond and not leave Dex hanging.

Okay.

Even more vague.

Dex's response was perfect. *I'll text at the end of the week.*

A smile spread across her face and she tried to push it away. She wasn't going to allow herself to act like a schoolgirl in love. *In love?* Where had that come from? She wasn't in love with Dex. And she certainly wasn't committing to anything. If the opportunity arose to spend the night with someone else, she'd do it. Wouldn't she?

An image of Dex's face in the glow of Christmas lights filled her senses. Remembering the soft feel of her skin and her touch sent a chill down Lucy's spine. She didn't know if she was in love or not. In fact, she knew she didn't even know what love felt like, but she did know she liked this feeling that Dex caused in her. And she looked forward to Dex's text at the end of the week. For now, that was all she could commit to. And for her… that was enough.

* * *

By Thursday morning, Lucy felt like she had been put through a wringer washing machine. She spent Monday, Tuesday, and Wednesday rushing from one location to another. As much as she loved Boston, she wasn't a fan of the airport. She was starving and trying hard not to be cranky. She knew the long waits in every line were due more to the number of people passing through than the staff's incompetence. There was only so much even the best customer service person could do to make that many people happy in one day.

She tried not to release her sigh again since the woman behind her was doing it for her. The young, purple-haired girl at the register was working efficiently taking orders, but it seemed the cooking staff backing her up might not be as quick. But then they didn't have to deal with the customers. Lucy had been dreaming for three days about a lobster roll, and it seemed no matter how long the wait would be her mouth wouldn't accept any imitation. She had passed all the traditional Boston seafood haunts, and there were a lot of them, for this version that came from a pub of sorts.

When it was finally her turn to order, she watched a young man scoop mounds of chunky lobster meat with a light coating of mayonnaise onto a New England style hot dog bun. A handful of crunchy fries and a small container of coleslaw completed her order. She gladly took it, stepping out of the line. She wondered what the others were waiting for since her sandwich had been prepped so quickly. Was she missing something even better than her favorite? She almost asked a man standing nearby but then decided she was happy with her selection, at least for this time.

She grabbed a few napkins and began the long trek back to her gate. At least she didn't have to change terminals. Having to leave one terminal and then clear security again didn't seem like an efficient process, but people seemed to make it work. Of course, she never had to stress about being late for a flight. Not that the flight wouldn't leave her, because they would, but she had only to call in that she was stuck at the security checkpoint line and she would be rebooked on the next available flight. She might end up going somewhere other than her scheduled location and, of course, it probably screwed up a large part of the Air Marshals' flight schedules, but adjustments were made.

She made a quick stop and picked up a few more magazines for her next flight before entering her gate area. As she passed beneath one of the hanging televisions, she heard the announcer's excited voice mention an emergency landing. Instead of finding her usual isolated seat to enjoy her sandwich, she plopped down in front of the TV. The headline in large letters across the lower half of the screen took her breath away—"Eastern Airline pilots prepare for emergency landing." She had to force herself to concentrate on what the news anchor was saying.

"After the pilot radioed air control to clear for an emergency landing, the ground crew went into action. Everyone is ready and standing by, even though the flight is still about twenty minutes out."

Lucy dropped her bag of food at her feet and waited for the announcer to drone through all the statistics for emergency landings at Los Angeles International Airport. LAX was second only to Hartsfield Jackson in Atlanta as the busiest airport in the

United States, and it was one of the largest international airports in the world. As the announcer was so clearly communicating, emergency landings happened there on a regular basis. The flight in question would fly low over the runway several times to allow the ground crew to view its malfunctioning landing gear. The filmed footage would be analyzed, and then the pilot would attempt a landing.

She rubbed her palms against her jean-covered thighs, only realizing after the action that her hands were damp and clammy. Why hadn't she asked Dex where she was going to be this week? She was pretty sure she was in the US but where, she had no idea. Was Dex the pilot flying the malfunctioning plane? She rested her head against the back of the chair and tried to take deep breaths. Dex was an experienced pilot, and if she was in the cockpit, she would know what to do. That thought did nothing to stop the queasiness she was feeling.

The announcer's bubbly personality was starting to get on her nerves, so she gathered her belongings and stood. Walking into the flow of passengers moving through the terminal, she dropped her food into the nearest trash can and ducked into a quiet alcove. Even though there was a good chance Dex was in the air and wouldn't have her phone on, she still typed out a quick message. Then as ridiculous as she knew it was, she dialed Dex's phone and listened to the recorded message, hesitating for only a second before leaving a brief and what she hoped wasn't confusing message. She couldn't say the things she wanted to without sounding crazy after all, given all of her insistence that nothing could happen between them.

The thought of Dex being on a plane that could potentially crash sent her mind reeling. She could still remember the number of high-risk landings quoted by the television reporter. Even she had her share of stories. Nothing serious and most of the time she didn't know any more details than the average passenger. Once the oxygen masks had even dropped from the overhead compartments. The plane had made a quick landing only to discover the masks had dropped due to a malfunction rather than a loss of oxygen in the cabin. Emergency landings happened somewhere in the world almost every day and in the majority of them no one was even injured. And yet she still would give anything to know where Dex was right at this moment and be reassured that she wasn't in the cockpit. Unfortunately that wasn't going to happen until Dex could call her.

Lucy returned to her gate and waited as patiently as she could for the boarding process to begin. The long-anticipated lobster roll was gone from her mind, replaced by thoughts of the woman who had taken her world by surprise. A woman who was so disarmingly unaware of her own beauty.

Basking in the glow from the restaurant candle, Dex had been a vision that Lucy was unable to get out of her mind. Dex had reached inside her and found the dormant feelings she had made an art of hiding. When they had met in Paris, the determination in Dex's eyes had been like a laser zeroing in on Lucy. Since then she had been doing her best to ignore the tingly feeling in the pit of her stomach and treat Dex like every other one-night stand. The ache in her heart said otherwise though. She wasn't sure what she had to give, but the way Dex looked at her it was clear she saw something in her. She wanted to be the only woman in Dex's life. The best thing she could do at the moment was try to occupy her mind with work even if that wasn't what she wanted to do. Dex would call her when she could and everything would be okay. She was ready to see where Dex wanted to go with what was happening between them.

CHAPTER EIGHTEEN

"The crew is briefing the passengers on emergency landing procedures," Dex said as she slid into the co-pilot's seat.

"Okay." Pilot Carl Tash nodded. "We've burned off enough fuel so that was our last pass. Let's take her in."

"Ready. Auto brake is off and there are no other system failures."

Carl calmly spoke aloud each step as he continued to move through their emergency procedures. "Still no response from the landing gear. We have a green light. Here we go. Disconnecting auto pilot."

Dex felt the rush of adrenaline as Carl guided their 737 onto runway 25L at Los Angeles International Airport. Her palms itched to be in control of the large plane, but Carl confidently followed through their action plan. He had excellent audible skills and she had no problem following his lead.

She could see the lights of the emergency vehicles flashing in the distance. Unlike today's emergency, emergencies with the Blackhawk happened fast. Lights flashed and alarms sounded making her blood pump faster as she raced to rectify whatever situation had been thrown at her. Today, Carl had identified the issue with the landing gear almost thirty minutes earlier. They had even silenced all of the audible alarms so they could communicate with each other and ground control. The silence was tranquil but she fed the excitement coursing through her to keep her mind at a heightened level should she need to assist him.

She and Carl had both reviewed the video ground control had sent of their partially extended landing gear. If the gear collapsed under the pressure when the 737 touched down, then they would be performing a belly landing. The initial touchdown was soft as Carl fought to hold the bulk of the plane off the ground. The landing gear held their position as more and more weight pressed down on them. As the plane slowed to a stop, Dex took a deep breath. Together she and Carl ran through the remaining emergency shutdown checklist.

Carl stood. "Let's go check on the passengers."

She followed him out of the cockpit and was immediately confronted by anxious faces.

"Everything is fine now," she assured them. "Follow the flight attendants' directions and we'll get everyone safely into the terminal."

She stood in the door with Carl and consoled each passenger as they used the bright yellow emergency slide to exit the plane. When the last passenger had cleared the door, she and Carl followed the flight attendants down the slide.

* * *

Dex gave the taxi driver the name of the hotel and then rested her head against the back of the seat. It had taken hours to file all of the paperwork required for an emergency landing. She and Carl had stayed with the passengers until they had all been released by the paramedics. There was one twisted ankle from the emergency slide and a few bumps and bruises. She was thankful for Carl's gentle demeanor in dealing with each person. He was doing what Eastern Airlines expected of them, but he wasn't doing it because it was in the manual. His sincere compassion was felt by everyone.

He had taken care of her too, talking her into having a quick bite to eat when they finally finished with all of the required paperwork. Neither drank alcohol and he didn't talk much about the landing, but it was clear he wanted to make sure she was okay. So had the airline, which had called in another pilot to cover her next flight. They also arranged for her to catch a flight a couple hours later to Denver, where she'd pick up her next assignment.

Even before today, it had been a long week; it had taken all of her strength each evening to not call Lucy. She wondered where she was now and if she had seen the emergency landing on the news. Tonight after she settled into her room she would text her. She was looking forward to it. Her vow that she would forget Lucy was long forgotten, but she wasn't going to push her either. She would make contact tonight as she had promised, but the rest was up to Lucy. Remembering that she hadn't turned her phone on since she landed, she pulled it from her pocket and pressed the button. It immediately dinged, letting her know she had a voice mail.

The cab pulled to a stop outside the Denver Airport SpringHill Suites, and she slid her phone back in her pocket. The voice mail was probably from Deidra, and coffee was required before she listened to it. Deidra only wanted to keep her informed, but it was painful to listen to the sadness in her voice. She realized how horrible that sounded. Deidra was the one dealing with their father every day. She was thankful to escape to work, even if it was only for a week at a time. Of course, Deidra might have seen the news too. She certainly wasn't ready to deal with her questions or anxiety about that either.

After depositing her bag in her room and changing clothes, she sent her uniform to be dry cleaned and decided to walk to a nearby Italian restaurant. She needed to decompress and let the events of today wash over her. When she had seen the flight schedule, she had hoped to be able to see some Colorado mountains. Unfortunately she was on the east side of Denver, and all the good views were on the west side. Denver had gotten its first snow of the season less than a week ago, so the patchwork quilt view from above was mostly white. Her flight out in the morning was too early to allow time to enjoy a hike either.

She would have enjoyed the walk to the restaurant if not for the fact the streets were crowded with traffic. Spotting the sign for the restaurant at last, she followed the sidewalk into the brightly decorated and well-lit lobby. Unlike the place she had shared pizza with Lucy, this Italian restaurant was anything but dark and quiet.

The lobby gave way to a long bar and open dining space. Stairs on the side led to party dining tables upstairs. She was taken to a small two-person booth on the side and given a menu. The authentic Italian murals and decorations gave the room an Old World Italy appearance. When the waiter, a middle-aged man in a starched white shirt and black pants, approached with a wine bottle, she nodded eagerly. After the day she'd had she didn't feel at all guilty about a splurge of one glass.

"I'm Anthony. I'll be taking care of you this evening. Have you made a choice or would you like to hear the specials for today?" he asked as he poured the wine.

"I was thinking about the spinach ravioli?"

"Excellent choice. Would you like mushrooms and artichoke hearts in the sauce?"

"Sure."

"I'll put your order in and be right back with a glass of water."

True to his word, Anthony's return was quick. She had barely taken her first sip of wine.

"Is the wine acceptable?" he asked.

"Yes."

"Very good. It's our house wine. We have it shipped from my cousin's vineyard in California. Have you been to Santa Rosa?"

"Not yet, but I certainly hope to one day. I travel for business but mostly only to larger cities."

"Pity." He waved his hand in the air as if to make her lack of seeing Santa Rosa disappear. "It is a beautiful place. Maybe you will see it one day."

She nodded and he was off to greet a new table of patrons.

He was back with her meal before she even had time to take in all of her surroundings. She ate slowly, sipping her wine while she watched the other patrons. Sometimes she liked to read an eBook when she was dining alone, but it didn't seem appropriate in this setting. She wasn't a big people watcher, but she found the dynamics of others' relationships fascinating. There was always at least one couple who never spoke to each other while they ate. She tried to imagine where they were going or coming from. Probably a forced family visit. Maybe a funeral or a wedding. Certainly not locals out for a night of fine dining. They didn't appear to enjoy each other's company and had probably been married for way too many years.

She was savoring her last bite when Anthony returned.

"Can I get you anything else?" he asked, laying her check on the table.

He had been the perfect combination of attentive but not annoying. She was pleased that he along with the enjoyable meal and some people-gazing had taken her mind off her day. "No, Anthony, everything was perfect. Thank you."

"Would you like a container to take your ravioli with you?"

"Not this time. I'm in a hotel and have to leave in the morning."

"Oh yes, here for business. You must be in sales."

"No, I work for an airline."

"Oh, did you see the news earlier? There was an emergency landing at LAX." He leaned toward her conspiratorially. "We watched it on the television in the kitchen." He stood straight again, glancing from side to side to see if anyone had noticed his departure from proper etiquette. "No one was hurt, so it all turned out okay."

She didn't see any reason to tell him she had been in the cockpit or even that she was a pilot. "That's good news." She stood and handed him the black leather book with her cash in it. "It's all set. No change."

"Thank you, ma'am. Enjoy your night."

Enjoy my night. That was something she would certainly like to do. But the first thing she had to do was listen to Deidra's message and then deal with her own anxiety over the emergency landing. It didn't matter how many near misses she had been through; each one was only a reminder of how short life could be. There would be no lingering aftermath for her, however. No hesitation about getting back up in the air. Although she had discovered as she boarded the plane to Denver earlier that she much preferred to be in the cockpit rather than a passenger.

She slowly wound her way toward the exit, enjoying the last few seconds of soothing atmosphere and smells. After she had consoled Deidra, she would text Lucy. Saving the more enjoyable part of the evening for last. No matter what happened between her and Lucy she would never forget her. Lucy had affected her more than she had expected. To the extent she could, she had kept her focus this week on work in order to avoid analyzing her trip to Niagara. She still couldn't believe she had followed her. It was so unlike her.

Ego? Was that what was to blame? She didn't think so. Watching Lucy pack and leave that morning had hurt, of course. She didn't like the vulnerable feeling. The truth was she didn't need Lucy in her life. Especially if Lucy didn't want to be there. She knew she would be saying those words a lot over the next couple weeks. Convincing her heart they were true wouldn't be easy. No. She didn't need Lucy, but she did want her.

She stepped outside into the cold air, sucked in a gulp of it, and felt it wash away some of her sadness. She would be fine. She always was. Through everything she had faced over the years, she always pulled through. This time, though, she felt the loss. The emptiness.

Her phone vibrated with an incoming call. It reminded her that she hadn't listened to the waiting voice mail. Deidra's name displayed on the screen and she swiped to answer.

"Hey, sis."

"Where are you today?" Deidra asked.

"Denver."

"Good. Did you see what happened at LAX?"

Could she lie? Should she? Deidra had enough going on in her life without worrying about her too. "Yes, I did." That wasn't a lie.

"I bet it's cold where you are. It is here too," Deidra paused. "I have a small amount of good news."

"Yes, please." She could use some good news. She had gotten used to Deidra's call always containing bad news about their father.

"Dad held his fork and fed himself lunch today."

"That's great. What did the nurses say?"

"They said there is occasionally an upswing before the last downswing. I'm not thinking about that, though. I'm going to visit him in the morning. You're coming home tomorrow, right?"

"Yeah, I'll be in about noon."

"Okay. I'll call you."

"Hey, Deidra," she said hastily before her sister could hang up. "I'm sorry I didn't call you back sooner. I saw the voice mail, but I was getting settled in for the night."

"I didn't leave you a voice mail."

"What? Okay. Guess I better check and see who it was then. Thanks. Talk to you tomorrow."

"Tomorrow."

Tomorrow. Her mother had started that when she left for the military. Never saying goodbye. Confident there would always be a tomorrow. She smiled at the memory. She hadn't noticed before that Deidra did it too, but it made her happy. There would always be a tomorrow. Even without her dad or even Lucy. Tomorrow would always come.

As soon as she entered the shelter of the hotel, she pressed the button for her voice mail. Hearing Lucy's voice surprised her. She paused in the stairway and replayed the message again. Lucy's voice sounded tense even though she didn't say more than for Dex to call her. There was a text message saying the same thing. She climbed the remaining stairs to Level Three and walked the short distance to her room. She wasn't sure she was ready to call Lucy back. Even though they had texted after they parted on Sunday and she had planned to call her over the weekend, she still was preparing for the inevitable breakup. If she could even call it that. They hadn't had more than a few nights together and that probably didn't constitute enough of a relationship to require a breakup.

She paced her room a few times, trying to settle her thoughts. She had too much energy and she needed to burn it. The back and forth of her emotions was making her jittery. She changed into workout clothes and found her way to the gym on the top floor. All of the treadmills faced a large glass wall, presenting their backs to the door. In the distance she could see the mountain ranges stretching toward the sky. She began running immediately, keeping a slow pace until she warmed up. Staring at the view, she felt a wave of resolve wash over her. She couldn't keep feeling this way. On again. Off again. She needed Lucy to commit and if she couldn't then that's where they would remain. Would committing to seeing each other again be enough? Yes, it would. She liked Lucy enough to wait for her if time was only what she needed. But that was the problem, wasn't it? She didn't know if time was all she needed. She didn't know at all what Lucy was thinking because Lucy didn't talk about it.

She sighed as she slowed the treadmill back to a walking pace. Her breathing was labored and she had only been running for twenty minutes. Was it Lucy or the high elevation? It didn't matter. She was ready for a shower and sleep. Morning would come soon enough. She walked for a few more minutes and then returned to her room. She felt better with a little exercise after the wonderful meal and a shower now would put her to sleep.

When she emerged from the shower, her cell phone lying silently on the bed began to taunt her. Lucy had sounded concerned when she called. Maybe it was something other than what she expected. Lucy had probably heard about the emergency landing. She dialed Lucy's number and was surprised when it only rang once before she picked up.

"Dex?"

"Yeah. Is everything okay?"

"You didn't see the news today?" Lucy asked with a sigh.

Dex was silent as she thought about her answer. It had been easy to evade Deidra's questions. Lucy wouldn't be as easy.

"I just got to Denver."

"There was an emergency landing at LAX earlier."

Dex was silent again.

"Dex?"

"It happens a lot."

"I know, but you weren't there right? You're in Denver."

"I'm in Denver."

"Damn." Lucy sighed. "You were on that plane, weren't you?"

"Yeah." What else could she say? Lucy sounded upset, but she didn't know if it was because of her or whether the incident had dredged up feelings from her father's death. She waited to see if Lucy would explain.

Lucy was silent so long Dex wasn't sure she was still on the line.

"Lucy?"

"Yeah, I'm here. I was worried and I didn't even know for sure you were on the plane."

Her heart did a little leap at Lucy's words. "That's sweet."

Again Lucy was quiet. Dex wasn't sure whether to push her or give her time. It was clear she had more to say. Things that might not be easy for her and Dex wanted to hear them. This could be the turning point she had been hoping for.

"I'm fine," Dex said softly.

"I know. After freaking out a little and leaving you a message, I realized how much I wanted to see you again."

"That can be arranged."

"Good, because I've arranged to be in Toronto for my days off. When do you get in?"

"Around noon." She couldn't believe Lucy was making the first plans for them to be together. For the first time it wouldn't be impulsive or a coincidence. They were actually planning a weekend.

"I'll arrive a little earlier. Text your flight number and I'll hang around your gate. I'm not sure where the Eastern office is in Toronto."

"Sounds like a plan. I'm looking forward to it."

"Okay. See you tomorrow."

Lucy hung up before Dex could say goodbye. She crawled into bed hugging her phone to her chest. Her stomach was churning and her heart wanted to leap out of her chest. No woman had made her feel like this. Especially not with so few words. She knew how big a step it was for Lucy to have made those arrangements. She had even admitted to Dex that she had been worried.

Dex snuggled into the covers, mentally planning what they would do for the weekend, what things she wanted to show Lucy and what places she wanted to take her. She knew the smile on her face would still be there when she woke up in the morning.

CHAPTER NINETEEN

Lucy paced the length of the seating area again. Dex's plane had landed almost thirty minutes earlier, and it looked like everyone had departed. Still no sign of Dex. What if this wasn't the right plane? What if at the last minute Dex wasn't on the plane?

She took a deep breath. When had she lost her composure? Dex would text her if something had gone wrong. Wouldn't she? She had almost worked herself into an anxiety attack waiting on the plane to arrive, something she had never had before. None of this seemed right, but then she remembered her time with Dex. That had felt right. She missed her touch, but she also missed being with her. Seeing her laugh and sharing a look. She turned and began the trek back across the room once more.

When Dex's voice caught her ear, she stopped and leaned against the closest wall, trying to look casual. Her heart raced. Dex emerged from the gateway with another pilot. Though she carried on a conversation with him, her head turned from side to side taking in the entire gate area. Lucy waited patiently until their eyes met. All the anxiety she had been feeling fell away, and she was filled with the warmth of Dex's smile.

She knew Dex would have paperwork to clean up from the flight so she fell into step behind them. She hesitated when Dex motioned her to join them. She said the appropriate things when Dex made the introductions and then walked beside her to the Eastern Airlines office. Motioning to the coffee shop across from the office door, she told Dex to take her time. She would be waiting.

Less than twenty minutes later, Dex emerged and dodged the flow of people to join her.

"Shall we go?" Dex asked.

She immediately stood. She didn't need any encouragement. She was surprised at how anxious she was to have Dex to herself for the entire weekend. Yesterday's fears still lingered, leaving her wanting to spend a significant amount of time just holding Dex in her arms. She had thought a lot about the words she would say to Dex when she had the opportunity, but now that she was here she wasn't sure she would be able to say them. She was confident she would be able to at least show her how she felt, though. Having finally given herself permission to enjoy Dex's company, she couldn't wait for their weekend to start.

As they made their way through the airport to the exit by baggage claim, she saw Dex was holding back something she wanted to say.

"What?" she finally asked. If Dex had changed her mind since they had last seen each other then she needed to know now. Changing her own thought processes had been hard enough, but she wasn't going to put her feelings and emotions out there now just for Dex to stomp on them.

"I don't know." Dex grimaced. "Okay, I do know. I'm not sure why I said that. I'm just wondering why the sudden change of heart. A week ago you were blowing me off and now you're here waiting for me. I'm not sure how I'm supposed to react."

She took a deep breath. She knew they would have this conversation, but she hadn't expected it so soon or in the airport with so many people around.

"Yesterday when I was watching that flight do an emergency landing, I couldn't stop thinking about what if it was you in the cockpit. How would I handle losing you? I realized I would regret losing the opportunity of spending time with you."

Dex grinned. "So you want to spend time with me?"

"Yes, I guess that's what I said."

"You want to date a pilot?" Dex joked.

"Now, you're just pushing it."

They maneuvered around other travelers and made their way to the exit doors.

"Am I safe to assume we're headed to my condo?"

Lucy grinned shyly. She was willingly returning to the scene of a previous one-night stand, something she was sure she had never done in her life. What was wrong with her? Is this really what she wanted? She glanced at Dex as they stepped outside the doors and the wind caught her hair. Dex was more than beautiful. Could she handle calling Dex hers? Yes. Yes, that was what she wanted. To belong to someone and know they belonged to her.

"Sounds perfect."

They walked together to the nearest cab. Lucy opened the door for Dex to slide in. Holding up her coffee cup she pointed at the trash can nearby so Dex would know where she was going. When she turned, a woman the same height as Dex had looped her arm through Dex's and was leading her away. As Dex climbed into another waiting cab, she turned and met Lucy's eyes. Lucy thought she could see confusion and maybe regret, but she wasn't trying to pull away from the woman.

Her heart collapsed as she watched the cab with Dex in it pull away from the curb and merge into traffic. She wanted to fall to the street and cry. What in the world had happened? Did Dex have a girlfriend she had never mentioned?

"Hey, lady. Are you coming or not?"

She slowly walked back to the cab she and Dex had picked and climbed inside.

"Head into Toronto. I'll let you know what hotel."

She knew she sounded a little rude, but she would make it up to him with the tip. She needed to make it clear she wasn't in a chatting mood. She began searching hotels on her phone and located one near the CN Tower and Blue Jays Stadium. She gave the information to the driver and then turned off her phone. There wasn't anyone she needed to talk with.

* * *

"What the hell!" Dex exclaimed.

Deidra looked at her in surprise. "What?"

"I was…We were…oh, never mind." Dex slouched back in the seat. Deidra wouldn't have come to get her unless it was really important. "What's going on?"

"Dad's asking for you. I thought you would want to get there as soon as you could. His clearness could vanish at any minute. He recognized me as soon as I walked in. It was like he had never been gone. He knew he was in the nursing home and that Mom was gone. He knew how old the boys were."

Deidra's voice drifted to the back of Dex's mind as she thought about having her father back again. She knew it wasn't going to last, but a few moments would be enjoyable. Her thoughts shifted then to Lucy and she quickly pulled her phone from her pocket. She couldn't call her with Deidra sitting next to her, but she could certainly text. Keeping it short, she explained it was a family emergency and she would call later. She watched the delivered tag on her text message and waited hoping it would switch to read. After a few minutes, she closed the screen and slid it back into her pocket. When she looked up, Deidra was staring at her.

"What?" she asked.

"Who was that?"

She shrugged. There was no reason to make Deidra feel bad now. "No one."

"Is it the new girl? The love of your life?"

"What are you? Five years old? She's not the love of my life." *But she could be,* Dex thought. Lucy was everything she had always looked for. Strong and kind. And so adorable. As soon as she answered the text she would make arrangements to meet her tonight. She groaned as she realized Lucy now had nowhere to go until they met back up. Damn Deidra's enthusiasm. If she'd had a moment to think, she'd have given Lucy the keys to her condo.

Seeing Deidra had surprised and scared her; her first thought had been that their father was gone. It had taken a few moments to realize there wasn't sadness on Deidra's face. Why had she let Deidra pull her away so easily? She had to tell Lucy to wait for her. And she had to do it now. She quickly pulled her phone back out and dialed Lucy. She hoped she hadn't reserved a hotel yet. Maybe she could reach her neighbor, Sharon, who had a key to her place for emergencies.

Lucy's phone rang straight to voice mail. Dex frowned as she left a message.

"I'm so sorry. It was a family emergency. My neighbor has a key so you can get in. I'll meet you there in a little bit."

She avoided looking at Deidra, but from the corner of her eye she could see her watching her. She hung up and sent a text to Sharon. Luckily she was already home from work and would be around all evening. She texted Sharon's condo number to Lucy and told her to grab the key and make herself at home. She slid her phone back in her pocket and finally looked at Deidra.

"What?" she asked again.

"What's going on?" Deidra asked.

"Lucy was going to stay with me and now she has nowhere to go. I was making arrangements with Sharon to let her in."

"Lucy was with you?" Deidra said excitedly, spinning around in her seat to look out the back window as if she could see back to the airport terminal.

"She was."

"Oh, Dex. I'm so sorry. I didn't even think about the possibility that you weren't alone. I was so excited to get you to Dad while he would still know you."

"I know," she said, all her previous anger at Deidra fading away. "You didn't know."

"Why didn't you tell me?"

"It all happened so fast. I was surprised to see you there and then you were pushing me in a cab." She looked around them as if seeing their situation for the first time. "Why are we in a cab? Where's your car?"

Deidra shrugged. "I thought it would be easier to find you if someone else was driving. I left my car at the nursing home."

"You could have called, you know."

She felt bad as Deidra sighed. It wasn't her fault. At least not completely. She should have kicked and screamed when Deidra pulled her away from Lucy. She could only imagine what Lucy must be thinking. She would make it up to her tonight, she resolved. Resting her head against the back of the seat, she thought about all the ways she could make it up to Lucy.

She had been shocked when Lucy said last night she would meet her in Toronto. Everything about that went against what she had learned about the woman so far. Sure, she had been shaken by the idea of Dex being involved in an emergency landing. But was that all? Enough to make her fly on her days off and not return to the cabin she was renovating near the town of Madison. She had mentioned it only fleetingly, but it wasn't hard for her to imagine Lucy enjoying the warm weather of northern Florida and the isolation the cabin offered.

"Dex."

Was it Lucy? No, she was with Deidra. She sat up and blinked her eyes. Had she really fallen asleep so easily?

"Sorry, but we're here. Are you ready to go inside?" Deidra asked.

She nodded, swinging her travel bag over her shoulder as she stepped from the cab. Together she and Deidra walked into the nursing home. The smell of antiseptic mixed with pine trees mingled with the scent of the fresh cut flowers sitting inside the entrance. As usual she wanted to stay right there and avoid seeing her father in such a vulnerable position. But she didn't. She followed Deidra to his door and waited while she slowly pushed it open.

Peering around Deidra, she saw him sitting in a wooden rocker facing the television. As soon as he noticed them, he immediately turned the volume down on the news station he was watching.

"Just catching up," he said. His voice was gravelly from the small amount of talking he had been doing over the last couple of weeks.

"Hey, Dad," Deidra greeted him, taking a knee beside his chair.

He patted her head and then motioned to the other two chairs in his room. "You girls take a seat."

Dex had seen nothing so far to imply he knew who they were, but the talking and watching the news was certainly better than he had been. His eyes looked alert as he scanned her face and then took in her uniform.

"How's the flying?" he asked.

She nodded as tears filled her eyes. He did know who she was. She stepped closer and gave him a hug before taking a seat in one of the chairs. Deidra sat at his feet with her legs stretched in front of her. Her arm rested on their father's knee and his hand was on her shoulder.

"It's been good. I'm still learning some of the ropes, but so far it hasn't been too much of a challenge."

"I didn't figure it would be. You were always the technical one. Deidra here," he patted Deidra's shoulder, "she was our emotional one. You girls brought such joy to your mother and me. Never forget how much we loved you and be good to each other."

She felt the tears well in her eyes again and quickly wiped them away. Deidra, too, was fighting back the tears that threatened.

"We won't, Dad. You and Mom taught us better than to take each other for granted," she said, smiling at Deidra.

When Deidra nodded her agreement, he lifted the remote and turned the volume back up on the television. She watched as he drifted back into his closed world. The pats he was making on Deidra's shoulder slowed and then stopped. His eyes slowly closed and his head fell to his chest. The rhythm of the rise and fall of his chest was hypnotizing; Dex couldn't pull her eyes away.

"How we doing in here?" a nursing home attendant asked as she walked in. Her hair was pulled back in a tight bun and her round body was covered in brightly colored scrubs.

"We're okay," she mumbled and Deidra nodded.

"You've been sitting up long enough, Mr. Alexander," she said loudly, ignoring the fact that he was asleep. "Let's get you back to bed."

She pushed his chair closer to the bed and easily pulled him into a standing position. His eyes were open, but Dex wasn't sure he was seeing anything. The attendant maneuvered him back onto the bed and then tucked him in with a sheet across his legs.

"Stay as long as you want, girls. We'll be bringing him dinner shortly." She bustled back out of the room as quickly as she had arrived.

"I'd like to stay and help him eat his dinner. If that's okay with you?" Deidra asked.

She nodded. How could she say no? She wanted to be back at her condo with Lucy, but she also wanted to be here.

"We can stay as long as you want."

Dex took up a position on the opposite side of the bed from Deidra as a male attendant delivered the evening dinner tray. It was still what Dex would consider late afternoon, but Deidra had explained they feed this wing early since they were early to bed. She tried her best to make Deidra laugh, hoping their father was hearing at least some of their conversation. Deidra worked her way through the tray of mashed vegetables and some unidentifiable meat. The attendant had called it chicken potpie, but it was too smashed for her to identify.

When Deidra was happy with the amount of food their father had eaten, she put down the spoon and pushed the tray away. Dex watched as she cleaned his face gently with a nearby washcloth. They each kissed him on the cheek and left together. Deidra barely made it to the lobby before dropping into a chair and putting her head in her hands.

A nurse Dex had seen previously approached quickly and took a seat beside Deidra, dropping an arm across her shoulders.

"Today was a good day," the nurse said softly. She glanced up at Dex. "I'm Susan."

"Nice to meet you, Susan. I'm Dex. Deidra's sister."

Susan nodded. "I've seen you here before. Your father had a good couple of hours today."

"Yes," Deidra sobbed.

"He'll be okay where he's going and you girls will be fine too. The cycle of life will continue to turn. We all play our part and there's nothing you can do to change any of it," Susan reminded them.

Although Dex didn't want to think about all of that, she agreed with everything Susan was saying. They were heartbroken when their mother passed, but life had continued to move. Deidra would be deeply saddened when their father passed and then her family would build her up strong again. Deidra had so much to look forward to in her future. Her sons were growing up and soon they would have families of their own.

What did she have to look forward to? She sighed. Life. Life was what she had to look forward to. Her life would be everything she made it to be. She didn't have to sit back and just let things happen. She could, would, make an effort to have what she wanted—a family of her own, someone to come home to every night or at least at the end of the week. No, not just someone. Lucy. She wanted Lucy in her life. Tonight, she would make sure Lucy knew that too. Doing her part and telling Lucy how she truly felt was the best thing she could do to move them forward.

And if Lucy didn't want to share her life?

She would worry about that when she had to, she decided. She wasn't ready to give up without a fight, though.

CHAPTER TWENTY

Lucy pulled the Niagara Falls moose from her suitcase and tucked it into the pillows at the head of the bed. She had done this every night since she bought it. Except, of course, the night Dex had stayed with her. She had also purchased another suitcase in order to be able to carry it until she returned home. To say she was disappointed at how things had turned out was an understatement. She wanted to curl into the bed with her moose and sleep away this nightmare.

Dex had been everything she had hoped she would be, but today reminded her that life seldom worked out the way she wanted it to. She refused to let today be another wash to the memories of the losses in her life. Her father's memory was always sitting at the edges of her mind no matter which direction she turned. She would always miss him, but the feeling of loss had faded slightly during her time with Dex.

Dex. She still wasn't sure what had happened at the airport. She sighed in defeat. There was a small part of her that was relieved Dex had walked away. She liked to think that would make forgetting her even easier. That didn't stop her from looking every few minutes at the phone lying on the top of the dresser. Had Dex left her a message? One that explained everything? Did it matter?

No, because relationships weren't for her. She knew that. At the same time, she knew she was a different person than she used to be. The new Lucy needed people in her life.

She turned on her phone and listened to the message from Dex. After reading the text messages, she stared at the phone trying to decide how to respond. Did she want to go to Dex's condo? Yes, of course she did. But the last twenty-four hours had taught her that maybe she wasn't ready to be in this type of a relationship. Her feelings for Dex were too intense. Maybe a little time would help her put things in perspective. And give Dex time to explain who the woman at the airport was.

For now, though, she would work on building the other relationships in her life. It was a weird feeling to want someone to be with, especially when what she was thinking about wasn't about sex or spending the night with someone but about hanging out and sharing a laugh. For the first time in her life she wanted companionship. She wanted someone in her life who wasn't a lover.

After making a few calls, she checked out of the hotel and took a taxi back to the airport. Her boss had been only too happy to give her two weeks off when she called, and so she was heading home. Sheila and Karen would be around for support, she knew, and Dan would arrive first thing Monday morning to begin the construction on her kitchen. She felt in control of her life again. Her final task was to send Dex a text message. Her words were simple. *My plans have changed.*

* * *

Dex waited until Deidra dropped her off that evening to respond to Lucy's text. Her sister felt bad enough already about pulling her from the airport. She didn't see a need to tell her that Lucy had decided not to spend the weekend with her. She dialed Lucy's number again as she dropped onto the couch in her living room, the words Lucy had said to her when they were in Niagara Falls echoing in her head: "People aren't dependable."

She couldn't help feeling that she had let Lucy down. Although she hadn't meant to walk away from her at the airport, Lucy had been left to fend for herself. Not to imply she couldn't. She had been doing that for years. Only counting on herself and no one else. But that was part of the problem. Lucy couldn't see herself with anyone else.

She wondered where Lucy had gone. Did she get a hotel room? Did she go back home? Their short conversation about where they each lived hadn't given her enough information to be able to track Lucy down. She wasn't sure she would if she could. After all, until Lucy told her how she was feeling, she couldn't do more than apologize again for what happened at the airport.

When Lucy's voice mail picked up she made a quick decision to leave a detailed message. Lucy deserved an explanation and if she wasn't ever going to be able to talk with her directly again then a message was the next best thing. She explained that Deidra was her sister and that their father had been ill. His good day had led Deidra to whisk her off to visit him. She was sorry and regretted immensely how all of that had happened. She asked her to please call when she could.

She waited all evening, hoping Lucy would call and they could work things out. She was more than willing to go to Lucy's hotel room to be with her. When she awoke the next morning still sitting up in the living room chair, she realized Lucy wasn't going to call. She had blown the chance she had with her without even meaning to.

* * *

Lucy waited until Dan was hard at work before leaving him to the destruction of her kitchen. Today he would remove all the old cabinets and the flooring. Tomorrow he would begin the installation. He estimated he would be finished by the end of the week and she couldn't wait. She was really glad he had brought another worker with him for the demolition today; it meant she didn't have to feel obligated to offer her assistance. She got out of the house and gave them space to work.

She had talked to Sheila when she arrived the previous night and Sheila was expecting her. Karen was at work and she needed some help with her garden. Though maybe that was only an excuse to get her there. She didn't care. She wanted to spend time with them. For the first time in her life she could say she had friends and it felt good. She had listened to Dex's message earlier and she desperately needed a distraction. Her head ached from trying to figure everything out.

Bogarts appeared at the fence as she got close to Karen and Sheila's house. She spoke softly to him and he brayed back occasionally. Having his large body walking beside her brought comfort and she reached through the fence to pet him. He stopped walking and pressed his body into the wire separating them. The fur on his back wasn't as soft as the short hair on his head and muzzle, but he seemed to like the backrub the best.

"Did you miss me, buddy?" she asked him.

He answered by pushing harder against the fence.

"I'm not sure what to do anymore. I was so close to having something with Dex. I don't know exactly what it was, but it was good. She didn't do anything wrong, but I ran. Just like I always do."

She scratched behind his ears. Resting her chin on top of her other hand that lay on top of the fence post.

"Do you think I should call her?"

Bogarts gave a soft bray.

"I thought so too. I've acted like an ass, though. I'm not sure I know how to apologize. And what if she won't forgive me? What if this time I've pushed her away for good?"

"Well, you won't know until you try," Sheila said from behind her.

She turned quickly, surprised to find another human listening to her conversation with Bogarts.

"Sorry, I didn't mean to startle you. I heard your voice from the garden where I was working and came to see what was happening. It seems you and Bogie are having an interesting conversation."

Lucy shrugged.

Sheila motioned toward the garden. "Want to come help me and get answers to your questions?"

She laughed. "Of course. What can I help you with?"

"My back has been killing me. Probably all the bending over in the garden. I need to get these bags of soil spread around. If you do the lifting and dumping, I'll do the spreading."

"Sounds like a plan. Just show me where to dump."

She worked silently, wondering how much of the conversation with Bogarts Sheila had heard. She expected Sheila to pepper questions at her, but she had remained silent too. For possibly the first time ever she wanted to share what was happening in her life and get someone else's opinion. She knew from the few times she had been around Sheila, though, that she wouldn't offer advice without an invitation.

"So how long had you been eavesdropping on me and Bogarts?" she joked.

"I heard enough to know there's a woman involved."

"Yikes. I hate the sound of that. But yes, my life has been reduced to figuring out what's going on with a woman."

"Want to tell me what happened?"

"We had planned a weekend together and she was whisked away by another woman. It turned out to be her sister," she added quickly.

"So what's the problem?"

Lucy sighed as she dumped the last bag of soil where Sheila directed. "When I heard her explanation about her father being sick, I know I should have called to see how she was, but all I could think about was the rug of happiness being pulled out from underneath me again. I was just starting to believe in the possibility of something good between us. How could I not have known something so important was happening in her life? I thought I knew her."

"My guess is that you don't."

She glanced in surprise at Sheila.

"Well, do you think you do? You just said you thought you knew her."

"No, I guess I don't," she said with resignation.

"Why does that make you sad? You might not know her right now, but that doesn't mean you won't get to know her. That's what the future is all about. Do you want to know her better?"

Lucy sat down in a grassy spot at the edge of the garden and Sheila joined her.

She did want to know Dex better. She had made that decision several days ago. Maybe everything that happened at the airport hurt more because she had made that decision. She had decided to allow herself into a position of vulnerability. And then she felt burned.

"Lucy?" Sheila nudged her back to the conversation.

"I do want to get to know her, but what happened at the airport reminded me what might happen between us if things go bad. That if I open myself up to her, she could hurt me even more. It reminded me of the mantra I have lived my whole life believing. You can't count on anyone. People let you down— even when they don't mean to."

"Oh, Lucy. That might be true, but it's also part of life. People aren't perfect. If you never take the chance, you'll never experience the joy of loving and being loved."

Lucy pulled her knees up to her chest and rested her head in her hands. How had she lived her whole life without facing this issue? She knew how. She had never met anyone she cared enough about to take this chance.

"I can't tell you that you have to take this risk," Sheila continued. "But I can tell you about the joy you'll find if you do. I can't imagine my life without Karen. She makes everything in my life better. Even the bad stuff."

"But what would you do if she left tomorrow? How would you survive? Especially since you've experienced things so good?"

"I'd be heartbroken and, honestly, I'm not even sure how I'd get through, but I know I would. That's one of the joys of life. It continues to move and evolve."

Sheila stood and reached out her hand to pull Lucy to her feet.

"Enough philosophy. Let's go get some lunch."

Lucy laughed. "That sounds great."

Sheila put her arm around Lucy as they walked toward the house. "Love is never easy and the sooner you stop expecting that the better off you'll be. But it's always worth it."

"Couldn't resist one last cliché, huh?"

"I swear to you it's the last one." Sheila laughed. "But seriously, it is the truest one. What you gain from giving your heart is more than anything that would be taken away from you if you lost it."

"How many times were you in love before you met Karen?" She was pretty sure she knew that answer since Sheila and Karen had begun dating in high school.

"Once. Believe it or not," Sheila said with a wicked smile. "I was in the sixth grade and he had the curliest hair I'd ever seen. His mom was in the military, so they were just passing through. He was only here for a few months. Our life together wasn't meant to be."

Lucy punched her lightly on the arm. "Seriously. I know you guys started dating in high school so how can you be so experienced about love?"

"Well, aside from the romance novels I read—lesbian, of course—I know that my life would never have been this good without Karen. In fact, I don't even want to consider what it might have been like."

Sheila pushed Lucy toward the kitchen table and began pulling food from the refrigerator.

"We had chicken last night, so how about chicken salad?"

"Sounds great. Thanks for feeding me. I'm not sure the amount of labor I've put in deserves food."

"Oh, don't worry. We still have a few hours to work this afternoon."

"What else would you like help with?" She knew she had dumped the last bag of soil.

"Bogarts needs a bath."

She raised her eyebrows. "That sounds like fun." She really wasn't sure what bathing a donkey would look like.

"It's not too bad, and I'm hoping with you there that he'll be much more cooperative. We'll scrub his body with some shampoo stuff and then brush his mane and tail." Sheila explained as she mixed the chicken salad and toasted the bread for their sandwiches. "Can I talk you into staying for dinner?"

"No, I guess not. I should get home before the contractor leaves so I can talk with him."

"Karen will be disappointed."

"Oh yeah, I forgot to mention that I'm here for two weeks. I took some time off to finish the remodel in my house and decided to take the week of Christmas off too."

"That's awesome," Sheila said excitedly. "Do you have plans for Christmas? We'd love to have you here."

She thought about what she would like to be doing for the holiday and then groaned.

Sheila patted her back as she set their lunch on the table. "Don't worry. We'll leave it open. Try to make contact with her and see how that goes. We'll understand if you go to visit her instead of joining us." Sheila turned back to the table with their drinks. "Does she have a name?"

"Dex. Her name is Dex."

"That's an interesting name."

"It's a nickname. Diane Alexander is her real name. I'm not sure where Dex came from, but it might be a military nickname."

"She was in the military? Cool."

"Yes, an army pilot."

"Well, I can't wait to meet her," Sheila said as she sat down across from Lucy. "Hey, did you see that emergency landing at LAX?"

"I did."

"You weren't on that plane, right?"

"No."

"I bet you've been through stuff like that a lot."

"Occasionally."

Sheila deserved more than one-word answers. Unfortunately the previous conversation had pretty much drained all of her energy. She was pretty sure Sheila understood that because she didn't ask any more questions.

They finished their lunch quickly and then went back outside. The day was cool, but the Florida sun was hot. Lucy rolled the short sleeves of her T-shirt up to her shoulders, hoping to avoid the dreaded farmer's tan. She discovered quickly her job in the bathing of Bogarts was to entertain the donkey. The scrubbing of his body went quickly, but the brushing of his mane and tail seemed to be more painful. After watching Sheila move in circles chasing him, Lucy moved in and cradled his head.

"That's working perfectly," Sheila said. "I'd have suggested a carrot next."

Bogarts's ears twitched at the mention of a carrot and he began trying to check every pocket on Lucy's pants.

"He knows what the word 'carrot' means, doesn't he?" Lucy asked as she pushed his head away from her hip.

Sheila's answer was a laugh. "You can grab one for him from the barn."

When she came back with the carrot, Bogarts almost knocked her down trying to get to it. She held the larger end and let him gnaw on the other. By the time he had worked his way to her fingers, Sheila was almost finished with both his mane and his tail. She passed the remaining chunk of carrot to him and followed Sheila back to the barn.

"I have one more task, if you're up for it."

Lucy glanced at her watch. She still had about two hours until Dan would be ready to call it a day.

"Sure. Let's hear it."

Sheila passed Lucy a round plastic bowl. "Let's pick some raspberries."

Lucy frowned at her. "It's December."

"We have a small greenhouse across the pasture. I use it mainly for herbs and such, but this year we decided to plant raspberries and spinach."

"That's an interesting combination."

"The raspberries were my pick and the spinach was Karen's," Sheila said, laughing. "Seems fitting, right? I'm sweet, and well, we'll just leave it at that."

They walked across the pasture to the small, enclosed greenhouse. Once they had filled both of their bowls, they returned to the house. Sheila handed her a small container of berries to take home with her.

"Thanks. I'll eat these for dessert tonight." Or maybe dinner, she thought, as she remembered her refrigerator was bare. At some point Dan would haul it away and bring her a brand-new one. She hadn't wanted to deal with trying to keep a bunch of food cool.

She left Sheila peeling potatoes in the kitchen. Dan was loading the last of his equipment when she arrived back at her cabin.

"Oh good. You're here," he said when he saw her. "I called in reinforcements and we were able to finish the demolition and haul everything away. I'll begin installing the cabinets first thing in the morning. Sorry, but you don't have a stove or refrigerator right now. I put everything from the fridge in a cooler and it's in your bathroom. One of the guys picked up some ice for you so it should stay cool until we get the new fridge installed tomorrow. I expect we'll be finished in a day or so."

She watched him climb into his truck and pull away. She was surprised he had called in more guys to help him, but maybe he was trying to get the job finished before the holiday. Whatever the reason she appreciated it. In only a few days, she would have a brand-new kitchen.

She stepped into her kitchen and stopped in surprise. She wasn't sure what she had expected, but the emptiness was stunning. The walls and floors were stripped to the wood beneath and there were no appliances. She slowly walked in a circle running her hand across the edge of the wooden frame where her new countertop would go. The room felt like her life. Gutted of everything it had always known. Tomorrow her kitchen would look brand-new again, but how would her life look?

She meant the words she had uttered to Sheila earlier, but now they felt hollow. The truth was she wasn't sure she could bounce back from the loss of someone she loved again. Images of her father played in her mind. So much time had passed that the things she remembered were mostly things she had pictures of. Birthdays, vacations, and special events were all well documented, but it was his words and his thoughts she missed the most. What would her father have told her when she graduated from college or when she took the job with the air marshals? What pieces of wisdom would he have to share with her right now?

She moved to the living room to get out of the gutted room and the emptiness that was closing in on her. Her suitcase caught her eye from the edge of the laundry room. She dumped it on the floor, throwing dirty items straight into the washer. She opened the second case and stared for a second at the moose, searching for the feeling of joy she had felt when she bought it. Its legs were folded on top of its body to make it fit in the small case and she pulled it out. She carried it into the living room and set it on the mantel over the fireplace.

She took a couple steps back, taking in the entire room. The moose looked lonely on the empty shelf so she pulled it down. Hugging it to her body, she walked around the edge of the room, keeping her back to the gutted kitchen. She set the moose on the couch. Its hands flopped into its lap. It looked comfortable there, but her body felt cool where it had been squeezed against her chest. She missed the comfort it had offered so freely. She picked it up again and moved to the chair. Throwing her feet across the arm of the chair and onto the couch, she stretched out with the moose on her chest.

Was she losing her mind? What thirty-eight-year-old would seek comfort in a stuffed animal? She had never really cared what others thought or followed the norms. She had moved through life on her own, never spending enough time with any one person to care what they thought or felt.

Dex had changed that, had begun to fill every part of her senses and she felt an incredible loss inside now. Her jaw ached from the stress of nonstop analyzing of what she could have or should have done and said. She knew her logic was fried and she was no longer making sense, even to herself. But she had been saying it for years and now she knew it was definitely true. She wasn't capable of a relationship. It didn't matter how much she wanted to. She just didn't have it in her. And now she knew the truth. It was her. She was the one who wasn't dependable.

It was better to make that decision now rather than later, when it could be even more devastating and painful. She rested her head against the soft fur between the moose's antlers. As she drifted to sleep, she thought, *My moose needs a name.*

CHAPTER TWENTY-ONE

Dex jumped at the knock on her door. She had taken her uniforms to the dry cleaner and picked up a few groceries earlier, all the things she would normally do on a weekend. *Lucy?*

Deidra held up a bag of takeout when Dex whipped open the door.

"Peace offering," Deidra said.

"How did you know I was alone?"

"When I stopped to visit Dad, the nurse said she'd spoken with you about visiting today. I was pretty sure that if you were entertaining you wouldn't be planning to visit Dad. Especially when we'd already planned to visit together tomorrow."

She sighed. "Yeah, I thought I'd drop by later and feed him dinner. He seemed to like it when you did that the other day."

"I'm sure he'll love it, but let's talk about why you're sitting here alone," Deidra said as she began unpacking food from the bag she carried.

"What did you bring?"

"Egg rolls, crab rangoon, fried wontons, dumplings, and chicken teriyaki. Stop changing the subject. Where's your girl?"

"That's all appetizers. Didn't you get any actual meals?"

"Of course I did. I have double chocolate chip ice cream. Answer the question. Where is she?"

Dex sighed again. "I don't know. She's only sent one text saying her plans had changed." She dropped into a chair at the table and began opening the containers Deidra had brought.

"That's terrible. I'm so sorry. I wish I knew how to make it up to you. What are you going to do?"

"First, I'm going to eat all this crap you brought, and then I'm going to visit Dad."

"And then?"

"I'll go back to work on Monday."

Deidra smacked the back of her head. "What's wrong with you?"

"What am I supposed to do? She apparently doesn't want to be with me."

"I don't think you really believe that, do you?"

"No, but I think she blames her lack of ability to even attempt a relationship on the loss of her father."

"Was it a painful death?"

She could see Deidra was thinking about their father.

"It was a surprise to the family. I don't think she's ever forgiven him for leaving."

Deidra frowned. "Was it suicide?"

"No, but he traveled a lot, and I think she feels like he chose to be away from her and then he was taken from her forever."

"It sounds like you have a lot of things to work through. How are you going to convince her to take a chance?"

"I'm not going to."

Deidra smacked the back of her head again before pulling two cans of soda from the refrigerator. "What's wrong with you?"

"Again, I ask, what is it you expect me to do?"

"I expect you to fight for her. Who told you love would be easy?"

"I don't love her," Dex insisted.

"Okay, whatever. It's clear you wanted something more than a one-night stand with this woman. You blew off your family to take a little vacation with her and now you're moping like your world will never be happy again."

"I'm not moping."

"Again, whatever," Deidra said, holding up her hand to keep Dex from saying anything else. "Relationships require work and if you aren't willing, then you're right, just let it go."

Deidra opened the container of wontons and pulled one apart, dipping it into the sweet and sour sauce before stuffing it into her mouth. She studied the table while she chewed and Dex could see the conversation was about to make an uncomfortable turn.

"I know the military doesn't make it easy, but did you date while you were in?"

"Not really."

"Why not?"

"Too many people in each other's business."

Deidra nodded. "I get that, I guess. Have you ever dated anyone seriously other than when you were in college?"

"I tried once, but when I came back from a weekend pass the locks on my housing unit had been changed."

"What?"

"My key wouldn't unlock the door where I lived. I went to the company commander and he sent me to the billeting office. They claimed all of the door locks on every unit in my building were being changed. I asked around but I couldn't find anyone who had experienced the same problem. I realized then the Don't Ask, Don't Tell policy didn't mean you couldn't be targeted for conduct unbecoming. It was scary. After that I never met anyone I was willing to risk getting court-martialed over."

"But didn't everything change when the policy was repealed?"

"By law we were allowed to serve openly but you have to realize there were and still are plenty of high-ranking officers and non-commissioned officers who don't agree with the policy. But once you're out, there's no going back into the closet."

"Were you out?"

"Kind of but not really. I would go out with a group of women together, but seldom with someone alone. Especially someone who had made their sexual orientation public."

Deidra looked surprised and maybe a bit overwhelmed, but she didn't ask any more questions, concentrating instead on the food in front of them. Dex realized her lack of openness about her life had made Deidra curious. She had always felt her private life was just that—private. Even with her family. Maybe she should have confided more in her big sister.

Dex bit into an egg roll as she remembered how paranoid she had been that weekend. As a new second lieutenant, she was still learning how the military worked and whom she could trust. She had gotten rid of everything in her apartment that even hinted she might prefer women. She even erased music by lesbian singers from her iTunes account. Her life was certainly different now. She could make her own decisions about her private life without the fear of career consequences.

"I'm willing," Dex finally said with a sigh.

"What?"

"I'm willing to do the work to have a relationship with Lucy."

"Then do something."

"Like what?"

"Find her. Convince her. You figure it out. If it's something you want, then you have to work it out. Maybe she's not the one for you, but if you give up without trying then you'll never know what you might be missing."

"Okay. I hear you. I didn't want to force her into something so I was going to back off. But you're right. I have to at least tell her how I feel and give her a chance to respond."

"You might be surprised with her response when you take the chance first."

She thought about their time at the falls. She had been the one pursuing Lucy and each time she thought she would walk away Lucy had surprised her. Maybe it all wasn't as clear-cut as Lucy had tried to make it appear. Maybe she felt the connection between them too.

Still, she never wanted to talk someone into being with her. She wanted her to want it as badly as she did. When she recalled the look on Lucy's face when they kissed beside the falls, her heart leapt and butterflies danced in her stomach. She had seen something on Lucy's face that day. Something that might be strong enough to bring them back together.

* * *

Lucy stepped out of her bedroom as the front door closed. After a second day spent with Sheila, she had decided to stay home today. She had spent the day in hiding from Dan and his crew. She couldn't remember the last time she had been able to enjoy a book without interruption. Of course, no interruptions meant ignoring the banging and clanging coming from her kitchen. The book had been more than enjoyable, though, and had served as a wonderful escape from the dilemma she was facing with Dex.

Every time she moved, the phone in her pocket reminded her she hadn't responded to any of Dex's texts or voice messages. After her conversation with Sheila the first day, she had come home and convinced herself to let things go with Dex. Pursuing something that would only bring pain later didn't seem the best move. Relationships weren't her cup of tea anyway, right? And yet, two days later she still felt the pull to hear Dex's voice again.

She froze in midstep when she saw her new kitchen. The floor was a mint green tile with hints of dark red mixed in it that matched the curtains already hanging from the window— which she noticed were now very dusty. The backsplash that lined the back and matched the brand-new counter was swirled with more red than mint. The sink was a deep maroon that highlighted the red in all of the tiles. Shiny new stainless steel appliances completed the newly designed kitchen.

She opened a few of the cabinets, finding all of her stuff back in place. She hurried out the door, hoping to catch Dan before he left. He climbed back out of his truck when he saw her.

"We're all finished. I hope you like it," he said with a smile.

"It's stunning. Better than I'd imagined. Are we still good with the cost?" She had paid him in advance based on the quote he had provided. She had thought the amount seemed low when he gave it to her, but now seeing how beautiful the kitchen was she was sure it was too low.

"Yep. With the discount I get from the supply store in town, I still had plenty to buy everything and pay for the extra labor."

"Thank you, Dan."

"My pleasure. Keep my number in case you need anything else and pass it around to your friends."

"I'll do that."

He waved as he climbed back into the truck. She sat down on the porch and watched his truck disappear down the driveway. She couldn't believe this was her house. It brought her such comfort to call it home.

She sighed. The only thing missing was someone to share it with.

As she stood to walk back into the house, she realized she could still hear the hum of a vehicle. She was looking down her driveway when a silver sedan came into view. She tried to see through the window, but the afternoon sun made too much of a glare. She tried not to be annoyed at someone invading her space the second it was perfect. It wasn't Sheila or Karen's car, and she couldn't think of anyone else who would be visiting her.

Lucy watched as her mother climbed out of the sedan. Eileen wore jeans and a yellow sweatshirt, even though the day was still warm. She couldn't help thinking she looked as good as she remembered from their last meeting. Eileen gave her a wave as she turned in a circle, looking at the property around Lucy's house. Her gaze finally stopped on the house, and she walked toward her.

"This is a nice place, Lucy. I'm so proud of you."

Lucy sank onto the top step and stared at her mother. Her ears hadn't heard those simple words from anyone, even her mother, in so long. *I'm proud of you.* She resisted the urge to jump to her feet and fall into her mother's arms. What if this new version of her mother didn't last? Hadn't she worked hard enough convincing herself she could count on no one?

Her mother kissed the top of her head and sat down beside her. "Go ahead and ask."

"Ask what?"

"How I found you or what I'm doing here would be a good start. At least we would be talking. I've called you a lot since we saw each other last."

"I know and I'm sorry," she sighed. She had wanted to call, especially after everything with Dex, but the fear of finding out her mother had drifted back into a shell had kept her from it. She didn't blame her mother for their lack of a relationship. She knew it was her fault too. Her mother had lost so much and instead of standing by her or helping her rebuild her life, she had run away. "I really am sorry."

Eileen gave her a quizzical look before her face settled into a smile. "No more 'I'm sorry.' Okay? I know your life is really busy and I don't expect you to drop everything when I call. What I do expect, though, is for you to be honest with me. Are you willing to let me back in your life?"

That was a question she wasn't expecting and she needed time to answer it. Or at least to answer in a way that wasn't going to hurt her mother's feelings.

"Let's be honest, Lucy. I haven't been here for you and now you aren't sure if you can rely on me. I get that. But I'm asking you for another chance. Can you give me that?"

"I want to," she said softly.

Eileen hugged her. "That's the best answer I could have hoped for." She stood. "Now, show me this house of yours."

Lucy held the front door open, allowing Eileen to enter first. She forced herself to make simple conversation as they walked through the house.

"Is that fresh-cut wood I smell?" Eileen asked.

"It is. They finished my kitchen right before you arrived."

"It's really lovely."

Lucy followed her mother as she walked around the kitchen, running her fingers across the brand-new countertop. She tried to see her little cabin through someone else's eyes. It was small, but its openness gave it a larger appearance. The large window behind the living room sofa along with the one over the kitchen sink brought more than enough light into the two rooms.

When they stepped into her bedroom, she saw the moose resting at the head of the bed where she had been using it as a pillow. She had woken up with it in her arms yesterday morning after falling asleep in the living room. She could blame it on the early arrival of Dan and his workers, but the truth was she had liked waking up with the moose in her arms. It certainly wasn't the same as a warm body, but it made her feel less alone.

Back in the kitchen, her mother added water to the teapot on the stove and turned the burner on under it. Following her mother's lead, Lucy pulled two mugs from the cabinet and several boxes of tea. They continued to talk about the house and the changes Lucy had made. It was an easier conversation than the one they had outside, but she knew more was coming. Her mother was back in the form Lucy remembered from her early teenage days. Eileen wouldn't push too hard, but she would be persistent. If you were holding out on her, she had an instinctual way of knowing it.

At the table with their tea mugs between them, Eileen focused on her.

"So, tell me about the important people in your life," Eileen asked.

Another question Lucy wasn't expecting. Should she confess she had not formed any lasting relationships her entire adult life? Say it or not, her mother was going to be able to tell.

"Sheila and Karen live next door. We bonded over a donkey named Bogarts."

Eileen smiled. "That's nice. What about a boyfriend?"

Lucy's insides froze. Of all the things she had thought about over the last twenty years, coming out to her mother was not one of them. She had dated her first girl in college and had still been coming to terms with it when her father was killed. Coming out to her mother after that had never even crossed her mind. Her mother was no longer present in her life.

She looked out the window at the setting sun and then took a sip of her tea. Why was she delaying the inevitable? Because this could be the moment that would send her mother away again. Wasn't it her mother who had said to be honest?

"No, I do not currently have a girlfriend."

Eileen raised her eyebrows, but said nothing.

"I've dated only women for the last twenty years."

"I guess I'm not surprised. You stopped mentioning boys before you left for college. We have a lot to catch up on. That's not a surprise either."

Lucy's phone rang and she glanced at the screen before swiping.

"Sheila?"

"Hey, Lucy. I wanted to warn you that Karen's on her way down."

"Okay."

"She's bringing you dinner, but her real reason is we saw the car go by. Is it her?"

Lucy stood and walked to the door. "No, it's my mother."

"Oh. How's that? I guess you probably can't talk, right?"

"Right."

"Call us later when you can. Just take the food from Karen and send her home."

"Okay. Thanks."

The cart roared into view as she pulled open the door. She turned back to her mother and shrugged. "Karen from next door is dropping off dinner."

"Well, that's nice."

Eileen followed her onto the porch and Lucy introduced them quickly before Karen could ask too many questions. She wasn't fast enough to keep her mother from hearing Karen ask if Dex was here before they could say goodbye to her. She carried the food back in the house and set it on the table.

"Do you mind?" Eileen asked as she began pulling food from the bag. "I was going to suggest we drive into town for some dinner, but this is so much better. Now you can tell me about Dex."

"She's a pilot I met a while back."

"But you're afraid to take a chance with her?"

Lucy shook her head. Was she really having this conversation with her mother?

"What then?" Eileen asked.

"I don't know, but why would you say I'm afraid?"

"Oh, come on, Lucy. I may not have been around, but I'm still your mother. What real relationship do you have in your life? Karen and Sheila, okay. But I know you haven't lived here long so unless you knew them before you moved here this hasn't been a very long relationship. So, go ahead and prove me wrong. Tell me who you have in your life."

Lucy shook her head again.

Eileen sat beside her and pulled her into her arms. "I'm not trying to be hard on you, Lucy. Neither of us have had anything permanent since your father died. I was scared too. I was scared that something would happen to you and I'd never recover. But guess what? I missed so much of your life protecting myself."

She could feel the sting of the tears starting to fall and she fought to hold them back, burying her head in her mother's shoulder.

"Life is short, Lucy. We need to live every day to its fullest or we miss out on so much."

"How can you say that? Dad was everything to you. You lost it all," she sobbed. She couldn't remember the last time she had cried. Maybe when the news of her father had come or maybe the last time she had tried to share a meal and a conversation with her mother.

"I didn't lose it all. I still have you. And I still have the ability to continue living. I miss your father more than I can ever tell you, but there is more to being alive. I promise you that if you take a chance on love you won't regret it. I certainly haven't. Your father was wonderful. He made me feel special every day, and his words will stay with me until I die. I have no regrets for my life with him. It was everything I wanted it to be."

"Until he died."

"We all die one day. Yes, your father was taken before any of us were ready, but it doesn't change the wonderful memories we have."

Lucy pushed to her feet, wiping her eyes on the sleeve of her T-shirt. "I don't want to feel that kind of pain again."

"You will. Whether you want to or not. So, why not live today exactly the way you want to. Or rather with the one that you want to. Tell me about her."

Lucy felt like a teenager as she watched her mother heap mounds of food onto both of their plates and heat them in the microwave. She told her how she had met Dex but left out their nights together. She did tell her about how Dex had followed her to Niagara Falls, though. Before she knew it their plates were empty and her mother had cleared the table.

"I should get to the hotel," Eileen said.

"Cancel it."

"What?"

"Cancel it. You can have my room. I'll sleep on the couch."

"Well, I haven't checked in yet, so I have my bag with me. Are you sure?"

Lucy took a deep breath. She was sure. She wasn't ready to let her mother go yet.

"I'm sure. Stay with me."

While her mother called the hotel and canceled her reservation, Lucy carried her bag in from the car. She changed into sleep clothes and grabbed a few things from her room. She lay down on the couch with the moose as a pillow while she waited for her mother to prepare for bed. She remembered when they had met previously and she had done everything she could to avoid the awkward embrace they normally shared. That wasn't the way she felt tonight. She liked the comfort and strength her mother shared in her embrace.

"I think I'll go ahead and turn in," Eileen said when she returned to the living room.

She lifted her head and looked at her mother. Even though there were more lines on her face, this was the mother she had grown up with. Eileen pulled the footstool over to where Lucy lay on the couch and sat down. She pulled Lucy's hand to her chest and held it tightly.

"Our lives will change many more times over our remaining years, but I don't want anything to ever separate us again,"

Eileen said softly. "You'll learn to trust again if you let yourself. I promise to always be here to hold your hand when things hurt you."

Eileen ran her hand through Lucy's hair as she stood.

"I'll see you in the morning."

Lucy watched her disappear into the bedroom and she pulled the moose from under her head, hugging him tight. So many things had changed in the last four hours. She knew the past wasn't forgotten, but it would be. She had seen a transformation in her mother she never thought possible. She hadn't realized how much she had missed her mother. She had boxed up every emotion and carried it around like a treasure she was unwilling to share. She felt like her life was starting over again.

Where did all this leave her with Dex? She wanted Dex in her life, but she still wasn't sure she was willing to take the risk. She had never allowed anyone to get to really know her. What if Dex discovered she didn't like the real her?

She rubbed her face. Sleep would never come if she continued to think about all of this, but she couldn't seem to stop. She already knew she would give Dex the chance to get to know her—if Dex still wanted to, that is. She pondered the challenge of finding a way to connect with her again. It wouldn't be easy, but she had several options, one of which was appearing at the door of Dex's condo in Toronto. She began to contemplate scenarios of spending a Christmas in Toronto with Dex. Christmas Eve was three days away—and she wasn't sure what her mother's plans might be. Finding that out would be the first task of the day when she woke up. She'd figure out a plan. She still had over a week of vacation left.

CHAPTER TWENTY-TWO

Lucy awoke to a cramp in her back and the smell of coffee. It took her several minutes to realize where she was and who was making coffee in her kitchen. She groaned as she rolled to her feet and looked at her mother.

Last night had been like a dream. Her mother was back in her life—something she hadn't realized she had given up hoping for—and for the first time in her adult life, she felt grounded and secure. Maybe it was her mother or maybe it was her home. Either way she was happy. Now to make plans to fix things with Dex. She could send her a text or even call her.

She looked around for her phone. It wasn't within arm's length as she expected. Where had she left it last night?

"What are you looking for?" Eileen called from the kitchen.

"My phone. I can't remember where I put it."

"It's in your bedroom. I heard it ringing last night."

"Sorry. I hope it didn't wake you."

She jogged down the hall and grabbed her phone from the top of her dresser. She typed out a short text to Dex asking if they could talk. She didn't see a missed call so she checked her call log. Dex had called right after they had gone to bed. She hadn't left a message, though.

Eileen handed her a cup of coffee when she returned to the kitchen and they moved to the living room.

"Do you want to go and get some breakfast? There isn't any food in your cabinets or your refrigerator. I hope that's because your house was under construction and not how you normally live."

Lucy laughed. "I'm not home much—"

The sound of a car door closing interrupted her. She walked to the front door and opened it. Her pulse quickened as Dex climbed the steps to the porch.

"What...where?" she stuttered, trying to absorb what she was seeing.

Dex smiled. "Surprise."

* * *

Dex couldn't believe she had been able to grab a flight and was finally standing in front of Lucy. She could see how shocked Lucy was. She wasn't sure that was a good thing. She wished she had spent more time thinking about what she would actually say when she arrived.

"How did you find me?" Lucy asked.

Dex looked over Lucy's head to the woman watching her from the sofa. There was enough of a resemblance that she knew this was Lucy's mother. The woman gave her a small nod.

"Your mother answered your phone when I called last night."

She watched Lucy's eyes grow large as she turned her body and looked back and forth between them.

"How did *you* find me," Lucy asked her mother.

"I used my GPS. I did send you a housewarming gift, remember?"

Lucy shook her head as if she couldn't believe what was in front of her. Dex stepped inside the cabin, pulling the door shut behind her. She crossed to the sofa and stuck out her hand to Lucy's mother.

"Dex Alexander," she said.

"Eileen Donovan. It's so nice to meet you."

"You as well."

"If you're both finished," Lucy said sarcastically.

Dex glanced at her. Lucy leaned against the kitchen table wearing baggy sweatpants and a T-shirt, but she couldn't help thinking she was more adorable than ever. The look on her face, though, was a bit frightening. She knew she was taking a risk coming here. She knew Lucy might not be happy to see her. Her phone dinged with a new text message. She pulled the phone from her pocket and glanced at the screen. A message from Lucy was displayed on the screen.

She met Lucy's eyes. "You want to talk?"

"I thought we should."

"So I'm here. Talk."

Lucy looked at her mother and back at her.

"I was just leaving," Eileen said, disappearing into the bedroom. She returned a moment later with her overnight bag. She kissed Lucy's cheek and whispered something Dex couldn't hear.

Dex returned her wave as Eileen disappeared through the front door. For the first time since she arrived, she took a few minutes to study Lucy. There was no doubt in her mind she was the most beautiful woman she had ever seen. She felt her pulse race as she watched Lucy push back the hair that had fallen across her face. And sexy, so very sexy. Her heart skipped a beat when their eyes met.

"What did she say to you?" She couldn't help but be curious with the way Eileen's words had made Lucy's face grow hard.

Lucy shrugged, and for a second Dex thought she wasn't going to tell her.

"She said love was always worth the risk."

"It's an experience of infinity."

Lucy gave a chuckle. "Did you read that in a fortune cookie?"

"No, a teatag."

"Clearly a life lesson."

"Yes, it was. Love is an experience of infinity."

Lucy shook her head. "I don't think of infinity when I think about love. My dad is gone."

"Infinite love doesn't mean people we love won't leave this earth. It means I'll love you more tomorrow than I do today. That there is no limit to the amount of love I can feel for you."

"You love me?" Lucy asked.

"I think that might be possible."

"Why is it you seem to fit so seamlessly into my life? I've never had to try so hard to convince myself I don't do relationships."

Dex crossed to where Lucy stood, leaving a small space between them. "Maybe because now you do."

Lucy dropped her head, breaking their eye contact. Dex knew saying the right thing was important, but doing the right thing was what would convince this woman that she loved her. She gently touched Lucy's chin and lifted her head. Their eyes locked and Dex did her best to convey her feelings to Lucy.

"I *am* in love with you," she said softly. "So in love. I don't know how we'll work the living arrangements, but I know I only want to be with you."

A small tear escaped from the corner of Lucy's eye. "I never thought my heart would allow me to feel again, let alone that I would believe someone when they said those words. I want this too. I want you in my life."

Dex pulled Lucy into her arms and enjoyed the feeling of holding and being held. The comfort and strength that flowed back and forth between them was all she would ever need. There would be plenty of time to figure out what they would have to do to make this relationship work, but right now she only wanted to enjoy the thrill of being with the woman she loved.

Lucy pulled away, a small grin on her face as she pulled Dex toward the front door. "There's someone you need to meet."

She raised her eyebrows. "Someone more important than your mother? I already won her to my side, you know."

"I did notice there seemed to be a conspiracy taking place. But no, this is a great judge of character, and I need his approval before we can proceed."

She laughed. She loved this light, teasing side of Lucy. "Lead on."

"Oh wait," Lucy said, dropping her hand and running back inside the house.

"Now I'm intrigued," she said, glancing at the carrot in Lucy's hand when she returned. "I hope I can pass this guy's test."

Lucy smiled as she stared into her eyes. "I hope you do too."

Bella Books, Inc.

Women. Books. Even Better Together.

P.O. Box 10543
Tallahassee, FL 32302

Phone: 800-729-4992
www.bellabooks.com